Readers' c

'A fast paced, thrilling fantasy novel – I really hope it becomes very successful and you write many more.'

Tom age 13.

'I read it over three nights, really got into the action – would love to know more about the characters who live in Oeska.'

Vidhi age 15.

'Really enjoyed the theme. Nice idea. I read it in two sittings. I was tired on Sunday morning after a sleepover but the book woke me up with the excitement of the ending.'

Thomas age 12.

'Didn't put it down. A page-turner. I could really see it like a film.'

Sam age 11.

'Read it in three days. Found it very interesting. A very good, easy read. If there are future books I'd like to know how his dad got into that situation and to see more of the connection between their world and ours and its history.'

Andrew age 14.

for Tryphon
who breathed life into it
and for Lawrence and Emily
who believed in it

Geo Says No

Not a Dream

Geo Says No
Not a Dream

I Rosenfeld

Etica Press
2015

Published by
Etica Press Ltd
147 Worcester Road
Malvern
Worcestershire
WR14 1ET

A CIP Record for this book is available from
The British Cataloguing-in-Publication Data Office

ISBN 978 1 905633 21 0

Text design and typesetting by Etica Press

Cover design by Leyland Gomez

Cover illustration copyright © Emily A. Rosenfeld

Printed and bound in the UK by Short Run Press Ltd, Exeter

CHAPTER ONE

Black Dust

On the night of the earthquake George Cleigh was dreaming of a red guitar, when the noise of someone creeping around in his bedroom woke him up.

'Who's that!' he called out, convinced that somebody had broken in. Heart racing, he pushed his bedclothes aside, swung his legs off the bed and sat up. He gaped at the stream of moonlight that poured in through the glass door leading to his balcony. It was ajar, exactly as he had left it before he went to bed.

He sat in the dark, trying to still his breathing, listening closely for the sound of more footfalls. There were none. Starting to calm down, he focused his attention on the noises outside. They were just the normal sounds of a Greek island night in August, the hooting of owls and the tinny voices of crickets.

For a second he fixed his eyes on the gnarled branches of the olive trees, glowing eerily in the silver light of the moon. And then the floorboards squeaked again. His room filled with a deeper, denser darkness. A tall shadow towered up by the side of his bed. Where had it come from? He lay dumbstruck as the dark figure of a man sat down by his bedside and leaned slowly closer, lifting his hand.

'Geo!' he breathed, running his fingers through the boy's untidy hair and making him flinch. 'At last...'

Only then did George, who preferred to be called just 'Geo', recognise the warm tone of his dad's voice and the light touch of his hand.

'Dad? Dad!'

It had been almost seven years since Max Cleigh had disappeared. Geo had daydreamt his dad's return often enough. He had imagined the clink of keys, the turning of the key in the lock, the squeak of the hinge, the tread of his dad's foot stepping from the dark olive grove into the house – but not this.

He raised his arm and reached to flick the switch of his bedside lamp but just then his father's shadow vanished. Geo held his breath, slowly becoming conscious of other sounds. They started as muffled, muttered words that grew clearer – whispering, urging, spinning and swirling through the air, saying: 'Run outside! Get Leona. Run!' Then, with a whoosh, the whispers rushed out of the room, sucking every molecule of air along with them.

He felt like an insect trapped in a glass jar. Struggling to his feet, Geo stumbled outside to his balcony where he leaned against the railing, gasping for air. He'd lived here all his life. These hot summer nights were always the same, always filled with the voices of nightjars, crickets and nightingales, the hooting of owls, the scuttling of hedgehogs in the undergrowth. So why had they all, suddenly, stopped?

A heavy silence now filled the olive grove, flooding him with dread. He leapt back into his room, belted out into the corridor and rushed to his mother's bedroom.

The landing light hanging from the ceiling was swinging back and forth in its white silk lantern, and the floorboards began to creak louder beneath Geo's feet.

'MUM!' he shouted, bursting into Leona's room. 'Get up!'

'What is it!' his mum muttered grumpily, not making the slightest effort to sit up.

He flicked on the light switch and his heart sank as he spotted the freshly opened packet of sleeping tablets on her bedside table.

His mum buried her head under her pillow.

He grabbed her by the arm and shook her. 'Wake UP!' he shouted just as a ringing whisper rose up from the earth. It quickly grew louder, as though the voices of demons were muttering curses upon the old stone house.

With a sharp intake of breath, his mum sat up at last, swinging her feet to the floor. Geo ran out to the throbbing stairs, his mum on his heels. Tables, chairs, cupboards and bookcases shuddered and clanked in the dark. Vases, ornaments, glass and china rattled across furniture tops and smashed onto the floors. Halfway down the stairs, a hollow boom thundered up from the foundations, as if something that had been locked up underground had been set free inside the shaking house.

Walls cracked and split. Showers of black dust rained down on them from the ceilings. Pulling his mum behind him Geo leapt down the last few stairs and across the hall, undid the door latch and sprinted out across the patio. They dodged roof tiles that burst like hand-grenades on the flagstones. Hearing a great, vibrating snap, Geo glanced over his shoulder. Every wall of their home was twisting, ripping open and shattering, raising clouds of ancient dust.

Even when the trees around them stopped quivering they didn't stop running. The ground gave one last shudder; and then, nothing.

The earthquake was over but they kept running.

Not until they'd reached the end of the rose garden did they stop, spinning around and looking back, panting. In the growing light of the dawn, Geo saw all that was left of their house: a broken roof sitting on top of a mound of rubble.

'*That* got you out of bed, Mum, didn't it?' Geo said without thinking, and she gave him a startled, sideways look, eyes wide and cheeks smudged with the black, powdery dust that had poured down from the ceilings. Tears ran down her face, streaking the dirt. And before they knew it, they were both staggering about, laughing and crying like lunatics, hugging and almost unable to believe their lucky escape from the jaws of death.

They had not shown any affection for ages. A cold war of silence had raged between Geo and his mum for nearly seven years. It had erupted a few months after his father had left them. As the hostilities between them began to take root, Geo had learned to use the washing machine, forage in the fridge, and cross paths with Leona as little as possible. The reason for this rift was that Geo thought – no, he felt quite sure – that his mum knew what had happened to his dad, but refused to tell him.

'Geo,' she now said, stepping back, her chin still trembling from the shock. 'You saved my life!'

'It wasn't me, Mum,' he tried to explain, bending over to wipe a trickle of blood from the back of his heel. He felt dizzy as he stood up. The shock made him shake and sweat. He wanted to throw up. 'It was Dad. *He* saved us.'

Rising slowly behind her, the morning sun lit up the tips of Leona's hair as she stood stock-still in her white night-gown, her jaw slack.

'D-did you just say *Dad*?'

'Hey, Mum, don't faint! Come this way.' He tugged her towards an outdoor table and some chairs under a vine. 'I'm serious. Dad turned up in my room.' He flopped onto a seat.

She slumped into a wicker chair and opened her mouth to speak. At first nothing came out. 'R-really! Really?' she stammered, after a while.

'He woke me up and warned me to get you and run out – and I know it sounds mad, but then he vanished. I couldn't breathe. I had no idea what was going on. But I came to get you and, well, you know the rest.'

His mum closed her eyes and tipped her head back, breathing out a long sigh, nodding and smiling with a huge arched grin that made him think of a kid's drawing of a cheerful face. The moment didn't last, though. Leona opened her eyes and leaned across the table, staring at him. 'So you had a dream that Max turned up?'

'No - not a dream!'

'Tell me what happened again – what did you see?' 'Her face had become guarded again, defensive.

'He was just *there*, in my room,' Geo repeated more loudly, as though shouting might help her understand.

'Like a vivid dream?'

'No, I'm pretty sure I was awake!' He thought of something then; the stories his dad used to tell him when he was little; the tales about the Marshals of Tide and Time and the demon, Cromund. Tales so closely woven with surprise attacks, fights to the death, undying friendships, cunning acts of revenge, grief, love and dreamboarding, that as a child he'd always wondered if they were real. It was the dreamboarding Geo thought of now – the stories of people being able to infiltrate dreams, to send messages.

He leaned over and put a hand on his mum's arm. 'It was as if he gatecrashed my dream!'

Leona raised her eyebrows. 'Oh, a load of old tosh!'

'Really? But you used to tell me those tales too. And I can't think of any other explanation!'

'Don't be ridiculous.' Leona shook her head.

Why was she behaving like a total cow – pretending she didn't even know about dreamboarding? *Cool down,* he told himself. *Don't lose it. It only ever makes things worse.* He leaned a little closer to her and said, more softly, 'Mum, it's been tough on you, I know! But is there any truth in old stories? I need to know! Why haven't you told me the truth about Dad?'

'I never knew if Max was alive or dead ...' she cut in, her eyes brimming with tears.

'B-but now you do? Me seeing him … has that made a difference?'

She gave a wheezy cough, knitted her eyebrows, but didn't reply.

'Look, Mum, I'm nearly sixteen. And I'm not stupid. I mean – isn't it about time you told me everything?'

Leona opened her mouth to speak but, before she could, a black dust cloud that had been slowly rising out of the ruin like an evil djinni started to billow towards them.

CHAPTER TWO

Cromund

'Hey, don't just sit there, Geo,' she said, springing up from the garden chair, 'you don't want to breathe in that stuff, trust me.'

They sprinted off to the long drive, lined with oleanders and olive trees, where they slowed down. Geo was limping.

'So – back to Dad – don't you at least have a guess of what might have happened?' he asked. He had to stop for a moment to check his throbbing heel. A nasty bruise had already come up, but the cut only bled if he put his weight on it.

'Your heel needs bandaging,' his mum said. She began to tear a strip from the hem of her nightie.

'You are changing the subject.' First the dust cloud, now his foot. 'We were talking about Dad.'

'Let me sort this out first.' She steered Geo towards a tree trunk laid along one side of the drive and made him sit down.

Kneeling on the ground, she tore the end of her makeshift bandage into two strips. Geo exhaled with irritation as he looked down at her, mulling over all her faults. She was not a great cook. She hated shopping. In fact, if it weren't for occasional visits from a local cleaning lady, Geo was sure there would be no edible food in the house. And she was always warning him about being careful and not talking to strangers – like he was a six-year-old. Sometimes he felt a bit sorry for her. Once, when he had found her in her artist's studio sobbing and stabbing one of her own paintings with a kitchen knife, he wondered if she was crazy. This event had been upsetting, not only because it had given him a real fright but also because her art was one of the few things he liked about her. He often went to her studio just to look at her paintings. The ones he liked best depicted magical creatures that galloped towards the viewer seemingly from every wall. And she did have talent (he had to give her that), managing to make paint look like steam, vapour, sunlight, silver cloud – the stuff dreams are made of.

He shifted to straddle the tree trunk. As he turned, he caught a glimpse of something through the trees that made him catch his breath.

'Th-the Mandiballs' house,' he breathed. 'There's not one tile out of place.'

'What!' His mum, who was still kneeling on the ground, raised her head and followed his gaze.

They stared at it. Leona's jaw was hanging slightly loose.

All the colonial gables, chimneys, external staircases, arches and verandas of their neighbours' mansion at the top of the hill were completely untouched. How could this be, when their own house had been reduced to dust and rubble by the earthquake?

'Ah!' she doubled up as though someone had kicked her in the stomach.

'Are you hurt? Mum? Are you feeling sick?'

'Just a bit queasy.' She stood up unsteadily and took several deep breaths, then steadied herself against the trunk of a pomegranate tree on the side of the drive. She was muttering and swearing under her breath. Geo caught something about 'Cromund's spies'.

The name gave him a jolt. *Cromund.* Geo trawled through his memory for everything he could remember about it from all those childhood stories, so long ago. A hoard of words and images flashed through his memory in vivid, strobe-lit fragments. His father's voice: 'Nothing but a shadow, Geo, a sliver of mist, a disembodied spirit obsessed with slipping under the skin of any mortal corrupt enough to let him be his master.'

'So is Cromund real?' he now asked.

She didn't respond, just kept rubbing her temples in a daze.

'Mum, I'm not deaf! You were just muttering stuff about Cromund and his spies. What aren't you telling me? Perhaps I was too young to be told before. Perhaps you wanted me to have a normal childhood. But you know, when Dad told me the stories all those years ago, it felt like he was giving me coded messages – like I was supposed to remember them, and they might save my life, one day. And there's one character I'll never forget from his stories: the demon, Cromund.'

Leona stared back at him. The ancient olive trees seemed to crowd upon them on the narrow drive. The morning breeze lifted an eddy of dust and leaves that coiled round their ankles. Behind her, the green gate of the estate swung half-open on its rusty hinges. Her long hair writhed in a stronger gust of wind. Her eyes shone in the fluid light. And for a fraction of a second Geo thought he was looking at someone different – someone so unknown to him, it took his breath away. Then, turning abruptly, she marched up the drive.

As she walked towards it, the green gate creaked fully open and the grocer's van drove through it into the estate. It screeched to a halt and the delivery guy jumped out, almost dropping his armful of free-range eggs and goat's milk. Laying the delivery on the bonnet of his van, he gawped at the pile of rubble that had been Geo and Leona Cleigh's home.

'Your house!' he said, crossing himself and muttering some phrase in Greek. 'Y-you really got it, didn't you! Seen nothing like it – except down the bottom of the hill by Philip's café, where the lion fountain is.'

'The *fountain*, did you say?' Leona rushed over to him. She was flushed. Her eyes shone so brightly, she might have just heard that the Martians had landed.

'Yes, Mrs Cleigh! The fountain – saw it with my own eyes. You should've seen it!' He thrust his hands in front of him, his eyes glazing over as he relived the moment. 'I heard a loud "crack!" and the ground started to ripple – like a wave ... and the fountain just got swallowed up! And then a flat stone came up in its place. A nasty thing, pitted, dark! Really spooky.'

'Still got friends in high places!' Leona said, sounding relieved and raising her eyes towards the sky.

Geo gave a shudder. She seemed loopier by the minute – not that she'd ever been a shining example of common sense. But he noticed that her eyes stayed glued to the treetops; and they were growing wider.

Geo followed her gaze and his blood froze. There, at the intersection between a thick branch and the trunk of a very old olive tree, crouched a life form that could have jumped out of a nightmare. It looked like a shadowy yellow demon, rippling and wavering like thick, scummy water. Geo could make out two flame-red eyes leering at him, as though it plotted to suck away his last breath.

The delivery guy let out a terrified yell and leapt back inside his van.

Geo grabbed his still-gaping mother by the arm and pushed her into the van.

They slammed the doors and went swerving and screeching out of the estate. As the driver braked to avoid an oncoming car, Geo cast a quick glance behind him through the van doors. One minute the nightmare creature was there.

But he blinked. And when he looked again, it had vanished into a whirl of shadows.

– CHAPTER THREE –

The Fountain and The Stone

In the car, Geo's mother said she could do with a stiff drink and the driver said he could do with two, or three, or a dozen. Geo said nothing. He was staring at a vanity mirror fixed onto the back of the car's sun visor, left open by the previous passenger. Though it showed his face, he could hardly recognise himself. His skin looked almost mustard yellow and his eyes terrified. His pillowy lips were so pinched that he seemed to have aged twenty years in half an hour. The tuft of dark golden hair that normally fell over the side of his forehead stood up as though he had received an electric shock. And something had happened to it. He leaned closer, not quite believing his eyes: half of his fringe had turned white.

'Well, what do you know!' he exclaimed, slamming the sun visor shut. From age twelve to nearly sixteen he had suffered the indignities of greasy hair, bad skin and bunny teeth. He had just come out of this horrible phase with a good shampoo, a bar of medicated soap and an orthodontically reconstructed smile, which his friend Evangeli said was capable of melting any girl's heart. Geo had not really believed her because his mind had not quite adjusted yet to his supposed transformation from ugly duckling to the tall, tanned, good-looking boy she insisted he had become all of a sudden.

And now some of his hair had gone white! He was

swearing under his breath, thinking, *why me, what crap luck, how come I go from spotty mess to finished old man before I even hit sixteen …*

'What's the matter?' asked his mother, who sat between Geo and the driver. Then, noticing his half-white fringe she exclaimed, 'Oh! How did *that* happen? You poor thing!'

'I've no idea. And I'd rather not talk about it,' he snapped.

They gazed outside at the wooded hill, which soon gave way to sloping fields, a sunny meadow with a couple of scraggy sheep, a row of houses, garages, dog kennels and chicken coops. Finally they reached the bottom of the hill where the houses were more densely packed.

Geo couldn't think clearly – no – he couldn't think at all. *Zombie on parade* he thought, and the words somehow stuck to his brain and kept coming back to him in dizzying waves. *What's wrong with you, zombie, think, why can't you think – must be the shock – shockwave in your brain – earthquake – and your house just a pile of rubble.*

He made himself look out of the side window and name things, the twisting road that ran through the village … ah at the village, already! So they had arrived, though the driver went at snail's pace because so many people were milling about, most of them half-dressed, talking about the earthquake damage – all their jammed garage gates, rickety extensions, cracked window panes and roof tiles that had come loose.

The driver was telling them something. Geo turned and saw the guy's lips moving but couldn't focus on the meaning of his words. He wished he wasn't so muddled. *It's the shock*, he told himself again. Meantime, his brain had replaced the repetition of 'zombie on parade' with a longer but possibly less useless string of words. Over and over, a little voice at the back of his head now chanted, *come on now – you need help – why not go home to England – that's what you need – don't you see? – family – relatives – really – you so need help!*

Though they had lived in Greece for as long as he could remember, both Geo's parents were English. Geo knew only one relative living at home, in Brighton, his dad's brother, Ian. His uncle was a nice enough man, but married to the grumpiest, most unwelcoming of people. His wife, Linda, had a forehead permanently deformed by a fixed frown that had always made Geo think of an especially grouchy extra-terrestrial. As for her smile – actually, he had never set eyes on Linda's smile. It probably did not exist.

In spite of this, and even though his mother had not made any effort at all to keep in touch with Geo's uncle since his dad had disappeared, Ian was all Geo had in the way of a relative. No wonder, then, that all he could think of as they drove through the village was how soon they could catch a plane to England. He was about to share these thoughts with his mother, when the driver rammed on the brakes and let them out. Without even a 'thank you' to him for the lift, Geo's mum stepped out of the van and dashed off towards the main square. Geo couldn't believe her rudeness.

'Thanks so much for the lift,' he tried to make up for his mum and waved at the van driver as he jumped out and followed Leona through a small crowd of bleary-eyed, half-dressed locals, swapping news. A man was shouting down his mobile, already telling someone about the one house that had collapsed altogether. It had a painfully familiar address. *How come bad news always travels so fast?* Geo wondered.

The village square came into view at the end of the lane. His mother headed straight for the village fountain where the black stone was supposed to have risen out of the ground. Geo sincerely hoped that the van driver had been exaggerating. The idea of the fountain getting swallowed up by the ground and being replaced by a black, pitted, spooky stone! It had to be nonsense. Even so, a shiver shot down his spine as they got nearer. Through open windows, he could hear expert seismologists giving telephone interviews on breakfast shows about earthquakes. In the distance, a handful of journalists had arrived to interview local people 'live'. He could see a radio crew, setting up their recording equipment outside the church. The grocer's driver had already parked his van and taken his place in front of an enormous black microphone, telling the rest of the world about how he had seen the earth ripple like a wave.

The village square was framed by a row of houses on one side, a kids' playground opposite, Philip's café on the left and the wall of the village church on the right. Normally Geo would have been able to see the fountain against the church wall, where it stood at the foot of the clock tower. But even though it was only seven-thirty in the morning, a swarm of people, many of them still in their pyjamas, milled around the church wall, so Geo couldn't catch as much as a glimpse of the fountain.

He followed his mother as she jostled through a flock of old ladies and past another journalist – this one doing camera interviews. And then, squeezing through the last row of bystanders, Geo saw it: the marble lion's head that had always been fixed to the wall of the church had disappeared. All that remained of it now was a mossy, slightly damp outline, clear to see against the whitewash of the wall. And a stone really had risen from the ground. Flat, square, matt black, it stood at least two metres wide and long, and half a metre high. Steam rose from its wet surface in the heat of the sun, forming a tiny cloud in the perfect blue sky.

Geo gaped, not knowing what to think. His mother shuffled past a gang of kids who were jumping on and off the stone. She sat down on it with a sigh, running her hands all over it, stroking it, muttering to herself and occasionally looking up as if she was expecting someone.

Suddenly, she jerked her head towards a couple of bystanders and gave a muffled cry.

'Angelo! Sophia!' Leona said, looking furtively around her. She was speaking to the two people arriving in front of her through the crowd. 'Nice work! I knew something was up, the moment I heard about The Fountain and The Stone!' She had uttered these words with such awe, Geo could practically hear capital letters.

Geo looked more closely at the strangers and his heart sank. If he was hoping for someone ordinary to take charge of things, his mother's friends hardly fitted the bill. The man was tall, scrawny and unshaven. He wore a long scruffy coat, which, Geo thought, was pretty weird in the growing heat, and kept his right hand firmly inside his coat pocket. His hair was dark, unkempt, and it fell in tangles over his deeply tanned, lined face. The woman was dressed in biker's leathers and had spiky hair, piercing blue eyes and the abrupt manner of someone used to giving orders. Her skin was pitted and scarred as if she'd been in many fights. They both looked tough and, come to think of it, oddly familiar. The man – Angelo – pointed at the clock tower impatiently; almost ten to eight.

'But what are the charges?' Leona was asking him. She didn't look pleased any more. She seemed nervous.

Geo tried to listen in, but he only caught fragments of the woman's voice: '… without making a fuss, Leona. At least your son gets to claim …'

They crowded closer together, so Geo missed the rest of her words, and his mother's reply. But he could see she was agitated, arguing back and casting quick glances in his direction.

If Leona had bothered to introduce him to the strangers, Geo might have tried to do the polite thing and hang around – even tried to butt into their conversation to find out what they were talking about. But neither they nor his mother seemed in the least interested in including him. On the contrary, they huddled together in a way that made him feel like a spare part – no, worse, a nuisance. Well, Geo thought, so be it! He was too annoyed and hungry to care, not to mention barefoot, his injured heel throbbing with pain and a crimson blood stain spreading on his makeshift bandage.

'Mum! I really need to go to Evangeli's to borrow some shoes and stuff,' he told her, limping closer.

Leona grabbed him by the arm.

'Don't! Not now!' she said in a pleading voice. She turned to her friends: 'Wait for me right here.' She led Geo to Philip's café at the other end of the square, to an empty table next to the whitewashed café wall, as far as possible from the other customers. Geo sat with his back to this wall and she took the seat facing him, her long hair hiding the sides of her face from public view.

What's she going to come up with next? he wondered. And who were those people? He didn't actually remember seeing them before. But then, why did they seem so familiar? Maybe a memory from a long time ago? He couldn't quite put his finger on it.

'Geo, I have to go,' Leona announced. Just like that, out of the blue.

He could feel his hands, slippery with sweat, gripping the arms of his plastic chair. 'W-what are you talking about? Go where?'

'There's no time to explain – you must listen to me!' She glanced at the clock tower, leaned forward, grasped his hand and said in a harsh whisper: 'There's no choice, look, I've *got* to go!'

A wave of fury swept through him. 'Come on now, Mum! How can you say this to me?' he hissed, shaking his hand free. 'Really! Go *where*?' he added.

She looked at him with a steady gaze, her eyes serious and sad. 'Away,' she replied slowly.

A laugh of disbelief came out of his throat. 'What, just like that? Why can't you take me with you?'

The breeze lifted Leona's long hair. 'I haven't got the authority to take you.'

Geo's vision blurred, giving him only a very hazy impression of his surroundings. Without standing up, he kicked his chair backwards, so its back fell against the whitewashed wall. He crossed his arms over his chest and knitted his eyebrows. He'd had enough of this. 'Well, off you go, then! See you around,' he said in angry voice.

Her eyes glistened with tears. 'Do you think I want to go? I don't have a choice – I've done something arrogant and selfish and I'm being arrested for it. And now you must listen to me. Please.'

Geo ran his fingers through his discoloured fringe and looked back up at her cautiously, flattening the tuft of white hair over his left eye. 'Arrested!'

'Yes,' she replied with an impatient nod. 'And I don't want to leave you, but neither is it within my power to stay.'

'Really?' he said in a low, furious whisper, 'I don't see any uniforms, warrants and IDs! I can't even see any handcuffs!'

Leona looked at him in dismay. 'Geo, I could say "sorry" a thousand times and it still wouldn't be enough. I'm sorry I have to go. I'm sorry I've failed, so abysmally, to prepare you for this. I never could see how, when for years I was reduced to...' Her words drifted away to nothing. 'But you hit the nail on the head earlier, when you said I was protecting you from the truth.'

'Yeah? What truth? And why?'

'Well – so you could have a normal life. And the truth is about you, me, your family. Who we really are. I've tried, so – so *hard*, to live a normal life!'

'Well, you shouldn't have just tried, you should have *done* it!' he muttered furiously. He felt betrayed, disappointed and horribly tired. But he still didn't quite believe she was going to leave him.

She looked at the clock once more and gasped. 'We only have *seconds* left,' she said quickly. 'Look, I didn't plan this, Geo! I have no choice, but you're old enough now to... ' her voice petered out.

Geo looked at his feet, too miserable to say anything.

'In time you'll understand,' she added.

'No, I won't,' he said, refusing to look up. 'I'll never understand.'

'Just – listen to me!' she pressed, her voice now panicky. 'Do the one thing I'm about to tell you. Go back to the house. Look for the safe. It was in my room, above my bed. There's a dreamcatcher in it. You're going to need it. The safe combination is KZC followed by the date of your birth, backwards.'

The clock struck once. Leona leaned over, grasped Geo's hand and squeezed it against her tear-drenched face, then bolted off towards the crowd. Leaping after her, Geo grabbed her by the arm. With a cry of frustration she shook herself free and dived into the swarm of people. The clock struck again. Geo stood on tiptoe, looking for her in the crowd. The clock struck a third time. He thought he saw the back of her head by the playground. She was darting off towards the foot of the clock tower. He noticed Angelo and Sophia, furiously beckoning her. Four. He pushed and shoved his way through bodies, until, on the strike of five, he spotted her raised up, in a little huddle with the two strangers. They must be *on* the stone, he realised.

Six. Leona caught his eye with one last, tearful glance. She looked as if she wanted to jump off the black stone, but the man seized her by the waist with his left hand. With his right one, he pulled a wooden stick carved with two intertwined snakes out of his coat pocket and raised it above him. A light misty haze settled around them just as the scarred woman grabbed Leona's arm; his mum wasn't going anywhere!

Seven. Charging forward, blood pulsing in his ears, he shoved people out of his way, and reached the stone. There was only one thought in his mind: to free his mother from the clutches of these people.

But as he reached out to his mother, the children who'd been jumping on and off the stone, the old women, the workmen, the milling spectators, everything, went still – a picture frozen in time.

The clock struck eight.

As its echoing clang faded in the air, no one except Geo saw how his mother and her companions dissolved into slivers of thin mist that funnelled down into the black stone and were gone.

CHAPTER FOUR

Stainless Steel

Geo staggered around, thinking he might faint. His breath came out in gasps. He sat on the black stone, resting his forehead in his palms. It was too much. His mind kept going back to absurd, unrelated details – flashbacks of the earthquake – the safe – its password – Aunt Linda's frown – Angelo's snake wand – a tuft of white hair.

He had aged overnight.

Next to him, a couple of kids resumed their game of jumping on and off the black stone.

Who were his parents, really? They had always been a bit eccentric – no, that was a lie – they'd been quite isolated and secretive, like people living in hiding. And that odd advice his mother had given, 'go back to the ruin ... find the safe ... there's a dreamcatcher in it.' Not money? But he was homeless and penniless. Why would he want a stupid dreamcatcher? Surely, there must be something less useless in his mum's safe!

He felt weird, his thoughts scattered. Could he follow Leona into the stone? Could there be a passage under the ground – a passage leading to some other place, where the strangers had taken her? He got up and tried to push the stone aside. It wouldn't budge, squatting in front of him, immoveable, cold, giving off a musty smell of fungus and mildew. Was it, maybe, something supernatural? Not that he usually believed in such things. But his mother *had* disappeared – sucked into the stone. He paced around it one more time, when he realised that people were staring.

I must look a sight, he thought. He was a mess, wild-eyed, some of his hair gone white, wearing only a pair of shorts and a light tee-shirt; and he was still barefoot. He looked down. The cut in his heel had bled some more. A bright red stain was spreading on the bandage his mum had tied around it.

Get a grip on yourself, he thought. He didn't want to have to answer the questions of social workers, hospital doctors, the police. He had no idea what to tell them about his mum disappearing. He became aware of a woman staring at his bloody heel and talking to him. He could see her lips moving, her hand waving in front of his face.

'Hello! Hullooo! Do you need help?'

Ah, he recognised her as someone's mother from school. She looked unreal, like a puppet with invisible strings moving her lips upwards into a smile.

'Are you all right?' she asked, peering into his eyes. 'You look miles away.'

The smell of eggs frying wafted out of a kitchen window, making him feel sick. 'Yes, I ... I'm fine,' he stammered. 'Thanks – sorry – Mum's waiting for me round the corner.'

Time to push off, he thought, and fast, before the well-meaning woman found out that he no longer had a mother. He limped quickly away from her, trying not to put too much weight on his injured foot.

The crowd was slowly beginning to disperse. People were going back home to get dressed, have breakfast, go to work. He glanced at the radio crew as he went past. They were dismantling their gear and loading it into a van. His eyes moved from the kids' playground beside the café to the row of houses and the church tower. Everything looked familiar but distant, as though he were watching it through the wrong end of a telescope. His head wouldn't clear. He felt just as confused now as he had felt a few moments ago when he saw his mother disappear right in front of his eyes. He tried to remember something useful, like the number of the bus that went to his friend Evangeli's house.

If he visited Evangeli he could have a shower, a clean bandage and a good breakfast. Then he'd work out what to do. But he wanted to look for the dreamcatcher first. Getting to the safe seemed more important – his mum wouldn't have said it otherwise. He hurried out of the square, heading for the main road and back towards their wreck of a house. The August sun was climbing up in the morning sky and the tarmac started to get uncomfortably hot. He wished the soles of his feet were more tough. He wished *he* were more tough. Questions kept plaguing him: why would his mum keep a dreamcatcher in a safe? Could it be valuable? Made of gold and jewels, perhaps? But how come he'd never seen that safe? He could only remember one of her paintings hanging on the wall above her bed. Ah! That made sense. Her safe was probably hidden behind that picture.

He reached the main road and walked to the crossroads where he flagged down the car of the local garage mechanic. He was kind – even gave Geo a pair of old trainers he kept in the boot of his car. They were stained and a size bigger than he needed but if he tightened up the laces, they were okay. As the mechanic dropped Geo off, he noticed that someone had closed the gate at the top of the drive. Perhaps a kind neighbour, Geo thought, someone wanting to stop the curious from gawping at the ruined house – or looting it. Geo edged in through the gate and closed it behind him, grateful for the privacy. Under the canopy of the ancient trees – each more than six hundred years old, as his father had told him – he glimpsed the lopsided pile of rubble that had been his home only yesterday and his heart gave a jolt.

He saw a burly workman standing on a pile of broken wall pieces. He hadn't seen Geo who stood frozen on the spot, gaping, too surprised to do or say anything. What was the man doing here? How dare he? A knot rose in Geo's chest as he recognised the top of an old mantelpiece mirror that lay by the man's feet, together with fragments of their living room fireplace. The man looked sweaty and dusty, like he'd been rummaging and scavenging in the ruin for quite a while. Then a small, well-dressed woman emerged on what had once been the east-facing patio, holding a large map in her hands and directing the workman.

'Mrs Mandiball!' Geo breathed. She was the neighbour that had made his mum mutter "Cromund's spies!" What was *she* doing here?

Geo started to get a bad feeling about this.

But the Mandiballs were ridiculously well off! Mrs Mandiball didn't need to scavenge! Unless …unless – could the dreamcatcher be so precious that she wanted it? But how would she know of it?

He sprinted down the drive, yelling, 'Excuse me, but you are trespassing on private property!'

'Oh, is that so?' she replied coolly, without even bothering to look up at him from her map, which, he now realised was in fact an architect's plan. She raised her thumb at the man and nodded towards Geo.

The man jumped off the rubble to stand in Geo's way. He was in his mid-thirties, thick-set and stout with a short neck, thick black hair and a broad face – Geo now recognised him as the Mandiballs' gardener.

'Yes, you *are* trespassing!' Geo repeated, turning slightly to face Mrs Mandiball.

'Now, now, there's no need for rudeness,' Mrs Mandiball said, raising her eyes to meet his. She had a calming, quiet, almost girlish voice. 'Gosh! Aren't you a bit young to be turning white?' she remarked, staring at the snow-white streak that fell over Geo's left eye.

He stared back, not knowing what to say.

'It's just that your mother borrowed something that

belongs to us and I've come to take it back,' she explained, sounding so reasonable that she took him by surprise and he almost apologised. But when he examined her face, he saw that behind the pretence of a smile, her eyes were utterly expressionless. Or rather, they had the deadpan expression of an expert poker player. He stepped closer to the ruin, then spun around with his back to it, as if to protect it and folded his arms over his chest.

'So exactly what did my mother borrow off you?'

'Oh, I can't tell you *that*,' Mrs Mandiball replied with a patronising giggle.

'Why not?' he asked. 'My mother's in the village making arrangements,' he bluffed. 'She sent me home, to make sure there are no looters.'

Mrs Mandiball gave a loud laugh. 'Looters! Please, don't insult me.'

She glanced at her burly gardener and gave him the slightest of nods. Before Geo knew it, the man had stepped behind him, grabbed his neck from the back and held him in a painful head lock. Geo froze, terrified, knowing that he was millimetres from having his neck snapped.

Mrs Mandiball raised her hand. 'Not yet, John!' she said in her pleasant voice.

Geo raised his right leg and kicked backwards with his uninjured heel at the man's knee. Kickboxing was the only thing his parents had ever insisted he should master. John's knee sounded like a nut being cracked as his leg buckled and he screamed, falling backwards. Quick as a lizard, Geo rolled off him and leapt up.

'Stop right there!'

Geo's eyes widened. Mrs Mandiball had pulled a very odd gun from a backpack by her feet and was already aiming it at him. It made a dull, muffled sputter, but Geo jumped aside. A spring-loaded syringe missed him by half an inch, skidding against the double glazing of a window and clattering, unbroken on the ground. With a cry of frustration she fired again, but Geo had already thrown himself onto the ground and slid towards her feet across the patio paving. A second syringe smashed behind him against a broken wall. He saw her reloading and slid a couple more inches along the dusty patio floor, grabbing out for her ankle. But she was too quick for him, leaping to the side. With the advantage of being above him, she aimed at him again, pulling the trigger once, twice, three times.

Nothing happened. Perhaps her tranquiliser gun was stuck. And now she stabbed down at him, holding it with both hands like a bayonet. He had no time to roll out of the way, but he blocked her attack by kicking her hand sideways; then, grabbing her by the wrist he managed to hold on to the top of her gun-clutching hand and pull her down to the floor with him. Her angry scream tore at his ears. He felt her grip on the gun loosen, then a paralysing pain as she kneed him between his legs.

He doubled up on the floor, nearly passing out. He was conscious of her hand slashing down through the air, coming at him again with the syringe. But even though he was writhing with pain, he managed to roll away. Then, spinning on his back like a break-dancer, he used both feet to kick her across the chest. As she yelled in pain he saw his chance and made another grab for her armed hand. With her fingers still wrapped round the tranquiliser gun, he thrust the needle into her thigh and pushed in the plunger. Mrs Mandiball gave him a startled look, as if it were the last thing in the world she had expected. Then she flopped to the floor, limp as a rag doll.

But it wasn't over, Geo realised, as a brick smashed next to him and he heard the groan of her gardener, the man she had called 'John'. Spinning around, he realised he still had to fight the man, who'd managed to climb onto his good leg and now limped towards Geo, another brick in one hand.

Geo leapt to the side, knowing it would be harder for John to hit a moving target, but the man threw the brick anyway, grazing Geo's arm. Zigzagging between piles of smashed roof tiles and sections of broken balconies, Geo looked for the unused syringe which had fallen against the window. And there it was! He dived, picked it up, loaded it onto the gun he still held and took aim, though his hand shook so badly, he could hardly control it. John's face, a mask of pain, shock and hate, drew closer. He raised a third brick and hurled it at Geo; but Geo dodged it, pulled the trigger and ... nothing happened! John's fist came streaking through the air but Geo ducked and thrust the needle into the man's side. He pushed in the plunger. The anaesthetic took more time to work on the man, who slumped down, looking dazed and fumbling with the syringe, desperate to pull it out. But he was weakened already and Geo had the advantage. Trapping the man's arm with his foot to stop him from removing the syringe, he waited for the drug to take effect.

When the man was deeply asleep, Geo turned his attention to the ruined house. He had no idea how long the drugs would keep Mrs Mandiball and the gardener unconscious. He didn't want to be around to find out.

With the sun beaming down and the cicadas out in full force, Geo ducked under a section of the roof that had slid down to the front of the house, climbed up the lopsided end of a balcony that led, like a ramp, to what had once been the first floor of the old villa, and somehow scrambled through a twisted window frame onto a heap of smashed furniture, tiles, timbers and broken floorboards. There he began to throw off planks and roof tiles from the pile.

The idea that he might ever find the safe as his mum had urged him to, struck him as absurd, but he had to try.

He rummaged through shattered chairs and filthy curtains, terrified in case Mrs Mandiball or her gardener woke up. Weak with hunger, his heel aching, he worked harder and faster, burrowing through rubbish, chucking bricks, glass, pieces of furniture and smashed tiles out of his way. But he was getting nowhere. 'Like looking for a needle in a haystack,' he muttered, his eyes burning with the dust, his vision blurred with tears. *The safe. Stop feeling sorry for yourself and find the safe.* He kept searching through the wreckage as the sun rose higher in the sky. After what must have been at least half an hour, he stopped, exhausted, and sat on a broken slab of cement, arms round his knees, head bent, eyes shut. He felt defeated, and for some reason his dad's face came back to him – not the confident, handsome face he remembered from when he was a child but the one he'd glimpsed in his dark room at the start of the earthquake: older, thinner and drawn.

It's hopeless, he thought. *Hopeless!*

That was when he heard a muffled ring on his right. And then another. It sounded like his mother's mobile phone. She'd often left it on the charger, on the side table next to her bed. He dived towards the sound of ringing, picking his way through the wreckage. Coughing, his throat dry with the dust, he squeezed through a tiny gap between bricks and a collapsed ceiling. He could hear the ringing more loudly now, muffled but persistent. The gap got tighter and he had to scrabble on his stomach over a piece of wood. It looked like the door of his mother's wardrobe.

The gap narrowed even more and the ringing stopped but he kept going now. Inching forwards, he threw a few ochre-yellow roof tiles out of his way. He lay on his front, propelling his body forwards with his elbows. He hauled a heavy piece of ceiling cornice out of his way and skirted the side of a shattered curtain pole. Then the gap widened again, and there it was!

The ringing phone had led him to her upturned bedside table, though the entire section of wall behind his mum's bed had fallen backwards, forming a downward slope to the ground floor. Fractured and twisted, this piece of wall rested on the brick side of the conservatory which his mum used as a painter's studio, downstairs. The space was large enough for him to stand up again, but he clambered down the slope on all fours, hoping that its support would not give way under his weight. The picture Leona always kept above her bed was still fastened onto the piece of wall. Geo lay on his stomach, slid carefully downwards and began to unclip the picture from its stays.

It was one of her oil paintings, the sort where you can't make out all the details unless you stand away from it. Geo's heart boomed with hope as he yanked off its last corner. And there it was right behind his mum's artwork: a safe! He set it aside to get to the combination lock, but it slipped out of his reach, sliding down the side of the sloping wall away from him. As he watched the picture glide away, he finally understood its meaning: two people standing in profile in rich mediaeval robes, with wreathes of tiny flowers in their hair. Each of them held a graceful, long-stemmed cup made out of shimmering gold, which shone on their faces, making them look like kings of old as they inclined their heads slightly forward, about to drink from each other's golden cup – the Cup of Love, Leona had once told Geo. In spite of their old-fashioned clothes, the two figures looked not unlike his parents, Geo realised.

It made him unspeakably sad to see the painting slip away into the darkness below, but he had more pressing matters to deal with. He wiped his stinging eyes on his sleeve and refocused his attention on the safe. It was black and square, about two feet by two. He fed the letters and numbers his mother had given him into the combination lock. KZC – then his date of birth, backwards. Click, click, click, went the mechanism eleven times. His heart thumping, Geo turned the handle and the safe's door sprang open with a satisfying clunk.

Inside it, he found only a padded white envelope the size of a thin notebook.

He picked it up, expecting to find money and passports perhaps. But where was the dreamcatcher? He tore open the envelope, and there it was.

'Oh!' he said, feeling physically sick. 'Oh!'

If he wasn't worried about Mrs Mandiball and her gardener, he would have yelled with frustration. After all this! Yes, he had found a dreamcatcher in the envelope, but no money, passports or anything useful. And the blasted thing was far from valuable: a cheap-looking hessian trinket – the sort you might pick up in any tourist shop for less than a tenner. There was a folded note, as well, on some lined paper. He read it, his fingers trembling slightly:

> 'Dear Geo,
>
> If anything ever happens to me and you don't know who to turn to, go home to England and ask Uncle Ian about your dad. Find out everything he knows about a man whose name is James. I'm certain that they know something, though they would not help me; too many family tensions.
>
> But you are Max's son. And they owe you, xx Leona.'

'Oh, this is all so useful, dear Mother,' he spat out. She had no common sense, no common sense at all. A normal parent would have kept money and passports in her safe for an emergency. Even so, he had to agree with her note: under the circumstances, if his uncle knew something about what had happened to Max, then he really was Geo's only hope.

He glanced at the dreamcatcher, running his fingers over the hessian netting in the middle of the main hoop. This hoop was perfectly circular and bore three tiny charms, each no bigger than a grape: in the central, dominant position of the circle was a fierce looking wolf-head; on its left there dangled a tiny, tough spider-web made of gold thread and encased in a metal ring; a fluffy white chick's feather was suspended on the right of the wolf-head. Directly opposite the wolf-head on the main hoop was a clasp, as though the dreamcatcher could be worn as a necklace.

Geo's fingers brushed against the white chick's feather. At once, something both terrible and crazy happened: he thought he was flying, hovering around inside a cell with a narrow grey bed in its corner. His mother, still wearing her white nightie with the frayed hem was fast asleep on this bed. And in her sleep, she smiled, muttering, 'Ah, well done, Geo! So you can learn to dreamboard, now, like the rest of us.'

When he came round from this odd experience or dream – or whatever it was – he could hear a man outside, yelling to Mrs Mandiball and her gardener to wake up and get a grip on themselves. Geo swung around to listen, crouching down in the rubble.

'Hello, could you send in the Rottweilers,' the man was now saying in a different, business-like voice, and Geo guessed he was instructing someone on his mobile phone. 'That damn boy has gone in ... What ... No! Point blank no! I refuse to be the one who explains this bloody mess to Prince Cromund.'

Geo froze on the spot, not daring to make a sound. *Cromund! Again!* What was going on?

Geo slipped the dreamcatcher back in its envelope and slid down the rest of the sloping wall into what had been the conservatory at the back of the house. He crept out through one of its half-broken cast-iron arches, trying to make as little noise as possible. He glanced up the hill towards the Mandiballs' mansion and saw someone fling open a window. Its glass pane flashed, mirroring the sun like a signal. There was the jangle of stainless steel from inside the house, then he caught the distant rattle of chains and loud barking.

Clutching the envelope, he bolted across the back garden, sprinted to the bottom of the estate and clambered over a fence. Running full speed through a neighbour's lemon grove, he didn't stop until he got to the main road and flagged down a passing car.

CHAPTER FIVE

Runaway

'The only house on the island of Zonissos to collapse in yesterday's earthquake belongs to Mrs Cleigh, an English recluse, living with her teenage son. Several neighbours reported that Mrs Cleigh and her son were alive and well after the earthquake ...'

Geo hit the 'off' button on Evangeli's transistor radio. He was sick of listening to yesterday's news about the earthquake. He was even more sick of thinking about everything that had happened to him in the last twenty-four hours.

Not that he had done badly. He had managed to rescue his mother's dreamcatcher from the ruin. He'd persuaded Evangeli's parents to put him up for a short while, telling them his mum had gone to the mainland to try and sort out finances for a new home. And he had already planned how to get to England.

He had not dared to share the truth of his mum's spooky vanishing with anyone, not even Evangeli. The way she had evaporated in front of his eyes was simply too mad to be believed and Geo worried that if he told her the truth, his friend would think he was having a mental breakdown. And where would he be then? Probably in the care of the very social workers and doctors he'd been so keen to avoid. No.

He did tell her the truth about himself, though: the fact that he needed to be travelling to England and looking for his father.

For the time being, he was staying in Evangeli's house, in

a long, thin attic full of storage boxes. He'd slept on a creaky camp-bed as far as possible from a very old, pooh-coloured armchair which, rather confusingly, emitted the faint smell of wee.

He had been checking the local papers all morning, looking for work. Now that his mother had gone, he felt he had nothing else left except find a job, save enough money for a ticket to England and do everything in his power to find out what it was that his uncle knew about his father before he disappeared.

There were several problems, of course. Geo didn't know his uncle and aunt's address or mobile number. Their landline was not in the telephone directory – Geo had already tried to find it. All he could remember was that their house was in a little square on the Brighton seafront. On the other hand, he was sure he would recognise it, once he got there.

Another problem was that seven years had gone by since his dad's disappearance. There had been an investigation and a police report, but from what his mother had told him, it had uncovered nothing useful. Geo couldn't believe there was no trace of his father, but seven years was a long time.

Then there was the dreamcatcher he had found in the safe. He was still very puzzled about it. Why was it important? What had it done to him in the ruin, when he'd touched the fluffy feather next to the wolf-head? Could he do it again? He tried to reproduce the experience of communicating with his mother, but couldn't pull it off. Why not?

He put together everything he knew about dreamboarding; all the childhood tales his parents had told him; his dad's apparition on the night of the earthquake; and the way he had managed to speak to his mother in the ruin, the way she had appeared to be sleeping, yet they had managed to talk to each other.

'Ah,' she had said, 'now you can dreamboard, like the rest of us.'

He felt quite sure that his dad had gatecrashed his dream on the night of the earthquake, to give him a life-saving warning. This must have been why his mum had seemed relieved when he had told her of his father's brief appearance. Then, in the ruin, Geo had touched the chick's feather. Perhaps he had infiltrated his mother's dream. But it had been a one-off. He couldn't do it again. Perhaps there was a correct way to touch the dreamcatcher in order to get it to work. Well, that's what he'd have to work out.

He was still studying the dreamcatcher, examining the wolf-head and spider ring and brushing the fluffy feather with his fingers, hoping it might give him access to his mother again. But he was interrupted by a knock on the door of his bedroom. He stuffed it back in the padded envelope and stood up.

'Come in!'

Evangeli bounced in, looking small and mischievous, in her baggy summer dungarees, her dark fringe all over her eyes. A tomboy by appearance but soppy as a puppy by nature, she was panting loudly, her round cheeks a smooth, tomato red.

'I've brought you a change of clothes, shoes and stuff,' she said, shoving a black bin-liner into his hand. 'Got them from the local church. Finding you a passport's going to be tricky, though. Can't we go back to the ruin and look for yours?'

'Too dangerous,' he said, and she nodded, thinking that Geo meant that the ruin was dangerous. Of course the real danger was bumping into the Mandiballs and their charming Rottweilers. But he didn't want to talk about that.

'Mind you, there is something else you could do,' said Evangeli. 'Since you need to go to England, I've been asking around, and — remember Yannis's dad who works in the port?'

'Yes …'

'Well I went to speak to him. Asked him how do people manage to slip into a different country without proper papers? This kind of stuff. Tried to make it sound general, you know, like I was just curious — Not sure he swallowed it, really. But he told me anyway.'

'And?'

'He says security at the airport is crazy. But the port is easy, especially if someone's working on the boats.'

'So I could work on a ship to get away? Won't that take for ever to arrange?'

It turned out not. There was an employment agency at the port that recruited last-minute cleaners and kitchen-hands. There was always someone getting ill or having an emergency and rushing back home or even jumping ship. *Or dropping dead* – Geo thought with a shudder, reliving the awful moment Mrs Mandiball's gardener had nearly snapped his neck. But he didn't share that last thought with Evangeli.

He was changing, becoming tougher and older. The earthquake had changed him.

Geo had soon filled out an application form using a convincing fake ID bought from some shady characters who made a habit of hanging around by the employment agency at the port. He'd borrowed the money from Evangeli, promising he'd pay her back as soon as he found his dad. Thank god for Evangeli.

By six o'clock the next evening, Geo had said goodbye to Evangeli, thanked her family, and was on his way to the cruise boats section of the port.

– CHAPTER SIX –

Bob Noxious

Geo took another look at his fake ID as he hurried through the air-conditioned waiting room. The departure lounge at the port provided a welcome relief from the August oven-temperatures outside. He checked the departures board and had a quick read of his letter from the employment agency. He was supposed to be a cruise boat cleaner by the name of Mike Ansell. He had some sort of employment permit and an official letter certifying that he was to be a junior team worker on board the cruise liner *Queen Mab* for a probationary period of six months. At least, he thought catching his reflection in a glass panel, he was no midget. One more week and he'd be sixteen. And as long as he lowered the black, peaked hat over his eyes, walked with the confident slouch of a man and glanced at people with that cool, tough look he'd been practising all day, he knew he could pass for an older guy.

The cruising tourists had already boarded and a young woman with bleached hair was staffing Passport Control. Yawning and filing her nails, she glanced at Geo's letter and ID and waved him through.

He allowed himself a minuscule sigh of relief. He felt like he was one step closer to finding his dad, but how many more would there be? What if there was an infinity of steps ahead of him and he never found him? No, don't think like a loser, he chided himself, why expect failure when you haven't even started your journey? The clue had been in the safe: if anything ever happened to Leona, he was to travel to England and track down Max with Uncle Ian's help. His mother's message had been clear as daylight. Have faith, he told himself, have hope. Have patience.

The *Queen Mab* glided majestically from the quayside on her way towards Italy. The liner was only going as far as Venice – it was the best Geo had been able to manage with the agency at such short notice. But at least he was travelling in the right direction. With his fake ID, he hoped to use his wages from the cruise boat to catch a coach or train all the way to England. It was his only hope.

***

The chief steward introduced himself as Mr Dysoedema and waved at one of his minions, a bored-looking, spotty boy of about seventeen.

'Show Ansell to Staff Cabin Seven,' Mr Dysoedema ordered his boy, shooting a spiteful glance at Geo's white-streaked hair. He had spat out Geo's fake name like a cynical remark, fixing him with his tiny beady eyes under bushy eyebrows. An icy shudder ran down Geo's spine. *Did he know?*

'And I want him in the kitchens in twenty minutes,' the chief steward added, an odd grin curling up the sides of his over-large mouth.

Geo hurried after the boy along a labyrinth of corridors. 'What's your name?' he asked, hoping he might make at least one friend on this boat.

'Bob. Bob Knock-Shaws,' the boy replied with a scowl, and Geo thought he had said 'Noxious' and gave him a piercing look trying to work out if he'd been joking. But Bob glared back at Geo with such a cold and hard look that he realised Bob had already made up his mind to dislike Geo. 'Here's your cabin!' he added, pushing open the door of a starkly lit cabin.

The cabin was crowded with six bunk beds, and not a single window or porthole. Everything in it creaked, squeaked and rustled – doors, cupboards, bedsprings and the six plastic-covered mattresses. Men snored loudly in some of the berths. Empty bunks were strewn with the belongings of staff who were out working their shifts.

Geo was stuck with the only corner nobody else wanted: a top bunk sandwiched between the entrance door that would not quite close, and a cupboard that would not quite open. Like a joke advertisement, the slogan "Cabin built for maximum discomfort" ran through his mind.

'Nice,' he said with a cynical chuckle. 'Somewhere to sleep at least.'

'Don't think you'll be doing much of that!' Bob said. 'Now hurry up – we've got to get back to the kitchens.'

Geo climbed up to his berth, dumped his bag on the mattress and was about to come down when his bag shuddered and buzzed – as if there were a vibrating mobile inside.

'Weird!' he muttered, because he didn't have a mobile – he'd lost it in the earthquake.

'Come on!' Bob said angrily from the doorway.

'Wait!' Geo tipped his bag upside down on the mattress and rummaged through his stuff. The vibration seemed to be getting louder and more urgent.

'Are you stupid or something?' the boy yelled, his spots glowing like little oily suns. Stop mucking about! It really gets up Mr Dysoedema's nose when his boys are late.'

Geo stared; under a tangle of socks, he had found the envelope containing the dreamcatcher. It was vibrating. He turned away from Bob. He looked inside the padded envelope without taking the dreamcatcher out of it. A muffled gasp escaped from his lips. The eyes of the grape-sized wolf-head shone like fluorescent amber in the dark, staring straight back at him. And the whole dreamcatcher was juddering and pulsing more and more loudly, like one of those alarms that get noisier the more you ignore them.

'What's that?' Bob scowled, climbing up the bunk bed ladder to get a better view. 'What have you got there?'

'Just an alarm clock,' Geo replied nervously, leaning over his bag so Bob couldn't see what he was doing. He slid the dreamcatcher into his right-hand pocket. He couldn't leave it here, not if it kept vibrating like this.

Immediately, mercifully, miraculously, the buzzing and juddering stopped. *Oh, thank you god of dreamcatchers, thank you!* Geo patted the pocket of his light summer jacket and hurried after Bob to the kitchens.

CHAPTER SEVEN

The Queen Mab

As Geo followed Bob to the kitchens, he put his hand in his jacket pocket and touched his dreamcatcher. It was nothing more than an automatic gesture, like when you are in a crowded place and there are pickpockets about so you want to make sure your wallet is still where you put it. The moment he did this, he felt as if the seemingly pointless clasp opposite the wolf's head sprung open. What was it doing? He could feel no more vibrations, but what if it started making a noise again or some other weird thing that would get him into trouble? Hurrying after Bob, he ran his fingers over the clasp, and realised that not only had the clasp come undone, but something else had happened, too. He half-lifted it out of his pocket and took a furtive glance. He could swear that the mesh of hexagons that normally took up all the empty space in the middle of the dreamcatcher's main hoop was dividing itself into two halves and neatly folding itself into the hoop's two semi-circles!

Bob Knock-Shaws was still rushing him along the many corridors of the *Queen Mab*, but now Geo was desperate to take a better look at his dreamcatcher. He fell back a little, pulled the whole thing out of his pocket and checked it. He blinked; it was like watching some sort of an illusion. Geo saw the last of the mesh vanishing inside the sides of the hoop. His dreamcatcher no longer looked like the sort of trinket you might hang above your bed, but like a talisman you could wear around your neck. And from the middle of the main hoop, the wolf's eyes shone with tiny pinpricks of light, searching his gaze, making his spine tingle. Perhaps he was supposed to put the dreamcatcher on!

'Hurry up! Bob said looking over his shoulder and Geo's guilty hand shot behind his back.

The shouting and clanging of the kitchens was very close now. They reached a short corridor that stank of blood and raw meat. Through an open door Geo saw a whole skinned lamb and several piglets defrosting on metal hooks hung from the ceiling.

As Bob checked his watch, Geo took the opportunity to raise the dreamcatcher and align the two ends of the hoop at the back of his neck. It fitted snugly, with the wolf-head sitting comfortably at the base of his neck, under his Adam's apple. He pushed the two ends of the clasp firmly together and heard them click shut with a soft, satisfying snap. He buttoned up the top of his shirt so it would not be visible. And then he had the oddest feeling: his spine straightened and, at the same time, relaxed. His neck felt a little longer, his head lighter, his hearing sharp, and his feet more firmly planted on the floor. It was as though until now he had been half-asleep but had suddenly woken up and felt more alive than ever. He took a few deep breaths, letting this odd, blissful sense of confidence wash through him.

What IS this thing? he thought, running his fingers over the dreamcatcher. Through the material of his shirt, he brushed the wolf-head and the feather with his thumb. He even held the metal ring, squeezing the golden spider web, which was fixed inside it, between his thumb and forefinger. He found it oddly satisfying, the way it fitted so neatly around the pad of his right thumb. He couldn't understand why it felt so good to wear it, but he was glad he had put it on. It was meant for him. It made him feel less alone; no, more than that: it made him feel special.

Geo smiled at the amazing secret of it.

But he should have known it was all too good to last; the moment Bob pulled him into the kitchens the smile got wiped right off Geo's face. A gruff guy in a chef's hat stuck a cap over Geo's head. It was not as stupid as a bonnet and not as sweaty as a shower-cap, but it did nothing to contribute to his good mood.

'What are you waiting for? Get on with it!' he barked, showing him a chest-high mountain of potatoes. Then he added, pointing at Geo's cap from which a strand of white hair had escaped, 'And get rid of that skunky hairdo.'

'It's not a hairdo!' Geo protested.

'Oh. Nearly died of fright, did you?' the chef laughed.

Geo didn't bother to reply. He just tucked the stray white strand inside his horrible cap, washed his hands, picked up the potato peeler and got going.

It was seven-thirty when Geo started work. He finished peeling the potato mountain just before midnight, looking forward to getting to his bed at last. But the grumpy chef pushed seven buckets of vegetables his way.

'Wash, peel and chop!' he glowered, banging a two-foot bucket of sweet potatoes under his nose. Geo counted to ten to calm himself down, and resolved to be patient. He breathed deeply, trying to connect with all the amazing feelings the dreamcatcher had given him a few hours earlier. He also made himself remember his destination, holding in his mind everything his mother had written in the note he had found with the dreamcatcher.

Then he turned his willpower into a work rhythm and got down to it, thinking about England, thinking about his Uncle Ian and the man whose name was "James" and who might know something about his father.

At two, when Geo finished with the vegetables, the chef kicked a trolley in his direction with mops, buckets, scourers, sponges and cleaning fluids.

'Clean up!' he snapped.

By three in the morning, it was time to pack up. Geo staggered to the kitchen door, barely able to walk in a straight line.

'Back here on time,' the chef growled. 'Seven-thirty on the dot.'

Geo nodded weakly. 'Seven-thirty in the evening, right?' At least he could try to get some sleep during the day.

'Blimey,' the chef sneered. '*Morning*, you lazy bum, or Dysoedema will have your guts for garters!'

***

Geo stumbled to his cabin, his eyes stinging. That night he slept for three and a half hours. His dreams were more colourful and vivid than ever. He dreamt of walking through an eerie night garden. It was a place of dark pools and splinters of moonlight, when he felt the presence of a shadow lurking behind him. Even before it began to close in on him, it filled him with foreboding. A second later, he felt it reaching out for the top of his spine. He shivered in his sleep, trembling, unable to defend himself or run away or even lift a finger. He just dreamt on, petrified with fear, while the shadow touched the back of his neck with its cold fingers and, to Geo's horror, began to melt slowly into him.

All of a sudden, the trunk of a silver birch in front of him spit open and a long-haired wolf flew out of it, leapt past him and pelted into the shadow behind him.

He sat up in bed, gasping, to find Bob Knock-Shaws perched on top of the bunk bed ladder, shifty-eyed, his spots glowing red against his pasty skin. He was clutching his hand as though it had been savaged.

A primal, low-pitched growl came out of Geo's throat, in a voice he did not recognise as his own.

'I was only trying to wake you up! Creep!' Bob grimaced, shaking his hand, which looked like it had been bitten. Swearing, he climbed down the ladder and left the cabin.

A wave of confusion and fear tumbled into Geo's stomach. He felt almost certain that Bob had been trying to unclasp the dreamcatcher from his neck. He also thought that, somehow, the wolf had lashed out and bit Bob's hand. Or that he himself had lashed out in his sleep, which was even more worrying – was this what the dreamcatcher did? Make him do things like growl and bite people? Crickey!

Geo took a deep breath and tried to calm himself down. It took time, but he finally managed it. He was in no doubt that the dreamcatcher had some rather strange properties. It had definitely made him feel good; it had some sort of a built-in alarm; and it protected itself, even when Geo slept. But how did it work? In a bit of a daze, he dressed and went to the kitchens, where he withdrew into a brooding silence and got on with his work – fish-gutting, much to his disgust. As he worked, he thought things over and over. What was happening to him? What if this dreamcatcher was less of a blessing and more of a curse?

He did the breakfast shift until ten, and then was ordered to a training session with the chief steward in a remote, featureless chamber near the ship's engine. The room was hot, airless and would have been horrible enough without the engine vibrations making everything from floor to ceiling judder and throb like the inside of a giant drill. Geo and a handful of other new boys had to stand in line while Dysoedema paced in front of them in his chief steward's regalia – royal blue uniform with gold buttons – his hands clasped behind his back and a cane jutting out from under his arm. He inspected them with a spiteful curiosity that made Geo's stomach churn, one minute barking military-style orders, the next droning on about the stress and strain of having to train a troupe of gormless retards. After half an hour of this, Geo, dizzy with tiredness, felt a sudden stabbing pain between his ribs. He doubled up, gasping, and realised that Dysoedema was jabbing him with his cane.

Though he was shorter than Geo, the man's little black vulture eyes were almost level with his own.

'Watch your step, boy,' he said, flexing his cane. 'Your name!' he snarled.

'M-Mike Ansell!' Geo couldn't stop his voice from quivering.

'What … did … you … say to me?' Dysoedema slithered his cane across Geo's cheek.

'M-my name,' he stuttered.

'My name, *what?*'

Geo was sure he'd been found out. His heart was beating so hard, he was surprised Dysoedema couldn't hear it. The chief steward drew his lips back, revealing a row of pointed yellow teeth. Geo stared, mesmerised, at the man's mouth. Waves of nausea crashed into the pit of his stomach.

'What word do you use when you address me?' Dysoedema asked, his voice level and low-pitched.

'Sir?' Geo suddenly realised that was what he might want.

'Sir!' Dysoedema gave a flourish of his cane, moistening his lips with a flick of his dark red tongue. Relieved, Geo relaxed his shoulders a little. 'And just so you don't forget again, moron, you're doing the night shift in the kitchen tonight, *and* the breakfast shift tomorrow at seven-thirty.'

And so for his second night aboard the *Queen Mab*, Geo was once again penalised with only three and a half hours rest. When he staggered back to his cabin, he didn't even have enough energy to kick off his shoes. *I'll just lie down for a sec. I'll undress later,* he told himself, curling up on his mattress like an infant, his hand coiled under his chin. And like an infant, he soothed himself by brushing his fingers against his dreamcatcher. It was the only thing that reminded him of who he really was – George Cleigh, he thought dimly, as he began to sink in the blurred gap between sleep and wakefulness. 'Yes,' he whispered,' and Mum said that I too can go dreamboarding now.' Then he wondered if he could use his talisman to speak to his mum like he did when he had touched the white feather in the ruin. As before, he brushed his fingers against the feather. Nothing happened. He then grasped the tiny golden spider web fixed inside the ring. That too felt comforting, but as Geo let his mind empty, waiting for sleep to take over, he had the weirdest feeling that something alive and furry slipped into the space under his chin. His eyes flew open but there was nothing there, except the lingering feeling of the animal's soft tail as it dashed away.

CHAPTER EIGHT

Unknown Land

The slats of his bunk gave way with a thunderous RATATATAT, Geo clinging onto the sides for dear life. Row upon row, they collapsed like dominoes, until he couldn't hold on any more. He felt himself falling into the void, yelling and bracing himself for the inevitable crash into the guy who lay asleep on the bottom bunk.

But the crash never came. Geo fell and fell, swirling like a leaf. The wind whistled past his ears, his tee-shirt ballooned and his hair streamed behind him, until, like a landing parachutist, he stumbled onto a mound of grassy earth.

He lay for a moment stunned and panting hard, before sitting up to check for bruises. What had just happened? He looked around and realised he was in the same garden he'd seen in his dream the day before, the one with the silver birch and the wolf. But this time, the wolf was not there. And this time it felt different. Neither the silver birch, nor anything else he could see, hear, touch or smell, was at all dream-like.

Judging by the shadows of the moonlit cypresses around him, it seemed like some place in Italy or Greece.

His stomach tightened.

'No – not a dream,' he mumbled, making a quick list of what dreams feel like: vague, random, illogical, weird – things happen but you don't have much control over them except that you might make yourself wake up. Reality, on the other hand, was clear and familiar – things happen logically and you can control what goes on.

He pinched himself, just in case, but nothing happened. He still stood in the moonlit garden. How had he got here?

'This is mad!' he muttered. He remembered that he'd been clutching the spider web ring and that he had deliberately emptied his mind to get some rest. So had this triggered something in the dreamcatcher?

He made a mental note to himself to try emptying his mind always, before using the dreamcatcher. How would he get back, though? True, his life on the cruise boat was not exactly happy. But he had no idea what to expect here, although he comforted himself by the thought that his mother wouldn't have made him salvage the dreamcatcher if it would bring him harm.

He took in more of the view. The night sky was almost starless. Wisps and rags of cloud raced across the face of the moon, leaving only an eerie light in the swirling darkness. In the distance, he could make out hills and mountains.

The trees were alive with the song of night crickets. To his right, behind a screen of cypresses, he thought he could smell the salt of the sea and hear waves lapping a faraway shore. He ran uphill to get a better idea of his surroundings, hoping to catch a glimpse of a house or road – any sign of human habitation.

He brought his hand to his dreamcatcher. Without thinking, he stroked the tiny wolf-head and muttered, 'What now?' to himself. He was answered by silence, and the wail of the wind, howling through the rocky peaks up above him. A sudden gust ruffled the leaves of the silver birch. In his tense state of mind, he felt as though he was being told off by an invisible presence. *Have I fallen into a parallel universe where wolves and trees can talk?* He thought. He gazed at the dark mountain that had appeared on the horizon ahead, towering into the sky. It seemed to draw him near and, with one hand clutching his dreamcatcher, he strode towards it, all the time wondering how he would ever get back to the boat and to normal life.

CHAPTER NINE

Oeska

Geo struggled up a steep, narrow track, which followed the contours of the foothills. Higher up, the track turned into a crumbly ledge. He clung onto rocks and bushes on his left, trying not to look down into the abyss that gaped on his right. Slipping and sliding, he climbed on, weighed down by new doubts. How stupid, to go up this mountain! What was he doing here? How would he ever get back to the safety of his own world?

He stroked his dreamcatcher, comforted by the thought that at least that was still there. He gave it a little tug, half-hoping it might take him back to his bunk bed on the *Queen Mab.*

Nothing happened.

Higher up, the path eased off, leading him to a plateau hidden among rocky, barren mountains. A lake gleamed there, its waters shining in the moonlight with a cool metallic sheen. He skirted it and kept climbing, reaching denser trees until he discovered a path that led towards the dark mass of a forest. He had no idea where he was headed but he felt like he had to keep going.

The scuttlings of forest creatures sounded much louder here among the trees, making him nervous. Beams of moonlight filtered down through the leaves, casting spears of silver into pools of darkness.

His path, which until now had been wide and clear, began to peter out in the undergrowth. He wondered whether he should turn back, but what was waiting for him below? Nothing, as far as he could tell. Geo took a few uncertain steps into a clearing. He thought he had made a mistake and tried to backtrack, but it was too late. He was surrounded by stinging nettles, holly, hawthorn and thistles.

He looked for another way out of the clearing, thinking he was retracing his steps to the path, only to get boxed in again by a wall of bramble, towering up all around him.

Fear swooped down on him like a bird of prey.

'What now?' he cried out.

There was no answer except the rustling of leaves. How had he managed to get himself into such a fix? He reached for his dreamcatcher and stroked the tiny wolf-head for comfort, his heart racing, his mind blank.

All of a sudden, he noticed the shadow of an animal among the trees, about five or six strides away. The long-haired wolf who had guarded him from Bob's thieving hands! His pointed snout and untamed eyes glowed like beads of amber in the dark.

Geo's heart beat faster with two conflicting feelings: the fear of being attacked; and the excitement of knowing that the wolf had already protected him that morning.

The wolf flicked his head as if to signal, 'Come this way.' It appeared scary, but surely it couldn't mean harm – not if it had protected him a few hours earlier?

Yet Geo remained standing stock-still.

The creature made a barely human sound; a mixture of words and howl that sounded right inside Geo's ears. Something that sounded like 'him-al'.

Then, as though the creature could hear Geo's confused thoughts, he repeated, the sound, this time more clear: 'Hymal – the Hymalayan.'

Talking to animals had never been Geo's strong point. Dogs barked at him. Cats ignored him.

What on earth do you say to a talking wolf? Was this really what it was? After being dumped in this parallel world Geo wasn't sure what to believe but at least the wolf didn't appear threatening, yet he had the most piercing, yellow eyes in the world. Geo was in no doubt that Hymal – if that was his name – was neither cuddly nor fluffy, but a creature of the wild. The wolf gave him another angled 'come this way' sort of nod, put his head down and pushed into the brambles.

Geo watched him go for a moment, then began to pace after him. Anything had to be better than being trapped among the swathes of brambles that draped the trees like barbed wire. He trudged behind Hymal, past thorns that caught his clothes and dug into his skin. He felt one nick a gash above his eyebrow and the blood began to trickle over his eye. He mopped it up with his sleeve and managed a couple more steps.

'I can't see how ...' he started, then went quiet. Something was happening to the brambles: a gust of wind; a loud rustling noise. Their long, thorny fronds began to move, and it was like watching a spin-drier – one second full of clothes, the next with its contents flat against the sides of the drum. The brambles were turning into a tunnel of green. Hymal leapt into the tunnel and broke into a run. Geo sped after him, exhilarated, curious and heartened by the notion that something good might come out of this at last. He fell into a steady, slow, rhythmic jog until, after a sharp bend, the tunnel opened abruptly onto the side of a valley.

The view took Geo's breath away. On the opposite side of the gorge, a mountain peak rose. But it was what was above this peak that was astonishing. Tied to the mountain sides by colossal chains, a massive castle seemed to float in the star-studded darkness, swaying gently like a vast spaceship.

Geo stood still, listening to the boom of the chains as their links crashed and creaked eerily amid the silence of the mountains.

Hymal raced ahead, sniffing the air. Geo sprinted after him down the gorge and up to the other side of the valley, until they reached the peak where the chains held the castle, anchored.

'What *is* this thing?' he asked the wolf, panting as he caught his breath and craning his neck at the immense floating castle.

One paw already on the road of chains, Hymal's reply resounded in Geo's mind: 'The city on top of Olyska.'

Geo knew it well. This was the city of dreamboarders, ruled by the Marshals of Tide and Time: Oeska. The stories his dad had told him rushed back into his head once more.

Trembling with excitement, Geo leapt onto several parallel chains, which seemed to form a kind of road, on which Hymal already raced upwards. Geo followed, picking his way carefully, knowing that he must not stop to think about what he was doing, must not allow himself to listen to his fear, or even to glance below his feet. The chains swayed left and right in the wind like some primitive jungle bridge. It wasn't so much a case of climbing up to the castle as of clinging and scrambling as the chain links shifted, clashing and pulling under the strain of immense forces, as if the castle was trying to free itself from its bonds. Oeska looked like it was desperate to float away – if it wasn't for the size of the chains and the strength of their anchors, Geo was convinced the enchanted castle would have escaped long ago.

Only when they reached the top of the chains and scrambled onto a narrow ledge that went around the walls of Oeska did Geo stop to catch his breath and gaze down at the mountain peaks beneath his feet. They seemed miles below in the distance. Then he looked up at the huge rocks and boulders built into the castle's titanic walls, which were so high that Geo could not see the battlements at the top. There was no gate anywhere in sight. Now they were here, how were they going to get in?

CHAPTER TEN

Hymal

Geo balanced on the ledge and concentrated on not getting vertigo. He wasn't doing a very good job of it though, and soon began to feel nauseous. He kept his eyes fixed onto Hymal who was sniffing busily for something at the base of the wall. He tried to distract himself from retching by tracing the rocks with his fingers, studying the way their grey veins merged with swirls of sparkling crystals and wondering if they would ever, really, manage to break into the castle. Perhaps they'd have to climb back down again, although he really didn't want to contemplate that.

He felt the wetness of Hymal's snout nuzzling his right hand and heard the wolf's words directly in his mind: 'Use the spider charm! Here.' And he pointed with his snout at an oval bump in the castle wall. Set at knee level, the bump was slightly darker than the rest of the wall, and when he touched it, it felt like a small, smooth marble stone egg. If the wolf had not pointed it out, Geo would have never spotted it. He ran his fingers over it, Hymal's voice droning inside Geo's brain, its odd, wolfish chant forming into words: '*The spider knows nothing of closed doors. She will come into your house anyway.*'

'What do you mean?' Geo asked.

'Repeat the words.'

'What, the stuff about the spider?'

'Yes. Hold on to the spider charm first,' Hymal growled.

Geo gripped the small golden ring, squeezing so hard that he felt the golden net, woven in the pattern of a spider web, printing itself onto his skin.

Geo whispered, '*The spider knows nothing of closed doors. She will come into your house anyway.*'

Hymal looked up at him, bright eyed. A gentle arc of turquoise blue began to shimmer between Geo's left hand, resting on the marble bump and his right, which was still grasping the spider web ring. With a loud scrape, the whole boulder shifted and then moved a notch into the wall. Geo pushed with his shoulder, summoning all his strength and repeating the chant. At first nothing else happened and Geo thought he'd blown it. Perhaps he hadn't said the words right? But then the boulder gave way with a sudden jolt and uncovered the entrance to a short, low tunnel that led through the massive wall.

On the other side, daylight was shining.

He took a long, deep breath. 'Phew!' he said, his nausea giving way to relief. He could now see a stretch of scrubland at the end of the tunnel. He walked through, stooping slighty, for the tunnel would not take his full height, Hymal no longer in front but at his heel.

At first, he was too dazzled by the glow to see clearly. When his eyes adjusted to the brightness he stood, gawping. In front of him rose a city bathed in light. He could make out pagodas, church spires, obelisks, mosques, great tombs and formal gardens. He saw Aztec temples rising up undamaged and Chinese imperial palaces surviving intact; the Pyramids of Egypt and the Hanging Gardens of Babylon were there, perfectly preserved, untouched by war and time. All the domes, minarets and bell-towers of the city glowed in the light that seemed to sway lazily in the air. And everything seemed to be made of some white, glassy substance that caught the light and glimmered like crystal.

'Is this where my mother is?' Geo gasped, glancing at Hymal.

Hymal threw him a disgusted 'don't you know anything' sort of look, then leapt off towards the outskirts of the city. Geo rushed after him, trying to keep up. They soon reached a built-up area, finding themselves in a labyrinth of narrow lanes flanked by classical town houses.

But there was something cold and unearthly about this glassy city. Geo had seen no one, and heard no sound except an occasional gentle clang, like wind chimes tinkling in the breeze.

They came out of the lanes and entered a city square surrounded by grand buildings. Hymal slowed down, sniffed the air and meandered to the doorway of an Egyptian-looking building with tall columns and imposing stone sculptures of Pharaohs who stood guard at its gates.

The wolf turned to face Geo. 'Who is your target dreamer?' he growled in Geo's head.

'My target dreamer?' Geo faltered for a second. What did Hymal mean? The only person he really wanted was his dad – well, it was worth a try!

'Could you take me to my dad, Max Cleigh?'

'No,' Hymal answered flatly.

'Why not?'

'Because your mother has already tried to trace Max Cleigh in Oeska and failed.'

'Why's that?'

'It means he must be in another realm. There are seven.'

'Oh! Can you access my mother then?'

'She is in regeneration.'

'What does *that* mean?'

'Living in the earthly realm for someone like your mother has taken its toll. Her tissue, muscles, nerves, and so on, need to revive and renew.'

'Um, right.' Geo tried to process what Hymal had just told him. So his mother wasn't 'earthly'? 'But can I talk to her?'

Hymal gave a small nod. 'Oeska is for serious dreamboarding. For a close relative you could just use the feather method.'

'Serious dreamboarding!' Geo repeated. Like it was some kind of sport. 'So – umm, let me get this straight – Dad cannot be traced in Oeska. Mum is in regeneration. So I can't speak to either of them.' He nearly added, 'Bloody waste of time, then, isn't it?' but thought better of it. It would be better to wheedle a bit more information out of Hymal. 'I've already used the feather by accident,' he explained. 'When I was in the ruin I somehow gatecrashed Mum's dream.' Hymal nodded and his eyes grew brighter. 'But how did I do it? I've tried again but I can't get it to work,' he added.

'Empty your mind. Then it will.'

He laughed. 'Emptying my mind feels just about the last thing I could do right now.'

'Not now, next time you use the feather.'

'Right. How about now?'

'Who do you want to dreamboard now? In Oeska you can find someone in The Hall of Records by using the spider web ring. A much more powerful method.'

'The Hall of Records,' he repeated slowly, making a mental note of this name. 'Using the spider ring.' He fell silent for a moment. 'Well, there's this boy, Bob Knock-Shaws. He's a bit too curious about my dreamcatcher. I've no idea how he knows about it, I was very careful not to let him see it. So … erm … I want to know – what is it with this guy? Can you, maybe, lead me to *him*?'

Hymal blinked, his expression so attentive he looked almost human. 'To gatecrash someone's dream he must be asleep. Bob is wide-awake and planning to rob you right now. We have work to do.'

'Not again!' Geo gasped. A wave of frustration was sweeping through him, and something else, too, an instinctive and angry need to protect his dreamcatcher. The wind chimes suddenly grew so loud Geo had to stick his fingers in his ears. The crystalline columns and domes of the square around him blurred. Hymal seemed to increase in size and his voice in Geo's mind became urgent, commanding.

'Climb on my back!'

Geo did as he was told, putting his arms round the wolf's neck. The wolf ran, leaping so fast, the world around Geo turned into a blur of colour. He could smell damp fur, dank earth, rotting leaves and forest rain. All of a sudden he heard his bedslats slotting back in place and with an upward swirling motion his other reality reconstructed itself inside the crowded cabin of the cruise liner *Queen Mab.*

A raw headache thudded at the back of Geo's head. Something was wrong. He raised his hand to his neck.

His dreamcatcher was missing.

His eyes flew open.

Bob's face, twisted with pain, wavered into view. The right cuff of his white shirt was stained with fresh blood. And he was clutching Geo's dreamcatcher. Bob scrabbled quickly down the bunk bed ladder, but with a lightning move, Geo leaned out of his bunk and shoved his fist into his face.

'GIVE THAT BACK!' The growl that came out of Geo's mouth sounded not entirely human.

The boy yelled, his eyes pinpricks, full of fear. He instinctively raised his right elbow to defend himself, and leapt off the bunk bed ladder, but Geo had already seen his chance and made a dive for Bob's right hand.

'I'll break your every finger if you don't let go!' he snarled, bashing Bob's hand that held the dreamcatcher against the bed-frame. For a couple of seconds, Bob dangled there, offering no resistance. Then something gleamed and Geo saw a knife slicing through the air. Before its blade sank into Geo, he let go of Bob's right hand and grabbed the boy's other wrist. He now grasped Bob's knife-wielding left arm with both his hands, pulling and twisting so hard he actually heard the crunch of a bone coming out of its socket. Bob screamed in agony and his grip loosened on the knife. Geo pulled the knife away but he didn't let go until, still screaming, Bob dropped Geo's dreamcatcher on the cabin floor. Geo let go and Bob crumpled to the floor, clutching his shoulder with his good hand and crying.

– CHAPTER ELEVEN –

Thud in a Lifeboat

'*How come I fought back like that?*' was the question that rushed into Geo's mind the moment Bob pulled himself up and ran out of sight. He took several deep breaths to calm down. He picked the dreamcatcher up from the floor, relieved to see it hadn't broken in the fight, and fastened it round his neck again. He went off to the shower rooms – it was early, before six, and he had plenty of time before his morning shift at seven-thirty, but too much adrenaline raced through his bloodstream. The last thing he felt like was going back to sleep.

He took a long, hot shower, thinking about Oeska and Hymal. What a night it had been! Now he was back on the boat he could almost imagine it had been a dream, but he knew very well that it had not. He was sure that he had entered another world; and that this world offered the only explanation he could think of for his mother disappearing. Then he remembered Hymal telling him how to dreamboard his mother by emptying his mind first. Well, that was exactly what he intended to do at the end of this long, hard work day – unless he got in trouble.

He was pretty sure he'd dislocated Bob's shoulder. He just hoped Bob's own fear would keep him quiet. But what exactly *had* happened, he wondered, under the cascading water of the shower. Geo had seemed to *terrify* the boy. Was he turning into a wolf or something? This idea was so ridiculous it made Geo grin to himself, as he stepped out and towelled himself dry. He was sure that Hymal, being the spirit of his dreamcatcher – or so he guessed – had made him ruthlessly protective of his talisman.

But why did Bob want it in the first place, unless he knew about its powers? As an object, it was just a trinket, it had no value; it wasn't the kind of thing that he'd expect someone like Bob to go for. It was made of cheap materials, hessian, string, a tiny bit of fur for the wolf's head and a feather. Maybe the slim band of metal for the ring could be sold for money? Could the ring be silver? Geo couldn't imagine anyone going through all that trouble for such a measly gain. But then, he had not expected Mrs Mandiball with her mansion and fleet of gleaming SUVs to be interested in anything that he or his mother owned.

He pulled on his clothes, wishing it was already evening and he could use his dreamcatcher again. Instead he had a strong coffee and made his way to the kitchens. Even before he started work, he felt tired and worn out, but he kept himself awake through the breakfast shift with energy drinks. He was doing OK until Dysoedema dropped in to check up on him.

It wasn't in Geo's nature to find people hateful but it was hard not to loathe Dysoedema. Luckily for him, Dysoedema made no mention of that morning's incident with Bob Knock-Shaws, and Geo guessed that Bob had kept it to himself. But he cuffed Geo behind the ear and jabbed him twice with his stick, criticising his work. And when he found out that Geo had taken too long cleaning one of the larger cabins, he called him a 'lazy skunk-head' and pulled him down the corridor by the white bunch of his hair until his scalp stung and burned. Worse than all that, however, was when he hissed, 'And if you don't start working harder, like everyone else, you're getting dumped at the next port.'

Geo froze. He couldn't afford to be stranded on some island. He *had* to get to the final destination port –

Venice. Even if they refused to pay him his wages, at least he'd be near a train station for the next stage of his journey, to England.

But at least Bob was nowhere to be seen.

'Where's Knock-Shaws?' he asked one of the other boys when Dysoedema left.

'Off sick,' the boy sniggered, for Bob was Dysoedema's favourite and no one liked him much.

His day went by in a fog in which, like a sleepwalker, Geo cleaned toilets, polished sinks, rubbed soap-dishes until they gleamed, bundled up dirty linen and mopped floors, working his way along the gangways that stretched endlessly inside the cruise liner. It was ten in the evening by the time he fell on his mattress, too exhausted to even undress. He curled up, this time touching the feather charm, as Hymal had instructed him. He closed his eyes and tried to push all his thoughts out of his mind. It wasn't easy, but he made himself visualise a small white square with nothing on it, then did his best to push away any thoughts that came to him. He repelled every one, only paying attention to the blank square. He imagined it growing taller and wider until there was nothing else in his mind except this formless, white space.

Suddenly, his body filled with the sensation of flight and he was soaring like a bird, skimming the water above a large lake surrounded by grand, imposing mountains. He could rise up into the blue sky, turn, swoop down, skim the water again, roll, loop and even fly belly up with the sun on his face and the wind streaming underneath his back. He whooped, ecstatic at the marvellous wonder of it, turning with his arms outstretched, going faster and higher, so that he almost missed the rocky island in the middle of the lake. Almost, but not quite; as soon as he by-passed it, he slowed down and did a glorious, wide U-turn so he could fly back to take a better look.

The island occupied barely the area of a football pitch but its grounds were hilly, uneven and thickly planted with pines, bay trees, myrtles, pomegranates and cypresses. It even had a tiny bay and its own rocky harbour. A single rowing boat was bobbing in its crystal clear waters, casting a trembling shadow onto the golden sand at the bottom of the sea.

Geo hovered above a pebbly beach past the harbour. Scents of pine, thyme and oregano flooded the warm, sun-drenched air. He flew slowly over the hill in the middle of the island, to its other end, opposite the harbour.

And that's when he saw them.

He flew down, puzzled. Behind the screen of a dozen tall, dark cypress trees, their tips stroking the blue sky like green paint-brushes, lay three boxes made of thick, strong glass. Each was full of some clear liquid in which three people floated; two men, with a woman in between. All of them wore long, leaf-green cloaks. He didn't recognise the men, but the woman, he realised with a start, was his mother.

He landed at once, hitting the ground running, stumbling and nearly losing his foothold. He staggered up, reached his mother and knelt next to her.

'Hey! Mum! Are you all right?' he asked anxiously, lifting the glass lid of her box which was hinged and easy to swing open. But he needn't have worried. Leona was floating, fast asleep, with her face out of the liquid, breathing normally. Under her cloak she wore a long dress that drifted around her in many shades of green and looked like it was made of bright moss, ivy and acorn leaves.

'You made it!' Her voice reached his mind without her lips moving. 'Well done!' She smiled in her sleep.

'Come on then, Mum, wake up properly! We need to talk,' he said, his heart drumming.

'No, Geo, I must not. I'm in regeneration,' she replied softly.

'Yes – Hymal told me.' He thought quickly – there were so many questions he wanted to ask. 'So are you one of the Marshals of Tide?' He still found it hard to believe all this was really *happening*. But he couldn't ignore what his eyes told him.

'I'm in their retinue of followers and attendants.'

'What does that mean?'

She smiled. 'This answer would be too long and complicated for this type of contact.'

'What's that supposed to mean?'

'You used the feather, Geo, which is usually for a brief exchange.'

'Oh, right! So how soon can you come back?' he snapped.

'There's no telling. But you're doing fine. You are learning to dreamboard!' Her smile broadened and her eyes fluttered almost open.

'But really, Mum, why can't you …'

'Geo.' She cut right across his train of thought, her voice firm in his mind. 'You can't step in the same river twice.'

'What are you talking about?'

'Water flows. Time flows. Life changes and so do we. I've been waiting for you to visit before going into a deeper, dreamless sleep. After today, you won't be able to reach me for a while.'

'What, that's ridiculous!'

'Let's not waste more time. The feather charm works only briefly, for a message. This one says, "I'm fine, Geo. I've been acquitted. I'm getting stronger. I love you. Keep learning to dreamboard. Be well."' She turned her head towards him, and her eyes shot open. She looked at him with the odd, unseeing gaze of a sleepwalker. 'But whatever you do,' she added, her lips almost moving with the effort, 'don't look for your father.'

'Why not?' he asked angrily. What else could he do with her gone?

'Because of Cromund.'

Then Leona, trees, island, lake and overarching sky dissolved, and Geo was back in his bed, wide awake. He had dreamboarded successfully, and that should have made him feel good. But all he felt was upset and confused. Trust her to forbid the one thing he had planned to do, the one thing he wanted above everything else. Why should he listen to her?

But at least she was safe – or so it seemed – and had been acquitted, even though he still had no idea what she had been accused of, in the first place.

Plus, he had to admit, she seemed well – healthier than she had looked for years.

***

The next day, for the first time on board the cruise liner, Geo worked a normal day-shift, went to bed early and even managed to get a decent night's sleep. He felt terrific, his work improved and he treated himself to a stroll on deck seven, an area of the boat that staff favoured after work. It had an amusements arcade where many of the boys in Geo's team came to play games or lose their meagre wages to gambling machines that promised to make them rich overnight.

He bumped into Jamie, one of the nicer boys on his team and they played video games, shooting green gunk aliens on a 3-D screen. As they went out, the August moon rose from the eastern horizon, casting an avenue of brilliant light on the waters. That and the sea air brought memories of his home island and of happier times so that for a moment he forgot his troubles. But all the questions that had been bothering him since Bob had tried to steal his dreamcatcher soon came back. Was Dysoedema's bullying just the random whim of a sadist? If Cromund really existed, then could Bob and even Dysoedema be in any way linked to him? What was the reason why Bob wanted the dreamcatcher? And why, after Bob's failed attempts, had they let him sleep?

'Hey, did you hear that?' Jamie said, interrupting Geo's thoughts.

'What?'

'A thud. In that lifeboat!' Jamie pointed at a structure of metal bars, which held one of the lifeboats in place. Geo pulled himself up one of the bars, lifted the end of a canvas cover and took a peek inside; darkness. If anything had made a noise, it was silent now. But, just as he was about to climb back down, something in the shadowy space of the hull caught his eye. He saw – or thought he saw – a shape crouching in the shadows.

He jumped off the bar, his heart racing. 'There's something in there. Can't tell what – could be a dog – could be a stowaway. Have a look!'

'No thanks!' Jamie said, moving briskly away from the lifeboat. 'A dog will bite and a stowaway will bite even harder. We should just report it to Mr Dysoedema. Well, you should – you're the one who saw it.'

'Sure,' Geo lied. It was the last thing in the world he intended to do. Then he grinned. 'I was only joking!'

Jamie raised his eyebrows and chuckled. 'Ah! For a moment you had me worried.' He checked his watch. 'Oh no, got to rush. I got a shift.' And then the boy ran off while Geo walked slowly to his cabin, his mind drifting back to the shadow he had seen in the lifeboat.

CHAPTER TWELVE

Diamondheart

It was the middle of the night and deck seven was deserted. Up above, the Mediterranean sky was filling with clouds. The moon grew dimmer and the breeze chillier. Geo had lain in bed thinking about the thud in the lifeboat and the figure he had seen crouching inside it. He had tossed and turned, finding it impossible to stop thinking. Something was drawing him back to the lifeboat. Curiosity, he supposed. Or just the satisfaction of knowing he was about to do something that would infuriate Dysoedema if only he knew. But he would never find out.

Under cover of darkness, Geo made his way to the lifeboat, slipping through empty lounges and up deserted stairs. He hopped onto the metal bar that secured the lifeboat to the deck, picked up the flap of loose canvas and peered in the hull again, hoping to catch a glimpse of the crouching form and find out who – or what – it was.

'It's a friend!' he whispered into the darkness, a shiver of excitement running down his spine. He knew he was being reckless, but couldn't help it. He'd felt like a prisoner ever since he got on this boat, but at least he was doing something he wanted to do now. No one knew he was out here. Dysoedema would be fast asleep.

Geo waited a few silent seconds, then leaned inside the lifeboat and switched on a torch he'd brought with him. He swept the inside of the hull with the bright cone of light, examining each plank, crossbar, oar and hatch. Empty. He gave a sigh of frustration. The shape he'd seen, or thought he'd seen, earlier that evening, had vanished. There was nobody there.

But Geo wasn't one to give up at the first hurdle. His eyes could not have lied to him earlier that evening. He hauled himself in and picked his way to the prow, shining his torch into every nook and cranny. Still, he discovered nothing – no traces of leftover food or belongings; and definitely no stowaway.

Perhaps he had made a mistake.

He was about to give up when he noticed a faint, musty, human smell. He ran his torchlight all over the hull a second time, more slowly and painstakingly. This time, his patience paid off. He discovered a tight-fitting disc cut out of the prow, and as he ran his fingers over it he realised it was a small hatch of sorts. It took him a bit of time to prise it open with a coin. Stuffed under it, he discovered a frayed old sleeping bag.

It was then that he heard a soft footfall outside. Heart racing, he switched off his torch and gathered himself under one of the crossbars. He listened as someone stepped on the bar, pulled back the tarpaulin and slipped in nimbly, without a light. Geo lay in wait, trying to plan his next move, or rather failing to plan it because his brain seemed to have jammed.

How stupid! What was he thinking, coming here unarmed? The stowaway approached, silent and soft-footed. Geo heard the click of a switch. The light of a torch tore through the darkness; he heard a sharp intake of breath, then a muffled, furious scream.

A girl? Before Geo had a chance to spring up, she dealt him a sharp kick in the ribs. He yelped and keeled over, gasping for breath, then staggered up, but she carried on kicking him.

'Hey, hey! Calm down,' he shouted, trying to grab her by the leg. 'D-don't be stupid! Ah… OUCH!'

She had dealt him such a kick on the left shin that he

was momentarily paralysed with pain. She snarled like a cornered stray, hissing and trembling with fright. He spotted her about to aim between his legs and leapt to her left, making a grab for her, twisting his fingers into the long, straggly tresses of her hair and wrenching hard. She yelled.

'Are you mad? Someone will hear,' he said in a loud whisper.

'So stop pulling my hair!' she hissed back, and he felt the stinging lash of her hand across his face but managed to shove her off with his elbow. She stumbled backwards, dropping her torch and almost losing her footing. He stepped forwards and grabbed her by the shoulders, accidentally kicking her torch into the shadows. All he could make out was the oval of her face, framed by her long, unkempt hair.

'I'm not armed, all right? I'm a friend!' he blurted out while he still had the advantage. But with a sharp tug she managed to wriggle free and counter-attack, this time forcing something painfully hard against his side. A knife?

'Out! Get out!' she said, pushing him towards his only exit at the prow, and pressing her weapon harder against him. 'Slow and steady – and no funny tricks.'

Geo did as he was told, his mind racing. He tried to make a quick assessment of his advantages only to realise he had none. But there was no reason why he shouldn't try to wing it.

'Look,' he said very slowly, in his most reasonable-sounding voice. 'I'm sorry! Didn't mean to give you a fright! Why don't you check my pockets – see?' With his hands clear up in the air, he let her rifle through them. Out tumbled a cleaning rag, a chewed-up pencil and a few coins. 'I was only trying to …'

'Shut up!' she hissed. 'Shut up and get out!'

'Fine,' Geo said, but he had still not given up. He needed to get her talking. 'As I said, I didn't mean to …'

'And as *I said*, shut up! Prat!'

'Thing is, I can help you, see,' he protested. 'Get you food! In fact, here, have a look...' Without thinking, he fumbled in an inside pocket she had missed.

She grabbed his wrist, twisted it and pressed her weapon still more painfully against his side.

'Ouch! Let go! S-stupid girl!' he cried out.

Flick! went the thing she held against his side.

'Aaaargh! Maniac!' he spat out, pushing her away. She fell back with a shriek, giving Geo just enough time to feel for his wound, for the sticky blood oozing out. But there was none. Surprised, he picked up the torch that she had dropped from the floor, shone it on his side and then on her hand. True, her 'flick-knife' had opened. But instead of a blade it had released a black hair-comb. Geo stared at it, astounded, before doubling up and bursting into hysterical laughter.

'All I was trying to say,' he spluttered, 'is that I've got some ...' He fished out the object from his inside pocket.

'Chocolate!' she said scornfully.

'Who doesn't like chocolate?'

'Well, I haven't eaten anything else for five days!'

'Oh. Why is that?' Geo asked, frankly curious.

'Because I ain't *got* proper food. Idiot!'

Geo might have felt annoyed that she had called him an idiot, if the girl's voice had not sounded tearful rather than angry. He was also very relieved that she was not armed and he was not wounded, so he just said, 'Oh, fine then, be like that! Though, mind you,' he added, hoping to cheer her up, 'even a chocoholic would not say no to an apple after a five-day binge! Why don't you let me get you some decent food?'

This seemed to infuriate her even more. 'I know your sort,' she scowled, 'lounging about by the swimming pool all day before your game of tennis with daddy.'

'What? I'm just a cleaner – I'm broke and I'm a runaway!'

'Really? Running away from what? Daddykins?'

'B-but I don't even … '

She grabbed the torch and shone it in his face, trying to make up her mind. 'No!' she declared. 'You're just a private school mummy's boy out for kicks, and you look like your nanny still combs your hair twice a day. Now go away, pea-brain, and keep your blubbering mouth shut if you don't want a real flick-knife stuck in your side!' She shoved him away.

'OK,' he shrugged, obediently moving on. She was spirited; quite unlike any of Dysoedema's teenage slave zombies. 'Look, I'll do you a good turn anyway,' he told her, not entirely sure why. 'I'll leave you some proper food tomorrow – right here, in your boat – no strings attached. Look out for it, late evening. I'll nick some!' he added, thinking this urchin of a girl might have a bit more respect for thieves.

'Oh, piss off! I want no stupid food from you. Anyway, I've got to move out of here now, don't I? And all because of you, you snooping moron!'

He gave a shrug. 'OK! I give up!' he said accepting, finally, that it was no use trying to befriend her.

But something in his tone of voice must have made her waver. 'Wait,' she called, her torchlight flitting across his back. Geo turned round. Behind the dim light of the girl's torch, he could make out the outline of her body and the shape of her head, framed by her hair. 'Tell you what,' she said quickly, 'you leave your food under the tarpaulin as you said – I might pick it up when it's safe – if it's safe! But you try to snoop on me or tell anyone about me … then …' She shone her torch under her chin and made a sharp, throat-cutting gesture.

***

'I wonder,' he thought to himself as he lay in bed that night, 'whether it's possible to dreamboard the girl.'

He was answered at once by Hymal's growl: 'She's not asleep. But you could try remote viewing.'

'W-what!' Geo stammered. The intrusion had taken him by surprise. 'What's "remote viewing"?' he added in a whisper.

'It's when you can see something happening in real time, though you are not present,' Hymal answered, his voice resounding in Geo's head. 'Use the feather.'

'Does the girl have a name?' Geo asked.

'Try Diamondheart,' the wolf replied. 'Diam for short.'

Geo brushed the feather with all four of his fingertips as he had done twice already and did his best to empty his mind. It was not easy. His encounter with the lifeboat girl was still vivid in his mind, her dark silhouette, the long straggly hair and the tense, moody voice as she had made her throat-cutting farewell gesture. It took him a long time to push all the swirling thoughts out of his mind and imagine a white, blank space. But it was worth it. When he managed it, he brought the image of the girl in his mind and said her name: 'Diam!' he whispered. At once, he felt like he was flying again, spiralling down from the cornice of a large, empty, room towards its centre.

Diam was sitting in an almost empty bar lounge, pretending to read a magazine but casting anxious glances at the door. Now he could see her in a properly lit room, he noticed that she had a straight, rather classical nose, jet-black hair, a fine, oval face, and the swarthy skin of an Indian or sun-tanned Greek girl.

He perched on the seat opposite her wondering if she could see him but she took no notice of him. He said 'hello' but she didn't hear. He watched her with curiosity. Diam's fists gripped the straps of a small mustard-yellow backpack that looked like it contained everything she owned. She seemed poor and unhappy and out of place in the opulent lounge, and she probably thought so too, because she suddenly got up and went outside. She climbed up a metal staircase to a remote corner of one of the outdoor decks near the ship's towering funnel.

She unrolled her sleeping bag, behind a bench and curled up inside it. 'I'm sick of tramping around looking for a good spot,' she said to herself. 'My lifeboat was luxury compared to this. What gives you the right, to take away my home, you stupid prat!'

'That's me she's talking about,' Geo realised with a pang of guilt, watching her toss and turn, as she tried, unsuccessfully, to doze off; but the wind changed and Diam's sheltered spot got blustery. She sat up, rubbing her upper arms and hugging herself, looking like she was about to cry. Trembling, she repacked her sleeping bag and started to wander around again, looking for a better place to sleep. She stopped outside a pizza restaurant on board the ship, closed her eyes, sniffed the air and sighed. She stepped away quickly, found a vending machine and stared at a large bag of dry-roasted peanuts, licking her lips. But when she dipped her hand in her pocket and counted the few coins she pulled out of it, she dropped them back and moved on without buying anything.

After more trudging around, she found an almost empty cinema where a bunch of bored teenagers were watching a free film about a lost fish with a bad memory. She picked up a half-eaten bag of popcorn someone had lost on the floor, and munched through it at the back of the cinema. Once it was empty she closed her eyes and drifted off to sleep.

Her image faded and Geo hung his head. He was tired and he felt guilty to have added to her troubles. That was when he resolved to find a way of feeding her the next day. With this thought, he drifted into sleep.

***

As he wolfed down a hurried breakfast the next day, Geo's eyes fell on a large clock at the far end of the canteen – a grey digital display of the time with that day's date underneath. It was in the middle of the busy, echoey canteen, among the harsh clatter of crockery, the scraping of chairs, the loud voices of people exchanging gruff words, the smells of fried eggs, toast and steamy tea, that the significance of the date slowly sank in. His own sixteenth birthday had, finally, arrived.

– CHAPTER THIRTEEN –

Cabin 19

He gulped down the rest of his breakfast and rushed off to his first assignment, polishing the state room corridor toilet bowls – and very elegant toilet bowls they were, too, though unfortunately no less smelly than their less magnificent counterparts. But the job had a definite advantage, being mindless enough to give him time to think. The old questions about his mother and her world flooded back in. Who were the Marshals of Tide and Time? What had his mother done wrong? What, exactly, was the danger of tracking down his father? And how about Diam? Would he be able to help her?

At the end of this unwholesome shift, he went on to scrub and mop corridor floors. From time to time, he brought his hand to his neck and touched his dreamcatcher stealthily, wishing that it was already bedtime. Now that he had caught up with sleep and felt less exhausted, he was looking forward to revisiting Oeska.

That morning the boat reached Trieste, at last; their last stop before Venice. Geo's intention was to collect his first wages, disappear into the crowded streets of Venice and find some way of crossing Europe by coach or train. It was a tall order and he knew it. But Uncle Ian, he regularly reminded himself, was his only hope.

At lunchtime, he stashed away as much food for Diam as he could – uneaten rolls of bread, packets of butter, triangles of cheese, biscuits, hard-boiled eggs and a couple of apples. At teatime he helped himself to a plastic bag from one of the duty-free shops and bought a blueberry muffin and a couple of grossly overpriced bottles of water with what little money he had. He added a small, sealed carton of orange juice, which someone had left unopened on a canteen table, put the whole lot away in the bag and waited until nine in the evening, when the outdoor decks would be less busy.

He went to the lifeboat on deck seven where he'd first met Diam. He had a quick look around in case anyone was watching, lifted the canvas flap and lowered the bag inside the hull. Would the girl reply to his note, left among the bread rolls? It said: 'Is this ok? Do u need anything else? If so leave me a note in the Games Rm on Deck 7 behind the Mad Rhino pinball machine.'

He made his way to his cabin, a little disappointed, but not surprised that he had not managed to bump into Diam all day. The girl was obviously terrified of being caught. And from what he'd seen of her, she was tough, determined and nobody's fool.

He lay in bed, stroking the feather with his fingertips, wishing he could see whether she had found the food. He managed, once more, to empty his mind of all thoughts. All of a sudden, with stunning detail that made him gasp, Diam turned up in the blank screen of his mind.

'Wow!' he mumbled at the clear, high-definition 3-D image of the girl. She was hiding behind a metal column from where she could watch the lifeboat on deck seven. But this odd kind of 'remote viewing,' if you could call it that, didn't last; he was back in his cabin staring at the ceiling. *What was going on?*

It took him several moments to empty his mind again, but he had not missed much. Diam had not moved from her hiding place. Geo realised she was waiting for the last few people to leave the deck, so she could check for the promised food. And there! The last family of four walked away, at last. Diam waited a bit longer, her eyes darting about. When she was sure that everyone had gone and it was safe to come out, she made a dash for the lifeboat, lifted the canvas flap and looked in.

'Great,' she said, seeing the bag of food Geo had left. She hesitated, glancing behind her. She looked worried, like she thought it might be a trap, but made a grab for the bag and darted back to her hiding place in the shadows. Her hand rummaged, seizing, snatching, tearing wrappings, filling her mouth with everything all at once and swallowing, almost without chewing, the food.

Geo watched her, grimacing, happy to see her eating, but suddenly embarrassed to be snooping on her.

When she had gorged herself, she drank the juice and rubbed her tummy. 'Hm,' she muttered. 'Maybe he *was* just a good guy. Who knows? Maybe they still exist.'

She rummaged in the plastic bag once again and saw Geo's note at the bottom. She pulled it out but to Geo's horror, ripped it into tiny pieces, walked to the railing and threw the bits overboard. She watched them, smiling, as they flew in the slipstream of the boat like a little trail of confetti.

'Why are you being such a cow?' Geo said, though he knew that she couldn't hear him.

'It's late,' she whispered to herself, and Geo noticed that she was stroking a little velvet pouch that she kept on a string around her neck, 'and I can't face another night outside.'

The pounding sea wind lashed her face. She tied back her straight black hair in a ponytail, collected her belongings from the floor and went to look for a place indoors. She strutted around the decks and passageways, head held high, obviously trying to look stylish and carefree, making herself smile, though Geo guessed that it was just a show to stop people noticing that she didn't belong.

Her eyes darted about. Geo couldn't tell what she was after, until she stopped in front of a small, unlocked cupboard at the end of a first class corridor. 'Great,' she muttered, shining a torch inside it. Two stacks of winter blankets, piled on either side of the cupboard, made it look like a nest. 'Shame it stinks of mothballs,' she added. But just as she settled herself on the blankets and fell asleep, the clattering and banging of mops and buckets startled her awake. She looked out through a crack, clutching her mustard-yellow backpack. Two boys had arrived – Geo recognised them as two young cleaners from a different team. They were talking about an elderly couple who'd occupied cabin 19 opposite Diam's cupboard and had just left their room to be picked up by helicopter.

'An emergency,' the taller boy said.

'Yeah, I heard, their son's been in a motorbike accident,' the other one said.

'Daughter,' the first one corrected.

They cleaned out the cabin and someone arrived to check their work.

'Out of my sight!' Dysoedema – of course. He cuffed the smaller of the two boys behind the ear. 'Off to the kitchens.'

'Yes, Mr Dysoedema, sir,' the younger boy said, scuttling off.

'And you,' he said to the older boy, who was clumsily pushing the cleaning trolley. 'Go clean the Steakhouse Restaurant toilets. Shoo!'

'Yes, Sir!'

Dysoedema, however, stayed behind and now turned towards the cupboard. For a moment, Diam stared at him, transfixed; then she withdrew from the crack and buried her head in her arms. Geo could swear that Dysoedema had stared directly at Diam with narrowed eyes, sniffing the stale air like a bloodhound on the scent of a rabbit.

Then, to Geo's relief, Dysoedema turned and strutted away.

Diam crept out of the blanket cupboard, took a small screwdriver from her bag, inserted it gently between the door and the doorframe, and wiggled, pulled and pushed until she managed to prise open the door to the cabin.

'Yesss!' she sang triumphantly, sneaking into the empty cabin. 'At last!'

With the door closed, she did a silent dance of victory, fists up in the air in front of an enormous mirror.

She leapt on top of the bedsheets. She didn't even bother to take her clothes off or get under the duvet, but buried her face in the plump feather pillow and fell asleep almost immediately.

Geo blinked. The image dissolved and he was back in his bed. Grasping the tiny golden spider web fixed inside the ring, he held it between the pad of his thumb and forefinger. As before, he had the weirdest feeling that something alive had slipped into the empty space between his chest and the dreamcatcher. It passed by in a flash, soft, furry and too quick to see, stroking the underside of his chin like the fluffy tail of the wolf, Hymal. Then, as he had hoped, the slats of his bunk gave way with a thunderous RATATATAT and he felt himself falling into the void.

CHAPTER FOURTEEN

Dreamboarding Proper

Hymal had been waiting for him in the night garden, next to the silver birch. Everything happened more quickly this time. In the star-studded darkness above the mountain peaks, swaying gently like a vast spaceship in the moonlight, the castle of Oeska awaited their entry. But this time, Hymal led him through the crystalline city to a different city square. There, the wolf slowed down, sniffed the air and meandered to the doorway of a striking building with gothic windows and long colonnades. Shallow, semi-circular steps made from white marble led to the main entrance. An uncanny scent of rosewater lingered at its doorway. With a flick of his chin and a flash of his amber eyes, Hymal pointed out the large ring door-handle. 'There!' the growl sounded inside Geo's head. 'Your starting point.'

Hymal turned tail and ran off, disappearing around a corner. Startled, Geo made to dash after him, but he was too late. The wolf had vanished like a ghost. Geo had no idea which way he'd gone in this mystifying city.

Geo wandered back to the doorway of the building, butterflies in his stomach. He had been ditched! Why had Hymal dumped him like that? He looked over his shoulder, hoping that the wolf would come back. For a few moments he sat waiting on the top step next to the door, feeling like a stranded tourist, before finally deciding to go inside. Mouth dry, palms sweaty, he got up and reached for the handle on the studded door. There was no knocker or bell, so he rapped on the wood with his hand, but got no reply. He turned the large ring, took a deep breath and pushed. The door squeaked and swung open.

Inside it was so quiet you could hear a pin drop. The only sound was a faint buzz, like the sound of electricity going through wires. The walls and floors were luminous white, as if made of frosted glass, and lit from below by hidden lights. But instead of being inside the hall of this building as he had expected, he recognised the rows of numbered cabins and now realised that he was inside the cruise liner *Queen Mab*. And not just any part of the cruise liner. He was standing right in front of cabin 19.

'What!' He grimaced and stepped out of the building. Immediately, he found himself back in the city square. He did the same thing a couple of times, getting in and out of the building, trying to work out what was going on; but the same thing happened each time. One minute he was standing outside the building; the next he was in the cruise liner, in front of cabin 19. Except that it was a different version of the corridor, with all the colour drained out of it and only this luminous whiteness shining all around him.

What was he doing, standing outside Diam's stowaway cabin? Was he meant to go in?

Like the front door, the cabin door was unlocked. He slipped inside and glanced around. The brilliant whiteness was stronger here and so was the electrical hum he had heard in the corridor outside. On top of the bed, Diam provided the only splash of colour: blue jeans, sleeveless green tee-shirt, black leather sandals and long black hair, streaming across her white pillow. Fast asleep.

He tiptoed towards the bed. The scent of rosewater seemed to waft up from her pillow. Geo felt a bit guilty, like a thief lurking around in a room full of unguarded treasure. Could it be a trap? Was someone about to rush into the room and arrest him? Why had Hymal told him this was his starting point? He took another step. Diam was breathing evenly, frowning in her sleep, her dimpled chin thrust forward, making her look dangerously wilful. The scent became stronger, reminding him of Turkish delight. He debated whether to wake her up. He wasn't sure what else to do.

His mouth felt dry. Bracing himself, he coughed loudly and tapped her on the shoulder.

'Hello!'

Diam stirred. She opened her eyes, stared at him blankly and raised her head from the pillow. At first he thought she was merely waking up, but then – Geo yelled and leapt back; the girl's body was dispersing like steam rising from a boiling kettle. Worse than that – as he stared, the cloud that was her body began to re-form. Its particles joined up and within seconds she was back on the bed, fast asleep. Geo reached out and tapped her – she felt real enough. But when he poked her, his finger went right through her ... not 'body' exactly but ... well, 'spectral body' would be a better word to describe it.

Actually, his father had told him a story about this when he'd been a kid. It had been about one of the Marshals of Tide boarding the dream of a mortal and how when a mortal dreams, his sleeping spectral body appears in Oeska so that the Marshals of Tide can board his dreams. "Dreamboarding proper" Max had called it. So this was it!

Hymal had brought him here for a reason. This was the spectral body of the girl he wanted to make friends with. He supposed the real girl was hiding in the real cabin 19. He unclasped the dreamcatcher from his neck and studied it. He grasped the golden spider web ring with his right hand, and placed his left on the girl's forehead, between the eyes. He wasn't sure why he chose the middle of her forehead, but it felt right. '*The spider,*' he chanted softly in a monotone as Hymal had taught him, *'knows nothing of closed doors. She will come into your house anyway!'*

At first a faint rainbow flickered between his hand and the girl's forehead. Then, a tiny tornado of gleaming silver spun between her eyebrows. In a heartbeat it grew as big as Geo. A short-lived wave of panic hit him as the silver whirlpool twirled faster and faster, moulding itself into the shape of his body. Gently, as if he was being swaddled in a silk cocoon, the whirlpool drew him in. He felt himself spinning, and at the same time shrinking to the size of a doll, a thumb, a pin's head, an atom. Then there was stillness.

***

He hit the soft ground spinning, still caught inside the whirlpool, wondering what was happening. Gradually, the swirling motion eased off and he was let out of into her dream.

He sprinted like crazy along the side of an impossibly long swimming pool, with Diam running next to him and Dysoedema chasing after them, shouting, 'Stowaway! Thief! Catch the thief!'

Diam looked scared out of her wits. They both knew there was nowhere to hide, but Geo grabbed her by the wrist, yelling, 'Faster! Follow me!'

'What?'

'This way!' he barked. 'Hurry!'

They did a crazy turn and belted down a remote gangway, managing to shake Dysoedema off for a moment, but they came to a dead end and there was nothing in front of them except the side wall of the ship's huge, white funnel. They could hear Dysoedema just round the corner, panting and shouting, 'Stowaway! Thief! Catch the thief!'

'It's a trap, fool!' Diam hissed at Geo, looking furious. She gave him a shove but instead of defending himself he ducked, fell to his knees and shook open a door at the foot of the white wall. But the door was so tiny, only a kitten could have squeezed through it.

'Great!' she spat out, aghast at the size of their only escape route when, instinctively, Geo slammed it shut again and gave it an almighty kick. The whole of the funnel wavered, like a mirror made out of shimmering water. With a sudden lunge, he pushed her through the wavering wall and jumped in after her. They both fell down, shrieking, for it felt like being thrown in cold water. As Geo slid deeper into the funnel, he caught a glimpse of Dysoedema up above sniffing around the funnel's base like a big, stupid hound who'd lost the scent of his prey.

But they were already out of Dysoedema's reach, gliding down a grimy chute, deep into the entrails of the ship. The noise of the engines came closer as they plunged deeper still.

'Dysoedema knows this boat like the palm of his hand, he'll soon suss out where we are,' Geo told her the moment they reached the bottom of the chute, their clothes black with soot.

'Look at you!' she laughed, gasping for breath. A fine, powdery black dust gave her a coughing fit.

'Look at *you*!' he coughed, shaking the soot off his hair. A puffy dust cloud formed all around them.

They slapped each other's clothes, spluttering and wheezing.

'That man – Dysoedema – we can't stay here!' Geo said.

Diam cleared her throat. 'I know a couple of good places.'

'Where?'

'TV lounges and a cinema?'

'That's the first place he's going to check now he knows there's a stowaway about,' Geo scoffed. 'He's not stupid you know!'

'Well, you find a place then!'

'Sure! Come!' Geo grinned and led her away to the bottom of a spiral staircase where a busker was strumming 'Stairway to Heaven'. Just then, Diam's dream began to waver as she started to come around from sleep.

***

Geo hit the cabin floor at speed. The immense, wheat-coloured field around him turned into a carpet. Pin's head, thumb, doll, boy: the gigantic pieces of furniture fell back, shrinking to a less scary size.

He looked around, dazed, and immediately knew that he was not in Oeska any more, or in Diam's dream. The luminous whiteness of floors, walls and ceilings had disappeared. Everything had returned to its normal colour and the eerie, low-pitched electrical hum had gone. All he could hear now was the distant drone of the ship's engine.

He was pretty sure that he had gate-crashed Diam's dream and was not in his bed, in his own cabin but in cabin 19 with the girl tossing and turning as she came around from sleep. Outside, through a large, square window, he could make out part of the deck. Beyond the ship's railing, the night sky and sea stretched as far as the eye could see.

'Ugh! Wake up!' Diam muttered to herself, yawning and shaking her head.

'G-good morning,' Geo said, his voice strangled with nerves.

She jerked her head towards him, her dark eyes as large as saucers, her jaw slack.

'You! How did you find me?' she shrieked jumping out of bed, her fists clenched and eyes blazing.

'Erm ... that's a bit hard to explain.'

'Will you stop *spying* on me!' she snarled, her face twisted with fury. Then she added, 'You ... you didn't get in my bed, did you – oh my god!'

'Don't flatter yourself! Stick-insect!' he blurted out, regretting it as soon as he'd said it.

She glared at him, blinking hard.

'Don't you remember anything?' The temptation to tell her about dreamboarding was suddenly overwhelming. 'I was helping you get away from Dysoedema – I mean in your dream – I mean …'

She blinked twice and Geo held his breath, hoping that she might remember their escapade. But she just gave Geo a withering look, then burst out laughing. 'My god, s-so you think you can get into people's dreams, do you?' She grabbed her bag. 'Just my luck to bump into a flipping nutter!' Sticking her nose up in the air, she pushed past him, flung open the cabin door and stormed out into the corridor. She stopped dead.

'You!' Geo heard Dysoedema bark, outside. 'What were you doing in that cabin?'

Geo peeped through the crack between the doorframe and the door, not wanting to come face to face with Dysoedema. He saw him making a grab for Diam, but she was too quick and managed to slip out of her denim jacket, wriggle free and bolt off in the opposite direction – but then she skidded to a halt. The corridor there came to a dead end. Between the dead end and Dysoedema, she only had one option left. She ran back towards Dysoedema, gave him a sharp kick and dived back into cabin 19.

The instant she darted back into the cabin, Geo slammed the door shut and locked it. On the other side, he could hear Dysoedema in a blind fury, whacking the door, shouting, clanking and rattling his keys, trying to find the right master. Geo knew they only had seconds before Dysoedema found the one he needed. His eyes darted around the room, looking for a heavy piece of furniture with which to block the door. In the meantime, the girl had made a dash for a large, rectangular window at the other end of the cabin which overlooked one of the outdoor decks. She was already unscrewing a couple of wing-nuts that held it in place, while Geo fell with his weight against the door. He could find nothing useful to block it with, but across the floor he spotted a thick rubber wedge that staff used to prop open bathroom doors when cleaning cabins.

'Quick!' he called out to her. 'The wedge! Kick it over!'

She threw him a contemptuous glance, but kicked the rubber wedge over anyway. Geo rammed it under the door just as Dysoedema found the right key and turned the lock.

Across the cabin, Diam finished undoing the two bottom wing-nuts and shoved the window open – a narrow gap, just enough for her to wriggle out to the deck. But the door now vibrated with Dysoedema's kicks as he snarled, 'I'll skin you alive when I catch you – do you hear me?'

Inside the cabin, Geo put even more of his weight against the door. He could hear passengers outside, coming out of their cabins to complain about the noise. That was when Dysoedema finally stopped pushing the door and Geo heard him on his walkie-talkie calling for help. Seeing his chance, Geo relocked the cabin door. With a sharp kick, he rammed the rubber wedge as hard as he could underneath it. Then, with two flying strides, he leapt across the room to the open window and ran after Diam.

CHAPTER FIFTEEN

The Jump

'Diam, just think of it as a night swim,' Geo said for the fifth time.

'Yeah, right!'

For the last twenty minutes, Geo and Diam had been arguing about how to leave the boat without getting caught. The more they argued, the more worried Geo got that if they delayed any longer, they would either be discovered or remain trapped on the cruise liner and end up going back to the Greek islands.

In those all-important twenty minutes they had arrived in Venice and the *Queen Mab* had just dropped anchor at the port.

'Look,' Geo repeated, trying to catch Diam's eye, 'there's no way that we can walk off this boat. Dysoedema will not let it happen. We can only *swim* away from it.'

'No way! This ship is as high as a tower block.' She took a step back, her eyes transfixed to the dark waters below.

They were standing at the edge of one of the decks next to a lifeboat launch platform.

Geo laughed uneasily. 'No, it's not that high, and anyway, there's only *water* down there.'

Diam looked down, her bottom lip twitching. Then, she drew back. In the light of the setting moon she looked a paler shade of green. There was no railing at that point. Only a tiny step separated them from the abyss of chill night air and black water below, a step as tiny as it could be deadly.

'You *can* swim, right?' he tried to peer into her face, but she turned away from him, hiding behind the drape of her hair.

'Yes.'

'And you're a good swimmer.'

'Mmmm?' Her voice wobbled so badly, it made Geo think of a sheep's bleating. 'I'm all right.'

He took her by the arm, trying to reassure her. 'Close your eyes if you don't like heights,' he said.

'What I mind is not knowing what's down there.'

'Diam, there's only water down there,' he repeated. 'Come on! We'll dive feet first. Trust me! We'll be fine,' he added, putting his hand round her shoulders. She shoved it off.

Geo wasn't sure he could call it 'friendship,' this thing that was slowly growing between them. All he could say for sure, since their hair-raising escape from Dysoedema earlier that night, was that she had stopped treating him like some infuriating stalker. But she still seemed wary and had not said a word about their joint dream. Perhaps she had forgotten about it, or if she remembered it she didn't want to bring it up.

It was now almost four-thirty in the morning. Geo knew that passengers were due to disembark after breakfast.

'When I was young,' he persisted, 'my dad used to take me for night swims. You just take the leap – it's the best way ...'

'And if the water is too shallow? What then?'

'I grew up on an island – I know a lot about boats, believe me!'

Diam stepped back even further from the edge. The more Geo tried to talk her into it, the worse she got. Suddenly, he stopped. A distant babble caught his ear. Above it rose the drone of Dysoedema's voice.

'Listen!' Geo said in a hoarse whisper. 'Dysoedema!'

'... checking every man, woman and child getting off this boat – personally going to scour every square centimetre of lifeboat, deck, cabin and hold. Nobody gets a free ride.'

'Except us!' Geo murmured, taking Diam's hand in his. 'When I say "Go", point your toes. Deep breath.'

Diam squeezed his fingers so hard it hurt.

Time had run out. A beam of torchlight flitted around their feet.

He tugged her hand. 'Go!' he whispered.

They jumped through the night air, into the shock of cold, pitch-black water. As he resurfaced, Geo thought he could hear Bob Knock-Shaws a long way above them saying, 'Sir, sir, I think I heard a splash!'

***

They swam until they reached the first empty dock. There, they pulled themselves up by climbing onto a rusty mooring ring for cargo boats.

On land again, Diam shuddered, wringing out the front of her sweatshirt. They had come out to the wrong side of a long fence in a port area probably given over to local traders with small cargo boats. Geo took shelter between two bales of hay and several bags of cement before taking off his dripping sweatshirt.

'You could always take some of your clothes off,' he suggested, stripping down to his boxer shorts and wringing out everything else.

'And you could always put some of your clothes back on,' she snapped, doing star-jumps to warm herself up.

Although it was summertime, a brisk breeze blew. Half a mile away the *Queen Mab* floated, its lights blazing, jewel-like, against the dark. Geo didn't think that Dysoedema had seen them, but he couldn't be sure.

'Better get going,' he said. With a shudder, he put his damp clothes back on again.

'That was a waste of time!' Diam gloated.

'No it wasn't. You look like a drenched cat, but *my* clothes are wrung out.'

They found a tree right next to the twelve-foot fence, climbed it and managed to use one of its overhanging branches to scramble over the wire. Then they put as much distance as they could between themselves and the controlled port area of Venice.

They left the busy, well-lit road that ran past the port, running across a flat bit of scrubland, over a modern bridge and through a couple of large car-parks, avoiding lights and police sirens. After ten minutes of steady jogging, they felt warm enough to huddle up on a bench between some houses and a quiet canal, where they managed to get an hour's fitful sleep. After daybreak they made their way towards the back streets of an area signposted 'Dorsoduro'. Both were desperate to locate the railway station, Geo because he wanted to find a London-bound train as soon as possible and Diam because she said she had to collect a bag from the station's left-luggage. They had spotted a railway track and followed it, in the hope that it would lead them towards the station, but to their disappointment, it only led to another part of the port. They were going around in circles.

'I wonder how far we are from the station,' Geo said, dismayed at the labyrinth of back streets and canals where they seemed to be already lost.

Diam nodded. 'We need a map.'

'Shall we look for a tourist office?'

But it was too early in the morning and the only people they could see were workers delivering food, collecting linen from hotels or rushing off to work. They asked around in English and when their efforts failed, resorted to any old rubbish they could think of or invent ("Scuzi me, but canne you telle us la derectiona to la staziona?"). They soon worked out that the part of the port where they'd come from had been much nearer the station than they had realised, but they had walked away from it and now they were lost in a maze of backstreets. The quickest way to get out of the maze would indeed be to get hold of a map, preferably a free one, from one of the tourist areas, near the Grand Canal.

Dog-tired and starving, they trudged along in the direction someone had pointed. They counted up all their money – ten and a half euros between them – waited a bit longer until the shops began to open, and bought a loaf of mouth-watering olive bread and a carton of cold orange juice. They were looking for a place to sit and share their breakfast when Diam pointed at a broken doorway wedged between a crumbling, uninhabited house and a building site.

'This way,' she said, 'We may find some stairs. Even without a map we'll be able to see more of the city and hopefully spot the station.'

They managed to sneak up to the building site and from one of the half-finished balconies of the top floor it was only a short leap onto the terrace of the old, empty house next door. The view from the roof terrace of the old house was breath-taking. They leaned over the railing. Bells were ringing and the sky lay all around them, blue and empty. Venice was at their feet with its red and ochre roofs, faded domes, bell-towers and houses the colour of hand-made paper. Geo squinted in the sun and he soon spotted a bridge over the Grand Canal and the roof of what could only be the station, with a long railway line bridging the lagoon between their island and the mainland of Italy. He smiled, already imagining himself crossing Europe by any means possible and trying to work out whether it would be easier to stow away on a train or a coach.

Satisfied at last, they sat on the tiled floor, warm in the morning sun, and tucked into the fresh olive bread.

'So … how will you pay for your ticket to get out of this weird place?' Diam asked, glugging her drink thirstily.

'Pay …' Geo echoed. He had no real answer. He had expected at least *some* wages for his horrible job on board the cruise liner. Jumping off the lifeboat deck in the middle of the night had not exactly been in his travel plan.

'You think Venice is *weird?*' he asked, diverting the conversation.

'Sinking, isn't it? And sooo old!'

He laughed. 'It may be sinking and old, but just look at it,' he replied, opening his arms. The city seemed to float in blue space all around him. Water shimmered everywhere in the morning light. The ringing of bells filled the air. And every moment felt razor-sharp and theirs for the taking.

'Yeah, it's spooky, don't you think?' Diam pointed at a nearby canal they could see from their vantage point. 'Look at that boatman in his pitch-black gondola with the plastic flowers and the red pom-poms! He looks like he might lead you straight through the gates of Hades to the realm of the dead.'

'Oh, very funny.'

'I didn't mean it as a joke,' she chortled. 'So – where are you heading for, then, after gloomy old Venice?'

Wondering how the same place could seem so different to each of them, Geo said, slowly, 'I'm heading for England. To talk to my Uncle Ian – my dad's brother. Though we haven't spoken since my dad disappeared …' he added.

'Your dad disappeared! How?'

'Nobody knows really – last we saw of him was in a blurred picture from a security camera in Cairo Airport. The police investigated, of course, but found nothing – or so they said. The ground might as well have opened and swallowed him.'

'What was he doing in Cairo?'

'Travel writing.'

'So why are you going to England? Shouldn't you head for Egypt?'

'Well, what's the point turning up in Egypt without any information? And the only information I can get my hands on is with my Uncle Ian.'

'Oh? How come?'

'Because Dad stayed with my uncle before he went off on his travels.'

'So?'

'So,' Geo said, getting a bit frustrated, 'Uncle Ian is the only person who would know who Dad went with, why, what his plans were … and I need a lead.'

'But didn't you say there was a police investigation?' Diam pointed out.

'Well, it wasn't a very good one, was it?' Geo snapped. 'Or else they'd have tracked him down!' They both went quiet, after that. Geo could tell from the way the girl looked at him, with a mixture of fascination and disappointment, that she didn't think much of his plan.

Well, perhaps she was right, perhaps it wasn't much of a plan, he thought with a sudden stab of anxiety. But it was all he had and he was determined to go through with it.

He looked away, suddenly aware of the cries of swallows circling the sky above. They reminded him of his island home, and his chest felt tight with homesickness.

He brought his hand to his dreamcatcher. He found it comforting, the knowledge that it was still there, firmly clasped around his neck. He had nothing, really, apart from this talisman, the clothes on his back and his fake Euro ID which he was pretty sure he could use as a passport. *If* they let him into the UK with a rubbish ID. And to think he had a real British passport, with his true name, buried somewhere in the rubble of his house! If it wasn't for the bloody Mandiball woman and her Rottweilers, he might have scavenged for it. But it was too late now.

They got up, climbed down the building site and made their way through the narrow lanes of Sao Polo towards the train station. Geo was determined to find a way to get to London. He might have to hitch-hike or find a way to board a train – jump over a ticket barrier? Hide in the luggage compartment of a coach? Board a passenger train and lock himself up in the toilet every time a ticket controller came along? He had no specific plan except to do anything that would get him to his uncle's house in Brighton. But Diam was heading for the station first. Geo knew that she had her small velvet pouch which she wore round her neck; and that whenever the railway station was mentioned, she smiled vaguely, brushed the velvet pouch with her fingers and looked rapt in her own daydream.

– CHAPTER SIXTEEN –

The Velvet Pouch

On the way to the station, Diam finally told Geo something personal about the bag she was supposed to collect from the train station. 'I've got to find locker 302,' she said, pulling a small key out of the little velvet pouch she always wore on a string. 'This is the key to locker 302, but I have no idea what's inside it. My granny – well, my adopted granny, technically – gave it to me before she … well – died.' Geo realised that Diam was having trouble even saying the word. 'All I know,' she carried on, looking a bit flushed, 'is that I'm supposed to use this key and look after it and not let anyone see it – especially not Anthon.'

'So who's Anthon? And why did you just show *me*?' Geo chuckled.

'I guess you're not as bad as I first thought; and Granny Zaira always said I'm a good judge of character.' She hesitated. 'Anthon's my adopted grandmother's son. If we were blood relatives he'd be like a dad or uncle to me …' she petered out.

Geo nodded. 'But if it was Zaira who adopted you, why don't you call her Mum? Why Granny?'

'Because she was old enough to be my granny and when you're adopted you don't want to draw attention to yourself.'

'Right. But why did you have to keep it hidden from Anthon?'

'Well, Zaira, she was quite an old lady, see. Towards the – erm – end, she got very ill. She gave me this key and told me to find the Stazione Santa Lucia in Venice and "claim what is mine".

'And then?'

' … she died,' Diam replied, her voice cracking a bit.

Geo waited for the moment to pass then said, 'So what did you do next?'

'Then I found out just how much of a pig Anthon could be without his mother around. So when the *Queen Mab* docked in Salonica just a few days later, I realised I was in luck. The ship was headed for Venice. I packed my things, went down to the dock, spotted a loud Italian family with lots of teenagers, jostled my way into the middle of the pack and sneaked in the cruise liner!' She gave him a smile. 'That's where you found me.'

'So how come you speak such brilliant English?' Geo asked her.

'I was practically brought up with three English children,' Diam smiled. 'Zaira's doing – she volunteered her services to a family of English missionaries in the slum where we lived and asked if I could play with their kids every afternoon. Best way to learn.'

'True,' Geo said. 'That's how I learned to speak Greek – though I'm still rubbish at writing it.' His stomach grumbled as they walked.

'I'm still hungry,' Geo said, 'and we've hardly got enough for a decent meal.'

'Let's go to the station first, then we can think about food.'

'When I'm at the station, I'll only be able to think about stowing away on a train to England.'

'Why train – if you're that desperate, why not go to the airport?'

'Last time a boy stowed away in the hold of the plane with the luggage, he froze to death. The hold isn't heated like the cabin is. I'm not risking that!'

'What if you had the money for a proper ticket?'

'Then I wouldn't risk it for other reasons.'

'Dodgy papers?'

'Exactly,' he replied.

'Wise move,' she said. 'We'll find a way of getting you on the train to England.'

'Even if it means hanging like a monkey on the underside of a carriage,' he laughed.

'Or hypnotising the ticket office clerk into giving you a freebie.'

'Oh, that *would* be nice!' Geo chuckled, liking her more and more. She was sharp and funny and he felt lucky to have her as an ally. 'Right,' he added cheerfully, leading the way towards the station. Let's collect your package from that locker first. Then we'll see.

'Good.' Then, out of the blue, she added, 'Can I come with you?'

'Sure! Why would you want to go to London, though?'

She gave a surprised laugh. 'Why would I not!'

***

Only a couple of streets away from the Stazione Santa Lucia, Geo felt someone watching him. He turned around and saw the shadowy figure of a man slip out of a dark doorway.

'Dysoedema!' he gasped. 'Just what we need!'

Diam glanced back. With a sharp intake of breath she broke into a run. Even though the man's face was obscured by the shadow of a Panama hat, it was unmistakeably Dysoedema. Somehow, he'd tracked them down. Though he wasn't running so much as walking behind them at a steady and slightly robotic pace, yet he managed not to fall behind. In fact, he seemed to be getting closer.

'Too slow!' Geo grabbed Diam by the wrist and they sprinted around a small crowd of children, a street performer, various stalls selling trinkets and across a canal bridge. Fear stirred in the pit of Geo's stomach; each time he turned around in the hope that they had shaken the man off, he was there. Closer. They were sprinting at full speed now but Dysoedema walked relentlessly on, at the same, steady, rhythmic pace, closing the distance between them. Geo's lungs ached and a stitch throbbed in his side. He didn't think they could keep running for much longer.

They hared through a passage cobbled with granite stones, under a crumbling arch, through a maze of lanes, and still, every time Geo looked behind him, the man had got closer – within just a few metres now.

'This is mad,' Diam panted as they dashed over a rickety old bridge and round a corner.

'Faster!' Geo urged.

'Well, what can he do to us?'

'I don't want to find out!' He pulled her on, and they stumbled round a corner into another narrow, cobbled lane. Immediately to their left he saw the door of a tiny, scruffy old church tucked away next to a fruit shop. Without even looking behind him, Geo saw his chance, grabbing Diam by the wrist and making a dive for the church door. Dripping with sweat and almost doubled up with pain, they hid around the back of the crowd – it was a christening, Geo realised, casting nervous glances towards the door.

He looked up at the statue of a small, friendly-looking mother in a cornflower blue dress. It wasn't his style at all, but probably for the first time in his life, he squeezed his eyes shut and expressed a sincere readiness to accept any help from anyone, anywhere and at any price. No help arrived of course, so he took Diam by the hand and they jostled their way into the middle of the crowd as close to the child as possible.

A dark shadow passed overhead, casting a chilly gloom over the entrance – then lifted slowly, until sunlight bathed the doorway once again.

Geo and Diam waited until every last member of the colourful, noisy congregation had gone away, before peering cautiously out.

'The coast is clear!' Geo laughed, almost in surprise. 'We've done it.'

Somehow Dysoedema had never made it inside the building.

CHAPTER SEVENTEEN

Locker 302

As it was August, the station was very busy.

'What I don't get,' Diam said as they walked through the low-rise entrance, 'was the way we kept running and he kept walking, but he was always getting closer!'

Geo nodded. 'I don't either, but then there's an awful lot of stuff that I don't get.'

They found the ticket office and Diam asked where she could find the left-luggage area, while Geo kept scanning the station for Dysoedema, unable to fully believe they'd got rid of him – *once and for all*, he kept repeating to himself, though a little voice at the back of his head insisted that he could be wrong. Desperate to get on a train to London, he said, 'Why don't I queue up at the ticket office while you look for your locker? Just to find out ticket prices – you never know, there may be a special offer.'

'Special!' she scoffed. 'Are you kidding me? There's no chance we've got enough for tickets to London. If you don't mind, I'd rather you came with me.' She led him to a bank of lockers on the ground floor of the station and stopped in front of the one labelled 302. Curious about what was inside it, Geo tried to keep a polite distance, pretending to read a discarded newspaper even though it was in Italian and he was holding it upside down.

But he needn't have bothered. The moment Diam inserted her little key in to the lock, she beckoned him over. 'Stand next to me,' she said quickly. 'Hide me from view and keep an eye out for prying strangers.'

Frowning and pursing her lips, she turned the key. The locker door swung open with a clang. Her face lit up as she pulled out a travel bag. Unzipping it, she rummaged around at the bottom, pulling out several rectangular packages wrapped in newspaper that looked, to Geo's eye, like wads of money. At the bottom of the bag she found a small blue package in a turquoise silk cloth. When she unwrapped it, she found a blue cardboard box labelled 'REALITY CHECK CARDS' and under the cards she discovered a letter that she browsed quickly, then stuffed in her pocket. She looked up at him, her dark eyes sparkling. 'A letter!' she told him. 'From my real mother! Un-believable! And money too. And the cards!' she nodded, smiling. Opening the blue box, she had a quick look inside. 'Nice!' she added. Geo wondered why he had never heard of this game before. Then she unwrapped a couple of the newspaper-wrapped wads.

It really was money.

'Yay!' She gave a laugh. 'Zaira did keep her word. I mean, it may not be much by most people's standards, but to me it's a fortune.' She held up the creamy envelope made of expensive-looking parchment. 'My mother says we'll meet when the time is right – and other stuff. Oh, I hope it's true.' She hugged him and Geo felt two little circles of wetness grow just below his shoulder from her tears.

'Feel free to blow your nose on the sleeve,' he teased.

They laughed and separated.

'Well, it looks like we can buy our fares outright – no need to be stowaways!' Diam said.

'What?'

'I mean, there's no need for you to hang from the underside of a carriage all the way to London,' she chuckled.

'But I …' He could feel his eyes widening.

'Oh, stop it!'

'I don't know what to say…' Geo said, touched by her generosity.

'How about "Great" or "Thank you"? Take your pick.'

'Thank you, of course, but …' he gave a big smile. Now London really did feel within touching distance.

'What does it take for you to accept?' Anyway,' she added, 'perhaps that uncle of yours will let me stay too when we get to England.'

Linda's exceptionally ugly extra-terrestrial-style frown came to his mind. He didn't want to make empty promises on behalf of his uncle and aunt. 'But why do you want to go to England?' he asked, frankly interested.

She scratched her head. 'Why not? Anyway, isn't that where *you* are going?'

'Yes.'

'So? Why can't I come with you? Unless you'd rather I went back to Salonica and Anthon.'

'No, of course not! I mean, I can't guarantee that Ian and Linda are still going to be at the same address. But if they haven't moved on, well – I will definitely talk to them. And they've got many more rooms than they can use.'

'Lovely. It's a deal then! Though my aunt *is* a bit of an ogre,' he added as an afterthought.

'I can handle an ogre!'

'… and their house is a bit of a zoo!'

'What, smelly?'

'No; just too many pets.'

Diam laughed. 'Oh, I don't mind – as long as they don't feed me to any crocodiles!'

***

Although they now had money, they stuck to their decision to travel by train, still hoping that it would probably be easier to get through passport control by avoiding airports. They also avoided the faster routes via Switzerland, deciding instead to cross the smallest number of borders even though it meant using slower, local trains.

Their journey from northern Italy across to south-east France would have been pleasant enough if it wasn't for the weather, which was stifling hot and humid. On board the train, it was like being in a steamy kitchen with all the ovens blazing – and Geo had enough recent experience of that in the cruise ship's kitchens. The skies boiled with steel-grey clouds, occasionally exploding with thunder and lightning.

They changed at Marseilles and headed inland, chugging through tunnels and up hills, across plains, into green valleys, over bridges and through sleepy towns, fragrant with geraniums. Booking a cabin seemed like a waste of good money so they slept in their seats instead. Geo was careful not to touch his dreamcatcher in his sleep because he didn't trust himself to dreamboard in a public place. He hadn't talked to Diam about it – not yet, not until they were some place private.

Perhaps because the weather was humid and their train air-conditioning system didn't work very well, he was plagued by nightmares of being trapped in a greenhouse where everything was rotting and there was never enough air to breathe.

In Lyons they boarded a train bound for Paris and from there they zoomed across Northern France towards Britain. But even before they had a chance to go across in the Channel Tunnel, a passport controller came to check their documents. Diam was given her passport back at once, with a brief nod. But Geo was asked to follow the controller to an area of the train where there was a small queue of passengers in front of a desk.

'What is the purpose of your visit?' the man asked Geo once he finally reached the front.

'To visit relatives,' Geo replied politely, trying to still his shaking hands.

The man asked Geo plenty of questions about the names of his parents, his school, his address in Greece and the

UK address he was heading for. Geo replied maintaining eye contact and hoping to god that no actual record of Mike Ansell – which the man was searching for – would turn up on the man's screen. While they spoke, Geo managed to control his quivering voice and gave the version of the truth with which he was most familiar. Too many lies would have him blushing and unable to keep track of it all. He told him that he was the son of Leona and Max 'Ansell'. He gave the name of the Greek school he had gone to, told them that his parents were English but permanent residents in Greece and that he was being met by his uncle and aunt at the station, his mother having made all the arrangements in advance.

His ID was checked, re-checked and scrutinised until, in the end, to Geo's great relief, the passport controller waved him away.

He went back and collapsed on his seat, quietly hyperventilating for at least five minutes before managing to tell Diam everything that had happened. She squeezed his hand in sympathy, told him to wait right there, went to the buffet car and came back with a massive bag of chocolate buttons and two cokes.

And so they celebrated their ride through the tunnel and subsequent arrival in England.

They reached Brighton after lunch on a cool summer Friday afternoon, three hours after their official entry to the country. All Geo remembered of Ian and Linda's address was that they lived in a cavernous house not far from the sea front in Hove. And that it had a round turret jutting up on one side of the roof, which gave it a rather haunted look.

Geo and his mother had visited them after Max's disappearance. Their visit had been brief. Things had been said, accusations had been made and offence had been taken about Ian and Linda supposedly knowing more about his father than they let on. Counter-accusations had been made about 'it' being Leona's fault in the first place. Though what 'it' was, exactly, Geo had never found out.

His mum had lost her temper and shouted at Linda. Linda had shouted back.

They had not been invited to stay for tea.

Geo had deliberately blotted this incident out of his memory. If he had dwelt on it, he would have probably not bothered coming. And he would have certainly not brought a random guest he had discovered stowing away in a cruise liner.

He spotted his uncle's house after walking around Hove for nearly an hour. The front garden was overgrown, the windowpanes dirty, the curtains drawn and the rubbish bin had been abandoned in the middle of the front yard. Exhausted and hungry, Geo and Diam rang the bell, rapped on the heavy door with its dusty stained-glass panels and then banged on it. But the door stayed firmly shut.

He threw a couple of pebbles at the first floor windows in case his uncle and aunt were upstairs and could not hear – he wasn't giving up easily. Nobody came to the door – until Geo aimed one last pebble at an upstairs window on the side of the house. Only then did he hear someone storming down the stairs.

The door was yanked open. A furious-looking woman glared out at them.

CHAPTER EIGHTEEN

Linda's Welcome

'What do you want?'

Geo's aunt scowled as though she had found them not on her doorstep but in the dining room, stealing her silverware. Years of disapproval had drawn deep lines all over her thin, pinched face. Even her faded old tee-shirt and shapeless leggings managed somehow to look offended. But in her arms she held two beautiful kittens, all whiskers and big round eyes, peeping out of a cream towel.

'Aunt Linda, don't you remember me? It's me, Geo!'

There was an audible intake of breath.

'Ah! Didn't recognise you. So tall!' There was a pause during which her eyes darted around. 'Where's your mother?' She asked, giving a nervous laugh and craning her neck over the threshold.

'I'm afraid Mum's not very well…' Geo lied. 'She's staying with friends,' he added cautiously.

'What, here?' she asked. 'Is she in the UK?'

'Erm…in Greece,' he replied uncomfortably, and his aunt looked visibly relieved. 'Is Uncle Ian at home?'

'No.'

Geo waited for an invitation to go inside, but it didn't come.

'H-he's at work then?' he checked.

'That's right.'

'W-would you mind if we waited for him?'

Linda moved aside grudgingly and they followed her along a cold, dark corridor. Diam accompanied him in silence, her eyes taking in the ornate plaster ceilings and the tiled Victorian floors. At the far end of the corridor they were shown to a messy but sunny living room at the back of the house.

Geo would have loved to accost Linda with every question that had passed through his mind about his father's last visit. But his aunt carried on in the same grumpy, irritable manner and he realised that to pester her would do more harm than good. They both collapsed in a long, comfy sofa that overlooked the back garden. Geo fought back his frustration, and resolved to keep his mouth shut until his uncle came home.

Everything was exactly as he remembered it. The smell of damp dogs lingered in the air. Thick Persian carpets lay on the creaky floorboards. The deep, feather-filled sofas were covered with cat hairs and newspapers, and the coffee tables were stacked with books, bills, unwashed mugs and letters. Mysterious paintings, mostly of people wearing animal masks, hung on the walls. And through the wide-open glass doors lay a perfect English garden in full bloom.

Geo introduced Diam to his aunt. Linda put the kittens in their basket, made her visitors cups of tea and even managed to bring herself to offer them a tiny scone each. They scoffed the food like hungry pigeons, while Geo explained about the earthquake and the reason for his trip to England. But he held back his mother's disappearance – and of course anything about the dreamcatcher, Mrs Mandiball or Dysoedema. She'd just think he was crazy. As it was, Linda didn't seem curious or interested, not even when he described the house collapsing. She just sat there, straight-faced, stroking one of her golden retrievers. The dogs seemed to pay more attention to Geo's story than his aunt did. The only personal comment she made was when she suddenly fixed her eyes on the white streak in his hair and said, 'Trendy hairstyle.'

Geo thanked her, not knowing what else to say.

'Is it inspired by the skunk species?' she added, sounding truthfully curious.

Luckily, his uncle Ian was expected from work early that Friday afternoon. He finally arrived just after Geo's third pretend visit to an upstairs loo from where he sneaked around the various rooms, looking for – he wasn't sure what, exactly; pictures of his father? Stray clues about Max's last stay with Ian and Linda? Clues about "James," the man Geo was supposed to ask Uncle Ian about?

But he didn't find anything anyway and then he heard Ian coming in and dashed downstairs.

Geo had always thought Ian looked a bit Humpty Dumptyish, but nowadays he seemed even more egg-shaped than he remembered, having shaved his head and increased his girth.

'Geo!' Ian exclaimed, giving him a bear hug. 'What a surprise! What a fantastic hairdo, by the way!'

Geo patted down his hair, feeling self-conscious and giving Ian a half-hearted smile; no use explaining how he'd got his white tuft.

Not noticing his discomfort, his uncle carried on with more cheerfully personal comments: 'Now, I know no teenager likes to hear this, but you *are* the spitting image of your dad! It's great to see you. '

Then his uncle flopped down in an overstuffed armchair and was introduced to Diam.

'So where's your mum?' he asked and Geo repeated his story, adding that he had come to ask Ian a couple of questions about his dad. And so, in between Ian's offers of cold milk and cheese on toast, which they devoured ravenously, they got down to talking about Max Cleigh.

'I was hoping,' Geo started, deciding to ask about James last, 'that you and Linda might give me a lead, seeing as Dad stayed with you before his trip to Egypt … I've really got to find out what happened.'

'It's a bit late to be looking for that, seven years after the event, isn't it?' Linda cut in. 'We told the police everything we knew.'

'Right.' Geo stared at the bright patterns on the carpet, trying to think straight. Linda's dismissive tone was getting to him. 'Yeah, I suppose it *has* been a long time. Maybe we could just ... talk?' Geo pressed. 'About Dad, I mean ...'

'But Geo, talk about *what* exactly?' Linda interrupted again, struggling up from a low armchair to resume her kitten-mothering duties. 'There's nothing more to say!'

Ian mumbled something into his mug.

'What about equipment? Did Geo's dad take anything to Egypt?' Diam butted in.

'You mean pickaxes and spades and things?' Ian asked.

'Yes!' Geo nodded, moving to the edge of his seat. Any information seemed suddenly of interest.

Ian took a sip of his tea and told them about not only pickaxes and spades, but also ropes, specialist clothing and even a hot-air balloon that Max had shipped off to Egypt before he caught his plane.

'But we gave the *police* all this information. Wasn't there a *police search* after the event? Did the police not make their own *enquiries*?' Linda kept repeating like a broken record, shrugging and shooting them all poisonous glances. It just seemed as if she wanted them to go – the sooner the better. But Geo wasn't finished.

'Do you know why he took the balloon?' asked Geo.

Linda stormed off to the kitchen, supposedly to fetch more kitten milk. Geo watched, astonished. He had forgotten how awful she could be. No wonder his mother had not kept in touch.

'Explorers and archaeologists use hot-air balloons to survey areas they need to map out – you know, the sort of site difficult to get to by road or plane,' Ian explained, sipping his tea.

'But I thought Geo's dad was just a travel writer,' Diam said, 'not an explorer!'

'Well, yes, but Max liked to review the specialist, high-end of travel. He wrote for enthusiasts, not for the mass market.'

'And did you see any of the address labels for the packages?' Geo came in shrewdly.

Linda strode back into the room. 'Of course Ian won't remember details like that!'

Ian shook his head, as if to agree with his wife but next time she was out of the room he said, looking at the ceiling, 'There was this man, mind you, that Max used to phone from time to time – Jameson, I think, was his name.'

Linda who had padded back into the room with a packet of fish-food, shot her husband an exasperated look. 'Not Jameson, *James!*' she corrected.

Geo's heart gave a kick. Remembering that his mother's note had said "*a man whose name is James*", he suddenly realised that the name confusion was all because of Linda.

'Not James, Jameson,' Ian insisted.

'James, Jameson, what does it matter?' she snapped, trotting towards the garden. 'I told the police about Max's calls to James anyway,' she called out from the French doors and, nipping back in for a moment added, 'They noted it all down in their report! In fact, they went to great lengths to check every phone number dialled from our landline while Max was staying with us. They checked his emails, mobile calls, even web visits made while he was setting up his expedition, but nothing significant turned up. So you're wasting your time. If the police turned a blank, I just don't see how two teenagers can outsmart them. And now, if you'll excuse me, I have to feed the pond goldfish …' Her voice trailed off as she hurried to the end of the garden.

'Look, I'm sure the man's name was Jameson. Dr Jameson. Not James,' Ian told them when Linda was out of earshot.

'A doctor? Was Dad ill?' Geo fretted.

'On, no,' Ian gave a chuckle, 'I think Jameson wasn't a medical doctor, but an academic – you know, a PhD, doctor of philosophy.'

'Did you meet him?' Geo asked.

'I'm afraid not. I think Max spoke about him once or twice, that was all.'

'What kind of work do doctors of philosophy do?' asked Diam.

'Oh, anything,' Ian laughed, 'from being personal adviser to the Chancellor to cleaning loos in Leicester Square. Obviously, it depends on how useful your PhD is! But many of them become teachers. I think it was this man that Max was planning to travel with. Though we never heard of him after your dad disappeared...' He got up and began to pace up and down in the room. 'Linda does have a point, though, we did tell everything to the police. They never managed to track down this man ...'

'Well, of course they didn't, if his name is Dr Jameson and Linda told them he was just some bloke called James,' Geo snapped.

'Oh, but I would have put them right,' Ian said, avoiding eye contact. 'The point is, though, all the leads simply disappear in Cairo.'

'So who drove Dad to the airport from Brighton?' Geo asked.

'I did. Heathrow. Late September. I think that Max was planning to visit the Valley of the Kings, and then going to some inaccessible sites by hot-air balloon.'

'Like ... where?' Diam asked.

'He never said. He'd been waiting for the weather to cool down. He had sent all his bulky luggage ahead so when I drove him to the airport he only had a small bag with a few clothes.'

'And did you see Max meet Jameson at Heathrow?' Diam asked, her eyes narrowed.

'No – I just dropped him off at the terminal. He grabbed a trolley, dumped his stuff and waved goodbye. That's the last I saw of him.'

There was a pause.

'So does the name Jameson mean anything to you?' Ian asked Geo.

'Nope! But it all helps.' Geo smiled. A plan was slowly hatching in his mind. Let Linda treat him like the biggest pain in the neck. Let everyone say his search for Max was a waste of time. Let them all think him a nutcase for even trying. As long as he himself knew what he was doing.

He asked his uncle if he'd mind putting them up for a couple of nights and Ian went off to talk to Linda. After a few muffled bangs and crashes from the kitchen, accompanied by a few hissy expletives, his rather flushed uncle led them up the stairs to the top floor.

'Make yourselves at home,' he said, giving them fresh linen for the beds. 'But don't stomp up and down the stairs unless you want to get on the wrong side of Linda.'

Geo didn't think it possible to get any further on the wrong side of Linda, but he just nodded and surveyed the room. It was a sunny loft painted in pale orange and yellow, with a dormer window, big skylights and bunk beds. He was secretly pleased about the bunk beds. Having fallen a few times from a bunk bed to the foothills of Mount Olyska, he had developed a fondness for them. And this time Bob Knock-Shaws was nowhere in sight.

Before leaving them to unpack, Ian said slowly, 'Actually, there *is* something else that comes to mind about Max.'

Geo's stomach tightened.

'One evening Max and I went out for a drink and, well, he started chatting about his expedition.'

'And?' Geo said.

Ian lowered his voice and looked behind him as though expecting his wife to come tearing into the room, talons bared.

'Your dad told me that while sacred objects end up in museums, *supernatural* objects don't. He said that he was going to look for such an object lost for two millennia – a small inverted pyramid buried in a desert.'

'A *what* pyramid?' Diam wrinkled her nose.

'Inverted: upside down.'

'And? What does it do?' Geo asked.

Ian looked at a loss. 'No idea!' He gave a shrug. 'But you wanted to talk about your dad. So this was one of the things that came to mind.'

'That was sooo helpful!' Diam sniggered as soon as Geo's egg-shaped uncle had shuffled out of the room.

Geo looked out of the dormer window and said, 'At least we've got a name: Dr Jameson; and a motive: the inverted pyramid in the desert.'

Diam gave a chuckle. 'Yeah? But what happens when you find it? The heavens open? An extra-terrestrial comes down and wags his bony finger at all the naughty little earthlings? And what do we do now?'

Geo nodded absent-mindedly. 'Don't know yet. But tonight I want to have another go at dreamboarding proper…'

'What are you talking about?' Diam asked, her eyes suspicious. 'Has this got something to do with you ending up in my room on the cruise ship?'

'I think you'd better sit down,' Geo told her, sitting on the floor with his back against the side wall of the dormer window. Diam brought a cushion and made herself comfortable, settling with her back against the wall opposite.

And so it was that Geo tried his best to explain dreamboarding to his new friend.

At first she screwed up her face, unwilling to believe him, but when he showed her the dreamcatcher and gave her details about the dream of hers he'd gate-crashed she bit her lower lip and narrowed her eyes. 'So how do you get in people's dreams?' she asked, her eyes twinkling with curiosity. But she still looked suspicious, and something else, too; a little amused, like she thought Geo was pulling her leg.

Geo tried to stifle his frustration. He looked out through the dormer window at the sky, which was clear blue with sunlit white clouds floating across. Deep down he knew that only meeting Hymal and seeing Oeska with her own eyes would really prove to Diam that everything he had told her was the truth.

'Well,' he replied, turning to face her again, 'it's kind of, complicated. There are different ways to dreamboard – at least three and maybe many more that I haven't even found out about yet. But when I use *this* charm –' he touched the spider web ring – 'I can get into the city of Oeska, and dreamboard a specific sleeper.'

Diam gave a chuckle. 'Why should I believe you?'

'How would you like to dreamboard with me?' he said quickly. 'Tonight – that is, if I can take you – and if you want to try it.'

'Mmm!' Diam said, giving him another wary half-grin.

Geo suddenly felt excited at the prospect. 'Why not try it? Tonight. It might work with two!'

'Mmm,' Diam repeated, her face guarded. She got up and opened a cupboard next to the door. 'Oh, look, a sewing kit!' she said irrelevantly.

'So?'

'Just what I need.' She resumed her place by the window where the light was good and started fixing the hem of her jeans.

She was threading a length of cotton through the eye of her needle, when Geo said, 'Diam, there's something else I need to tell you.'

'What?' Diam asked, looking up from her sewing.

'You know how the police did all they could to trace Jameson, and failed?'

'Yeah.'

'Well, they might have failed – but what if there are other ways to trace someone?'

'Like what?' She looked up at him again, the sunlight pouring from the window, illuminating the ends of her hair.

'Like tracking down Jameson in Oeska and boarding his dreams. It's clear that my dad saw quite a lot of him before he disappeared and I have a strong feeling that he was involved in my dad's disappearance.'

'Funny you should say that.'

'Why?'

'Well, I wondered about that, too. And also why your aunt didn't want you to even know Jameson's name – I mean all that weird "James not Jameson" palaver.'

'Yes, I wondered about that too.'

Diam put down her sewing and stared at his face. She looked very serious. 'But if you can board dreams as you say, why not gate-crash Max's dream directly? Why Jameson's?' she asked.

'Well, obviously, I would, if it was possible. But it isn't. I've already tried and – and it isn't.'

'Why not?'

'I don't really know but it's something I found out last time I went dreamboaring.' He paused and touched the tiny wolf-head that rested just below his Adam's apple, his mind back on Hymal. 'I reckon Dad is in some other … erm … *realm* – or so I've been told.'

Diam sighed. 'And who told you that?'

'Hym-' he stopped himself, suddenly not wanting to talk about Hymal. 'My mother,' he lied.

'Your mother,' she echoed, and resumed her sewing.

'Yes.'

'You're sure she's not, you know…' She hesitated.

'What?'

'Well, just – I mean – not in her right mind!'

'How can you say that to me?' An unexpected surge of anger took hold of him. 'You think my mother's crazy!'

Diam pursed her lips and gave a tiny shrug.

How dare she? thought Geo. For the past seven years he'd whispered that word himself often enough. But it made him angry. 'Thanks, Diam – and I thought you were someone I could talk to. Of course you'd know everything about ...' he burst out, then clapped his hand over his mouth. He had nearly said something cruel, something about Diam's mother that would really hurt.

But he stared at the lean, dark-haired girl, in her shabby clothes, sitting on the floor, sewing, and he softened. 'Sorry,' he said quietly, 'didn't mean any of that. All I'm asking is that you help me track down my dad. I want you to dreamboard with me.' Then he thought of something new. 'And who knows,' he added, 'I might even be able to help you trace your mother!'

This was when Diam pulled out of her pocket the creamy envelope that still held her mother's letter. 'Yeah, I could definitely do with some help,' she said, her voice a bit choked. 'I was wondering – would you mind reading my mum's letter? I'd like to hear what you think of it.'

CHAPTER NINETEEN

The Reality Check Cards

Dear Diamondheart,

I have always loved you and always will, but there are important reasons why, for so many years, I couldn't write. One day, when the time is right for us to meet, everything will fall into place. For the moment, all I can say is that when it's safe for us, we *will* meet, but you must let me be the judge of this. Please keep the little key safe and look in the locker again in a year's time.

The money is meant to give you a little help on your way.

I know that Zaira, being a gypsy woman, showed you how to use her Reality Check Cards and that you do enjoy 'reading' them. Apart from the money, you will also find a pack like Zaira's in the bag.

The cards may help you see certain things more clearly. But take care! I hope Zaira mentioned that they don't give a definitive picture of the future; nor can they tell you the ultimate truth. Nothing outside yourself can do this. But they do indicate some of the forces at play at a given moment in time. Please use them rarely and wisely.

Don't try to find me, but trust that we'll meet when the time is right.

With love,

Your mother.

Geo finished studying it, got up from the floor and paced up and down across the room. Diam raised her face and smiled, though her eyes brimmed with tears.

'So – what do you think I should do?'

'It tells you, doesn't it?' He scanned the letter one more time. 'Have faith that you and your mum will meet when the time is right. Check the locker in a year's time. And use your Reality Check Cards sparingly.'

'But if I *really* want to look for her?'

'Well, she says not to,' he replied, more bluntly than he'd intended. Diam's face flushed and her eyes reddened.

Deep down, he felt sorry for her. All he could think was, *What sort of a mother does this to her kid?* But he knew it would be wrong to tell her that, so he said, slowly, 'Well, she seems to care for you. She's written to you, given you the money and the Reality Check Cards. Maybe they can help?'

Diam shook her head. 'Like my mum says,' she waved the thick, creamy paper, 'the cards can only give you an insight, help you see things more clearly. I'll tell you what, ask me a question, then perhaps you'll see what I mean...'

Geo blinked. He had no idea what question to ask. Besides, he didn't believe that a pack of cards could tell you anything. But to please Diam more than anything else, he gave a shrug and said, 'Fine!'

Diam pulled the small blue glossy box out of the bag she'd picked up in Venice. It was longer and slimmer than a normal deck of playing cards, and about twice as thick. All it said across it in a medieval-looking script was 'Reality Check Cards'.

'So what's your question?' she asked. 'But remember! I'm good, but not *that* good yet – Zaira, who showed me how to interpret the cards, was an amazing reader. But I can only cope with easy questions, OK?'

He rubbed the side of his head. 'Can ... you tell me why Linda is being so mean?'

Diam made herself more comfortable on the floor, pushed the long tresses of her shiny, jet-black hair off her face, and took a couple of deep breaths like a swimmer about to take a long dive. She pointed at the space on the floor opposite her and he moved closer to watch her tip the cards out of the box. She shuffled them, her hands performing a dance of sorts, occasionally throwing the cards up in the air like a colourful streamer, and then making them glide from one hand to the other in an arc. Then she stopped, grew still and serious and sat in silence, gazing at the pack.

'Now: focus all your attention on your question while *you* shuffle and cut the pack!' She handed the cards to Geo.

He repeated his question about Linda silently, cut the cards and gave them back. Diam laid the top five face down and another four in a column. Then she turned the first one face upwards. 'This one,' she started, 'usually tells you about the question.' She pointed at the image of a stern woman on a throne with a black cat by her feet and gave a chuckle. 'That's spot-on! Here is a controlling, powerful woman, intolerant, and – looking at her cat – even shows your aunt's love of pets!'

She indicated the second card. 'The position of this card shows what gets in the way.' She turned it up and said, 'Interesting! Two beggars hobbling in the snow outside a brightly lit window. The meaning, I think, is clear enough: what's stopping your aunt from helping you is fear of losing everything. But why?'

She carried on in the same way with the reading, briefly explaining what the position of each card signified and then turning it upwards to go into the meaning shown by the picture on the other side. 'So,' she summed up in the end, 'something happened in the recent past and Linda has still not got over it. She and Ian used to be a lot better-off, but they've already made a big loss – of money, I think. Linda is not keen to lend a hand because she's probably scared of losing the rest. But she may have to take a risk,' Diam concluded, pointing at the last card, the Wheel of Fortune, 'because this is the card of change. And so Linda may have to give up being a scaredy-cat and do what is right.'

'Which is?' Geo asked.

'To change her tune and help you.'

'So she knows more than she lets on. I wonder how much more. Well, can you see anything else?' Geo asked.

Diam told him to pick up five more cards from the pack at random, and she held them close to her chest, like a poker player. Her eyes glazed over and she said, still keeping the cards hidden, 'Yes, there *is* something else! Because she is scared, Linda hides her true power and her true knowledge from you.'

The atmosphere in the room somehow changed. The air felt heavy; the light dimmed. Geo could hear his blood pumping. A floorboard creaked as though an invisible presence had entered the room.

'But why?' he asked. 'What is there to hide?'

Diam placed the cards on the floor and waved her hand over them, as if she were turning the front cover of a large book. 'Why?' she said dreamily. 'The reason is right here, behind the door to the forbidden realm where your father's trapped.' She bent over the cards, brushing her hair off her face, her eyes now staring at the cards, full of curiosity. 'There's your dad: tall, dark-eyed, unsmiling.' Her face grew serious and sad all of a sudden. 'Next to him is the card of guilt. There was a time when he missed you and your mother like air, water, sunlight,' she whispered, and Geo felt a knot at the back of his throat and a rush of tears crowding behind his eyes. 'Now he is too preoccupied with something else. I can't see what.'

She frowned. 'He is in a circular room that feels like a prison, only the door is not locked. He could easily walk out, if he wanted. In a different room in the same house is someone, more demon than man, vile, demented. Someone hell-bent on a terrible revenge.'

Geo felt the hairs on his back stand up.

'He challenges your dad to a game of strategy, an odd kind of chess. They play. I can't see the demon's face. How strange! He is holding a globe behind his back.' Diam bent so low over the cards now, that her long hair curtained them off. When she looked up again Geo saw that she was frowning, blinking and rubbing her eyes. 'Could it be that the demon is holding not a globe but *the* globe – the Earth behind his back?'

As Geo had no reply to this, she carried on. 'And now I see you, Geo, running towards the two players, brandishing a sword of fire. But there's a gulf between you and them. Grave danger. So *this* is the deeper reason for Linda's ways. Maybe she's afraid for … for your life.'

'My life!'

Diam looked up at him, her eyes odd; blank, unseeing. 'Immense danger,' she said. *'Offer two libations to the great mother. Seek her help,'* she added tonelessly.

A shiver ran down Geo's spine. Diam's eyes broke contact with his and she smiled. 'So! Does any of this make sense to you?' Then, looking as dazed as a rabbit caught in the glare of headlamps, she keeled over onto the carpet and fell asleep.

Geo was shocked at first, having no idea this is what reading the cards could do to someone. But after he'd checked her pulse – it was calm and steady – he began to pace the room, tormented by bleak thoughts. He remembered the yellow demon atop the gnarled olive tree, and it made his skin crawl. He could see him in his mind's eye, rippling like scummy water and leering down at him, seemingly greedy for Geo's very soul, his breath, his life. What *was* that thing?

Then he thought how he had expected Diam's reading to be a bit of joke, but it had been nothing of the sort. But that word she'd used, 'libation' – what did it mean? A row of yellowing novels and a dictionary stood on a shelf at the far end of the room. He got up and opened the dictionary: '*libation: liquid poured out in honour of a power beyond human understanding.*' *Whatever* ... he thought. It didn't make any sense to him, so he put it aside and focused on another, more pressing question: how could Diam have possibly known about Cromund and his father? He had not talked about Cromund to her! Yet she had somehow managed to 'see' the demon; 'vile, demented. Someone hell-bent on a terrible revenge.' Her words rang in his ears.

But Diam had 'seen' other things, too, that he himself had no idea of. Could she be right? If the demon from Diam's 'reading' was, in fact, Cromund, did his dad actually *want* to be with him? Was Max a prisoner or not? All Geo knew from dreamboarding his mother was that he should not try to find his father because of Cromund. But why? Geo imagined that his dad had been kidnapped by the demon. But if the prison door was unlocked, as Diam had said, why did his dad not simply walk out of it?

It was, of course, possible that Diam's reading was mostly wrong, but that it contained some random bits of truth, which, of course, made it all the more convincing. All the same, it had increased Geo's motivation. His fear that his dad was in serious danger made his urge to track him down overwhelming. Tonight he'd try out his dreamcatcher again, break into Oeska and learn how to locate specific dreamers: Max, if possible – though he doubted that it was; and Jameson if not. There had to be a way.

He looked at the dark-haired girl slumped on the floor, breathing softly in her sleep. His hand rose to his neck and he touched his dreamcatcher, thinking, despite everything, how lucky he was to have this extraordinary key to Oeska; and how lucky he was to be friends with this amazing girl.

***

Oddly, when Diam woke up she couldn't remember much from her reading. If a hypnotist had clicked his fingers and told her to forget everything, he couldn't have done a better job. No matter how hard Geo tried to remind her what had happened during the reading, she just said, 'Yep, I know; there's more to Linda than meets the eye. Quiet now! I've had enough freaky-deaky stuff to last me a lifetime.' And as if to make up for all that 'freaky-deaky' stuff, she refused point blank to chat about anything strange or mysterious, but spent the rest of the day talking about soggy sandwiches, damp rucksacks and dirty trainers – with the intriguing question of 'where do single socks always vanish to?' being the only mystery she was willing to debate.

Geo, on the other hand, tingled with excitement at the prospect of revisiting Oeska. He kept checking and rechecking the time, wondering whether all the clocks in the house needed new batteries when barely a minute had ticked by. But bedtime did arrive in the end. In the guest room, Geo let Diam examine the little wolf-head on his dreamcatcher.

'Interesting!' Diam made a face, running the pad of her finger across the soft fur of Hymal's head. 'He's got really fierce eyes, huh? Ouch!' She jerked her hand.

Two streaks of blood were running down her thumb.

'It's got teeth like needles!'

'I'd no idea!' Geo checked the wolf's jaw nervously and found it to be hinged, but as toothless as a baby's mouth. He daubed her thumb with a paper hanky, wondering how come he'd never caught his own finger in the wolf's jaw before.

When the bleeding stopped he made his way to the bunk bed ladder, tugging Diam by the hand. 'Come on then!'

Diam giggled. 'Should I be excited?' she muttered, looking thrilled and on edge, but also giving her lopsided grin, that made her look undecided. Geo climbed to the top of the ladder, flopped onto the mattress and lay staring at the ceiling, feeling awkward. 'W-when it happens,' he stammered, a bit embarrassed, 'I sort of fall down from the top bunk. Here. Lie next to me. Hold my hand. I'm hoping that will work. Now, do you know how to empty your mind?'

'I guess so. Like when you want to go to sleep?'

'Kind of. Let's do it together. Picture a blank square. Like a painting with nothing on it – just white canvas. Now, let this square grow bigger in your mind's eye until there's nothing else. Just a white nothingness. If any thoughts come into your head, stop them.'

'How?'

'Say, "Thank you, but not now." Then focus back on your blank square. Keep growing it until your mind is completely empty of everything.'

'Even songs?'

'No songs.'

'Tunes?'

'No tunes.'

'Pictures?'

'I said, empty it of *everything*. Keep going back to the white square until it's so big you can't even see its edges.'

The fall didn't happen immediately, but it didn't take long – the familiar swish of the wolf's tail under his chin, the crash of splintering wood as the top bunk gave way and row after row the slats collapsed. Pillows, mattress, sheets and bedding tumbled into the void, as Geo gripped Diam's hand firmly with his and they plummeted down, his heart beating like a jungle drum.

Somewhere to his right, he could hear Diam whimpering.

He lay sprawled on soft grass in the night garden, panting and winded. Next to him, Diam groaned and swore, her clammy hand gripping his. Up above, the sky was brimming with stars. The heady smell of the sea wafted up from a faraway shore.

Hymal leapt suddenly out of nowhere, fangs fluorescent in the dark, darting towards Diam. She shrieked, picked up a stone and scrambled into a half-crouch.

Heart hammering, Geo rolled in front of her, shielding her from the wolf. 'Leave her alone!' he bellowed. 'She's my friend. I brought her.'

Hymal snarled, lips drawn back, fangs bared. And then his growl came full of menace into Geo's ear, 'This is no kids' game!'

'Back off!' Geo shouted. 'Where I go *she* goes, and you must let us through!'

Hymal's yellow eyes narrowed. He hesitated, then turned tail and skulked off.

'You just growled at it!' Diam gasped, her eyes the size of saucers.

'What? I was just ...'

'No, you were definitely growling!' she shrieked, a note of hysteria in her voice. 'And he was growling back. No words. I'm not joking! You can talk to wolves? You're scary!'

'Look,' Geo said quickly, 'Hymal guards the dreamcatcher but he's letting you through and we need to follow him. Are you coming?'

White-faced, Diam straightened up. 'Depends whether he wants me for supper or for snacks,' she grumbled, struggling after Geo up the mountain.

With Hymal ahead of them, they climbed the barren slope, waded through the thorn-infested forest, and reached the road of chains. If it wasn't for Hymal snapping at their heels, it might have taken Diam a fortnight to climb it. But worried by Hymal and encouraged by Geo, she soldiered on until they reached the castle walls. There, Geo used his spider charm once again to break through the citadel's defences and, finally, they were inside, the crystalline city gleaming in the distance, bathed in light.

It was at last Geo's turn to chuckle at Diam – at the way she looked at Oeska, her jaw slack and her eyes popping out.

'Hm!' she finally said, grimacing like a child who couldn't work out a hard sum. 'I see!'

'You've seen nothing yet,' he laughed, pulling her along a narrow path that led towards the city.

Hymal sniffed the air, gave them a resentful look and led them as far as a fork in their path. There, he pointed out the left turn and abandoned them, rushing off towards a forest on their right.

'Grumpy old fleabag,' Geo said, following Hymal with his gaze. 'Brings you in, points you vaguely in the right direction and dumps you. Did pretty much the same last time.'

'Let's move on,' Diam said, her eyes fixed on the buildings in the distance.

The first time Geo had gate-crashed Oeska, it had been magnificent but cold, eerie and deserted. Today, it felt awash with life. The air was warm and scented. Lush trees bordered their path – oak, plane, horse chestnut, weeping willow, ash and silver birch. Geo hadn't noticed trees on his first visit, nor had he heard the rustling of their leaves, which made a noise as if they were telling jokes to whole flocks of birds that perched, tittering, on their branches. They carried on towards the glowing city, Geo explaining more to Diam about spectral bodies and dreamboarding, when they heard a soft thud from behind the trunk of an oak.

'Who's there?' Geo called out.

First, a wooden staff appeared. Then a rather odd man sidled out of his hiding place. His right eye, which was magnified by the thick lens of his glasses, resembled a hard-boiled egg tinted with blue and purple, as though he had been in a nasty fight.

– CHAPTER TWENTY –

The Guardians of Gaea

'Helooo!' the man said in a friendly voice, hurrying towards them. 'My name is Hiker,' he added, offering his hand.

'Hello.' Geo shook Hiker's hand, reassuring himself that he didn't look like a threat – just plain weird. He was dressed in a long, embroidered coat that stopped just above his ankles; though it wasn't so much his dress sense that gave him a strange look, as the shape of his head, which reminded Geo of a Halloween pumpkin with a flattened top, curved sides and a grin full of uneven teeth. Add a pony tail, short legs and a clean-shaven face with pitted skin, and the only thing that looked un-pumpkinlike was his square, black-framed glasses.

'So you are Geo and Diam, right?' Hiker carried on, while they gaped, wondering how he knew their names. 'Sorry,' he added, 'you don't know me but I know of you.' He gave them a lop-sided smile and blinked repeatedly with his good eye, which made him look like he was winking.

'Wh-what happened to your eye?' Diam stammered, seemingly too confused to ask a better question.

'Oh that,' Hiker said, bringing his hand to his purple eyelid. 'Nothing to write home about – just got into a spot of trouble with one of Dysoedema's boys in the engine room.'

'Y-you were on the cruise liner?' Geo asked.

'You bet! That Dysoedema and his obnoxious side-kick, huh? Two very nasty pieces of work, if you ask me. My theory is, they probably tricked you into getting that job with them.'

'So they are linked to Oeska? How? And how do you know all this stuff about me?' Geo demanded.

Hiker tapped the side of his nose. 'Ah, The Marshals of Tide always know things.'

'S-so a-are you one of them?' Geo stammered.

Hiker gave his uneven-toothed grin. 'Me? Oh no!' he replied, to Geo's relief. 'I've just been working as their envoy – you know, a bit like your mum has been.' He spoke quietly now, almost in a whisper. 'Cromund's agents, see, they're all over the place. A nasty bunch with no clue about the distinction between good and evil. I had been posted to your realm for years, trying to blow their cover. My last mission, before I got called back to Oeska, was to keep an eye on you on that cruise liner. Not that you needed looking after; in fact,' he chuckled, 'I ended up in more trouble than *you* did!'

Diam was staring at Hiker's coat, which looked a bit like a bridesmaid's outfit with floral patterns. She gave Geo a nudge between the ribs. 'But why is he wearing a dress?' she whispered.

'DRESS?' Hiker had heard her. The small man pulled himself up to his full height – which might have given him some dignity, if it weren't for the fact that he put too much weight on his staff and it got jammed in the soft, crumbling soil. 'This is a silk-embroidered 17th century Ottoman kaftan, if you please!' he snarled, yanking his staff out so hard that he lost his balance and fell backwards. 'Not that anyone cares for staffs and ceremonial robes any more,' he added, wrapping his floral garment around his hairy legs and springing up again. 'I *told* them I needed to change from this gear before coming to meet you, but no, it's all "Hiker this" and "Hiker that" and never a minute to get myself sorted. *And* they've gone and changed all the courtesy rules while I was away!'

'So who are "they", exactly?' asked Diam.

'He probably means the Marshals of Tide and Time,

Diam,' Geo replied, not wanting to seem totally ignorant.

'Yes, but who *are* these people?'

'My mum, and other people like her,' Geo explained. 'Not that she's one of the Marshals. She just belongs to their retinue of followers and attendants – that's what she said.'

'What do you mean "just"!' Hiker said, sounding miffed. 'We do one of the most important jobs on the planet, clearing the way for the Marshals to communicate with humans through dreams. You've no idea how important dreams have always been!' He drew himself to his full height again, puffing out his chest. 'Now, follow me this way, if you please.' He led them down a side-path that branched off through a woodland, towards a clearing covered in ferns and bluebells.

'Where are you taking us?' Geo asked.

Hiker turned to face him, his good eye glowing with pride: 'To meet Marshal Angelo, so you can get proper dreamboarding lessons and learn how to defend yourself and your dreamcatcher.'

'Angelo!' Geo repeated, much more interested in his plans than having 'proper lessons' about anything. The name rang a bell. Wasn't "Angelo" what his mum had called that gaunt, scruffy man who'd taken her away? 'Is he the same person who came to fetch my mum the morning of the earthquake?' he asked, his voice about an octave higher.

'Course he was!' Hiker's nodded enthusiastically. 'Angelo and Sophia always stick their necks out for your mother.'

'But they *arrested* her!' Geo snapped.

'Well,' Hiker's good eye winked half a dozen times, 'well, yes, it is true, they had to bring her in for questioning! No two ways about it. Had to! But better to be brought in by your friends, Geo, than ...' His voice petered out.

'Your enemies? So what did these so-called friends ever do for my mother?' he demanded.

They had reached the clearing now, and Hiker showed

them to a huge felled tree-trunk with his staff. 'Sit down for a moment,' he commanded, and stood in front of them. 'You don't know a thing, do you?'

'I know that Mum was apparently "protecting" me from the truth,' Geo replied, rolling his eyes. 'Anyway – you were telling me about Angelo and Sophia.'

'Yes, I was – and also about your mother. At first, Geo, your mother was like me – on a mission. But after she married your dad and had you, she became an exile – not really fit to live as a mortal woman, but with no power to come back to her world.'

'But exactly how did those two friends of Mum's help her?' Geo persisted. 'She didn't seem like she wanted to go with them.'

'Well I guess she'd have been worried about you! But Marshal Angelo had been helping her for years. Who do you think had woven powerful enchantments around the olive grove to protect your family from Cromund?'

'Really? And fat lot of good his protection did us,' Geo snapped.

Hiker gave him an astonished stare.

'That's not a very respectful thing to say,' he said in a low, reproachful tone. 'It was not Marshal Angelo's fault that the earthquake – or whatever that event was, which we are still investigating – breached the olive grove's defences. Nobody expected such a carefully planned attack. And nobody expected that the ruin would be crawling with Cromund's people later that morning when we were all working flat out making arrests and trying to make sense of what exactly had gone on.'

He slid his staff quickly upwards and held it from the middle. 'And now I'd like to take you to Marshal Angelo, if you don't mind. We mustn't keep him waiting.'

'Oh,' Geo said, intrigued at the prospect of meeting one of the Marshals. 'Great! But can you at least tell me where my dad is?' he added impatiently.

'I don't know that.'

'And Mum? Is she still in regeneration? Can I see her?'

'I doubt that, Geo, but, as I said, I'm taking you to Marshal Angelo. He might be able to help.'

Excitement stirred in the pit of his stomach. At last, he would get answers to his questions.

Hiker raised his staff above his head, parallel to the ground and called out, 'Bubnatch!'

Geo and Diam watched, wide-eyed, as a tiny soap bubble appeared at the end of Hiker's wooden staff, floated up into the air and instantly swelled up to the size of a minibus, though it kept the spherical shape and ever-changing colours of the original soap bubble.

It rose up into the air, did a wide swoop over their heads and came spinning down towards Diam. She shrieked and jumped out of its way. The bubble bounced off the ground like a huge beach-ball, but changed direction – towards Diam. It swallowed her up with a squelchy burp. Horrified, Geo ran under it, yelling and waving at Diam. He could see her trapped inside it, shouting and thumping its walls with her fists. But her voice could not be heard. The Bubnatch, he realised, must be totally soundproof.

He opened his mouth to ask Hiker what the hell was going on, but the giant soap-bubble bounced onto Geo's head before he spoke and engulfed him with a low-pitched sputter.

The ground was swept away from under Geo's feet and the bubble headed for Hiker next, swooping down and gulping him up with a muffled burr.

'Hiker, what is this?' cried Geo, falling on all fours inside the bubble, which yielded to his weight like the floor of a bouncy castle. Rising up into the air, it began to glide above the trees towards the centre of Oeska, as light as a dandelion seed in the breeze.

'It's just a bubble snatcher,' replied Hiker, giving it a sharp poke with his staff, which sped it up.

'Oh, I'm so reassured.' Petrified, Geo managed to get to his feet. He stood stock-still with his legs apart in the unstable, fragile-looking sphere, not daring to move a muscle as they floated through the air. He looked down through the transparent floor, feeling dizzy and sick. Diam had buried her face in her hands wheezing as if she was having an asthma attack.

'It's okay, you two,' Hiker chuckled, settling down cross-legged on the see-through floor and arranging his flowery kaftan over his short, muscular legs, 'Relax! Bubnatches are tough; you're not going to fall through! Just enjoy the view.'

By the time he finally dared to follow Hiker's example and sit down on the alarmingly flimsy floor of the Bubnatch, they had already crossed half the city. They were now flying over a green, where a ghostly version of the tower of Pisa stood like a multi-tiered wedding cake.

Feeling a bit calmer, Geo turned to Hiker. 'I think you should tell me everything you know about my mum.'

'I already have. Diam's mother, on the other hand, is a different matter.'

Diam's mouth fell open. 'What do you mean? H-how do you know about *her*?' she asked at last.

Hiker sighed. 'Has it not crossed your mind that when Geo took a stroll on deck seven and heard a thump in the lifeboat that perhaps it wasn't just sheer fluke? That you two were *meant* to meet so he could help you get into Oeska?'

Diam grimaced. 'What, you set us up?'

Hiker glanced about, looking worried. 'Don't say things like that around here. No! The Marshals were just puttin' you two on the right track. We're not supposed to interfere in the realm of Gaea.'

'The realm of Guy-what?' Geo interrupted.

'Guy-ah,' Hiker said clearly.

'Is that your word for the Earth?' Diam asked. 'But why

"Gaea", why not Earth?'

'Because,' Hiker said slowly, '"Earth" is stones and mud. While "Gaea" is the whole living planet and all who breathe in her mantle of air, light, weather and moon-tide.'

'I don't understand,' Diam said.

'Gaea is the great mother of all who live off her. This includes mortals as well as a handful of people like you two, who are not just common mortals. We call people like you 'gaea-borns'.'

'Meaning?' Deam asked, the colour draining from her face.

'Meaning that you have one parent from our world and one from yours, Diam. People over here are already gossiping about your gifts of insight, you know,' he added, giving her his crooked-tooth grin.

Diam was staring. 'S-so both Geo and I are gaea-borns, with one common mortal parent and one from over here?'

'That's what I just said,' Hiker chuckled, then, winking nervously with his good eye, plunged his hand into the folds of his embroidered kaftan and pulled out a couple of packets. 'Here, have a sesame snack,' he said cheerfully, tearing off the wrapping. 'Boost you up! We don't want you passing out!'

'Thanks.' Geo took a bite of his flat, honeyed biscuit. 'S-so Diam was always supposed to hitch a lift on my dreamcatcher to help her get into Oeska?'

'Ha ha! I like that.' Hiker slapped his thigh. 'Hitching a lift, huh? Yeah, that's about it!'

Geo looked down. They were just crossing a square surrounded by fine classical Chinese buildings.

'S-so is it possible to trace my mum from here?' Diam gave Hiker a nervous smile. Can someone help me do it?'

'Ah,' Hiker said, scratching his head. 'I hope so! But don't look at *me*! Been away in the earthly realm far too long. But … erm … I'm sure you'll get a chance to ask someone when we get there.'

'Where?' they both asked.

'You'll see. Not far now.'

They all fell silent for a while, looking at the city unfolding beneath their feet.

'So can gaea-borns live forever?' Geo asked, putting into words one of the many questions in his mind.

'Really, that depends whether they live here in Oeska, or down there in the realm of Gaea. So it's their choice. Of course, there's an advantage to growing up on Earth like you two. You can adjust to both worlds – a bit like amphibians living in water as well as land. People like your mum, on the other hand, who grew up here, need time to readjust.'

As the gorgeous city with its spires, domes, gardens, turrets and minarets now fell behind them, Hiker pointed at a woodland on their right. 'Nearly there,' he said.

After the trees, they travelled in the gorge of a long, steep valley above a snaking river. The Bubnatch skimmed across the river-water and rose abruptly upwards to the ridge of the valley.

'Wow!' Diam cried out suddenly, pointing behind Geo.

He turned and caught his breath. In the distance lay an azure lake surrounded by rugged mountains. And on the crest of a lower hill to its right, a graceful mansion glowed in the light. It had many marble steps, fluted white columns, green inner courtyards and lush gardens that sloped down the hill to the lakeshore.

As Hiker guided the Bubnatch towards the entrance of this mansion, all Geo could think of was his vague, scatty mother who could never quite cope with anything practical. The penny had finally dropped. If his mum came from this place, no wonder that seventeen years of washing up, chopping onions and pairing socks had still not turned her into a good housewife.

'Come on then! Marshal Angelo is expecting you,' Hiker said. 'You don't want to be late for your interviews!' He flicked his staff and the Bubnatch stopped ten feet above the front steps of the building.

'What interviews?' Diam breathed.

'Well.' Hiker's swollen eyelid seemed to glow brightly behind his glasses. 'You don't expect them to take you on at Silverfoot without a proper interview, do you?'

CHAPTER TWENTY-ONE

Silverfooted Selini

'Silverfoot ...' Geo said, looking suspicious. 'What is it?'

'The college!' Hiker replied, landing the Bubnatch at the bottom of the marble stairs.

'And what do they teach at this college?' Diam asked.

Hiker gave the Bubnatch a jab with his staff and it burst, releasing a fine, soapy spray. 'Everything you need to know about dreamboarding,' he replied. 'So you can learn it, practise it and get really good at it.'

A cooling breeze swept across Geo's face as he followed Hiker and Diam up the steps, towards the door of the mansion. He lowered his head and stepped up the long, marble stair.

'You look worried,' Diam said in a hushed voice, turning around and studying Geo's face.

'Yeah,' he whispered back. I was just trying to work out how to fail my interview.'

'Fail?'

'I don't want to be stuck in a college! Do you?'

'Can't say I've given it much thought.'

Geo glanced up at Hiker, who had reached the top of the stairs, and appeared to be tweaking the ear of one of a pair of stone sphinxes. 'All I want,' he carried on in a whisper, 'is to see Mum, then get some useful information out of Jameson, leave this place and track down my dad.'

Diam began to say something, but stopped as the panelled double doors of the college opened. Geo dawdled towards them, his brain working overtime. Dreamboarding, he reckoned, was all very well as a means to an end. But he had no intention of staying here. He only needed to find out how he could gatecrash Jameson's dream and get access to his mum. Interesting though it had been to get a spin over a city crammed with every famous building he'd heard of and many that he hadn't, Geo was keen to leave Oeska as soon as he got what he wanted.

'This way.' With a proud gesture, as though he owned the place, Hiker showed them to a huge circular lobby. Standing by the entrance door, Geo raised his face to the brightly lit ceiling, where a glass dome glittered in the sunlight. The dome was held up by a ring of tall columns and written inside its base, just above the tops of the columns, a circle of letters carved in crystal glimmered in the sunlight pouring in through the glass above:'*Silverfoot College – Main Hall – General Section and Library of the Recent Past.*' As Geo's eyes slid down again to follow Hiker and Diam who walked ahead of him, he realised that the single, curved wall of the room was lined with thousands of books.

In the circle of shadow between the bookshelves and the columns Geo saw several men and women sitting at desks and communal tables. Their ages ranged from around eighteen, he guessed, to, probably, one hundred and eighteen. They were dressed in modern clothes, mostly white but randomly dyed with every hue and shade of blue he'd ever seen. A few seemed to be studying or taking notes. Some were lost in thought, chewing their pens, muttering to themselves or staring vacantly into space, looking rather like composers lost in the throes of inspiration. The majority, however, huddled around crystal bowls set on tripods, which stood on the floor at the head of each table. These bowls were filled with a clear water while the students – if that's what these people were – peered into them, talking quietly among themselves. Whatever they could see in them made them point, smile, frown, laugh, nudge each other and sometimes stir the water, looking dismayed.

'What are those people up to?' Diam asked Hiker.

'Sssh! They're training for entry into various levels of the Dreamboarders' Guild,' Hiker whispered.

'But what are they looking at?' Geo asked, his voice louder than he'd intended.

'You'll find out when you join the college,' Hiker murmured, to Geo's irritation. The assumption that he wanted to study at Silverfoot was getting to him.

'And those bowls?' Diam asked. 'What are they for?'

Several heads turned.

'Shush! Can't you see this is a quiet area?' Hiker reprimanded. Cringing, Geo put his head down and followed the others who were crossing the enormous room quickly, in silence.

At the far end of the hall, opposite the entrance, they came upon three doors labelled 'Specialist Libraries,' 'Council Chambers,' and 'Tutorial Rooms'. Hiker raised his staff and rapped twice on the third door. Then he stood tall and waited.

The door swung open and a young woman with shoulder-length, shiny hair came out. She wore a short, high-waisted white dress with a lilac border. She had a startled expression, a bit like his own mother, Geo thought.

'Silverfooted Selini,' said Hiker, bowing his head. 'Master of Tides, Dreaming and Moonshin ...'

'No need for titles, Hiker,' Silverfooted Selini interrupted, smiling and tilting her head sweetly to one side. 'We've all switched to first names now, as you know. So who do we have here?' she added, with a glance at Geo and Diam.

'Sorry about the titles, Miss,' Hiker mumbled with an apologetic bow. 'I've been away for years serving in the earthly realm and I keep slipping back to the old ways. Anyway, your grace, I mean, ma'am, I mean Silverfooted Selini, your ladyship...'

'Just *Selini*, she reminded him, raising her eyebrows.

'Yes, of course.' Hiker took a deep breath and stood in

attention, staring ahead with a look of concentration. 'Introductions then! This here is George Artemidorous Cleigh, Geo for short, son of Leona and Max Cleigh, and the young lady over there is Geo's friend Diamondheart Katharophthalmi – Diam for short – adopted child of Zaira Katharophtalmi. Geo, Diam, meet –' he paused, clearly unable to call her just 'Selini,' then blurted out, 'the Principal of Silverfoot College, who will show you to your interview rooms.'

Then Hiker bowed and turned away. Geo and Diam exchanged glances.

A renewed wave of excitement stirred in the pit of Geo's stomach. He was about to meet Marshal Angelo. With a bit of luck, he was about to get answers about his parents!

Selini led them down a corridor with many doors. Each had a square plate engraved with the name of a college tutor. As they went past them, Geo saw that the plates gave not only the names of the tutors, but also their long, complicated titles and responsibilities, like, 'Room One, Marshal Delaciel, Master of Natural Justice, Chief Guardian of Gaea'.

But who had appointed these people to be the guardians of Gaea, Geo wondered, and what were they, exactly? Extra-terrestrials? Immortal beings, like Zeus, Thor, Venus or Freya? Or people like him and Diam, but just with more powers?

Halfway down the corridor, Selini looked at Geo with her slightly bewildered smile and said, 'I suggest that you two meet in the courtyard outside my office after your interviews. I expect they will be quite brief. We are all worked off our feet today. Go on then!' she nudged Geo, who was so restless now, he could barely speak. 'Knock on Angelo's door! This one, opposite mine. He's expecting you. And Diam, will you come this way, please?'

Diam winked at Geo with a nervous grin before

following Selini into her office. The plate on her door confirmed that Marshal Selini was Master of Tides, Dreaming and Moonshine and Principal of Silverfoot College.

Selini's door closed behind Diam, and Geo was left standing in the corridor, before Angelo's tutorial room. The plate on it said:

'Room 5

Marshal Angelo Master of Messages, Decrees and Healing. Chief Strategist Guardian of Gaea.'

Geo looked down at his grubby black and white trainers, the frayed ends of his jeans and his dirty fingernails, thinking he was in no shape for an interview. But so what? If this was the Angelo who'd come to fetch his mum on the day of the earthquake, he was a pretty scruffy character himself. And besides, Geo reminded himself, he wasn't here for an interview. He did not want a place in this college. He just wanted answers to his questions.

He cleared his throat and knocked on the door.

At first there was silence. Then a deep, resonant voice said, 'Come in!'

CHAPTER TWENTY-TWO

The Sealed Envelope

Geo blinked. There was so much light that for the first, confusing moment he thought he was outdoors. As his eyes adjusted he saw he had stepped into the tip of a triangular room with two white walls. At the far end – the base of the triangle, opposite the entrance – an enormous floor-to-ceiling pane of glass overlooked a lush garden. The ceiling was also made of glass, showing puffy clouds against the blue.

But he couldn't see Angelo anywhere. 'Hello?' he called.

'Over here!' The voice wafted up from one of two sofas overlooking the garden. Then an arm rose above it and beckoned him in.

Geo crossed the room slowly, distracted by the semi-abstract paintings on the walls. They showed ghostly shapes of telephones, high-tech satellites, wave patterns, coded signals and the outline of an angelic creature, carrying a wand carved with two intertwined snakes. With a start, Geo remembered he'd seen this wand before when Angelo had used it on the morning of his mother's arrest.

As Geo reached the two sofas, Marshal Angelo sat up, putting aside what looked like the latest games adaptor for an iPhone. 'Take a seat,' he said, waving him to the sofa on the left, his eyes scanning Geo's white hair-streak for only a fraction of a second. 'Nice gadgets,' he added in a slightly distracted manner, putting the consoles aside. 'Invented by a gaea-born nephew of mine...'

In the brief silence that followed, Geo sank into the soft cushions, desperately trying not to fidget, pat down his discoloured fringe, pick his nose and twitch – all of which he suddenly felt compelled to do.

Against the pristine whiteness of the room, Angelo seemed even more tanned and scruffy than Geo recalled. Unlike the others here, he was not dressed in light colours, but in the same long dark coat, slightly frayed trousers and dusty boots he'd worn on the morning of the earthquake. Perhaps, Geo thought, he'd just come back from another trip to the 'earthly realm'.

'So,' his host said, raising an eyebrow. 'The worst is over. You and your friend found your way to Oeska in record time.' He nodded approvingly. 'Good work.'

'Good work?' Geo echoed, not quite sure what Angelo meant.

'Really,' he carried on gently, his unruly hair falling over his eyes, finding your way to Oeska for a third time and leading Diam in as well, is as good as filling in an application form and passing every section of our entrance test. I hope Lady Selini mentioned that your interviews will be brief. I'm afraid both she and I have some urgent business to attend to.'

Geo gaped: *application and entrance test?* Was that what it had all been? He could feel his face flushing with anxiety. How was he going to wriggle out of all this? Were these people really expecting him to join their college? Did he have no choice?

After a short, tense silence, he resolved to play along with Marshal Angelo's expectations so he could get some answers for all the pressing questions he was hoping to ask about his parents.

'M-Marshal Angelo, c-could we maybe, erm … start the interview with a couple of questions I need to ask?'

'Just "Angelo", Geo. We're in the process of simplifying things.' He ran a hand through his unkempt hair. 'Well, what questions did you have in mind?'

'Why did my mother have to leave in such a hurry?' Geo asked.

'Leona,' Angelo replied, 'had a very narrow window of opportunity to – well, escape her fate and come back home with us. Seventeen years ago she broke an extremely important new law for which she got punished with exile and mortality. You must appreciate, Geo, that for someone raised with us in Oeska, exile to the earthly realm means becoming wholly mortal. As such, it is a death sentence of sorts …'

Geo sat on the edge of his seat. 'But what did she *do* exactly?'

'She was on a mission, Geo. Mount Olyska politics, I'm afraid. Let's say.' He sucked in his lips, as though he did not quite know where to begin. '… how can I explain – well, since ancient times our kind have often fallen in love with mortals and erm … procreated. That is – had children with them. I myself have had quite a few gaea-born sons and daughters.'

Geo nodded.

'But over many centuries of intermarriage, it became clear to us that many of the talents inherited from our side were being used for the wrong ends. Then in the past hundred years, humankind's assaults on nature began to affect even the finely tuned climate of the planet. And so, as an emergency measure and to reduce the risk of inflicting irreparable damage upon Gaea … well, these unions between mortals and us were banned. Unfortunately, your mother chose to disobey the new rules – you were born just one year after they came into effect – and so she was punished with exile and mortality. This is why she raised you on the earthly realm. However, on the day of the earthquake and … er … for very good reasons, Delaguerra, who oversees our security, needed to bring Leona in for questioning.'

'What reasons?'

'I understand that on the morning of the earthquake, Max sent you a warning.'

Geo nodded.

'Now – there were defences around your parents' olive grove. You may or may not know this, but I am a friend of theirs, a close friend. I had put them there myself for your protection. Just before the earthquake breached these defences, your father's unexpected "call" to you triggered off a security alert which we traced back to a London office. To Cromund, no less!'

'Cromund!' Geo breathed. 'So my father is his prisoner!'

'His message came from an office, not a prison.'

'Oh!' Geo could feel the blood pulsing in his temples.

'By the time we got to these offices, Cromund and his people had already fled without trace.

'Where were these offices?'

'Bayswater, actually, in London. Does it mean anything to you?'

'No, it doesn't.'

'Anyway, as I said – by the time we got there they had all gone; vanished!'

'So you suspect that my dad *works* for Cromund?'

'Well, I had my doubts. But it was widely felt among the Marshals that we had do some checks, including, question your mother. The trace we discovered to your father's whereabouts was too much of a security risk to be ignored. Anyway – your mother herself will explain.'

'Great!' Geo said, relieved.

'I hope you see then that she didn't have much choice on the matter. As you were nearly of age, she decided, quite correctly in my view, that she would be of more use to you if she agreed to help us with our enquiries. In return, we offered to give you some limited protection.'

'You mean Hiker?' Geo chuckled.

'Indeed,' Angelo replied, his face serious. 'Your mother

knew, of course, that around the time of your sixteenth birthday, and as long as you got your hands on a dreamcatcher, you'd have the opportunity to discover the means of entering Oeska for yourself – an opportunity which is open to all gaea-borns.'

'But how soon can I see her?' Geo said impatiently.

'You are about to *hear* from her, but as for seeing her …'

'Wait – why can't I see her?' Geo cut in. 'Is she still in … *regeneration?*'

'Ah, so you know,' Marshal Angelo said with a curt nod. 'Yes, that's the reason, Geo. Your mother needs to heal and … er … recover.'

Geo leaned forward, frowning. 'You make it sound like she's ill.'

'No, she's not ill, as such, but … um … let's say, not herself, either. How can I explain? Well, think about it. For seventeen years she had to live wholly as a mortal – a heavy price to pay for someone who grew up as one of us in Oeska. Now she needs time to, well, shall we say … acclimatise. You know, *adjust*. But have no worries. She is in safe hands. And I assure you, the less we disturb her, the speedier her recovery will be.'

'But how long will it take her to recover? A week? A month?'

Angelo frowned. 'Um … the only thing I can say with any certainty, Geo, is it depends on a lot of complicated factors that nobody can predict. But please don't hold your breath about having tea and cakes with Leona this afternoon, because it's not going to happen.'

Realising that it would be pointless to persist, Geo decided to change the subject to that of his father. After all, Angelo said he'd been traced – to London!

'Marshal Angelo,' he started.

'Just *Angelo*, please, will you?'

'Right.' He took a deep breath, bracing himself for the

lie that he was about to tell. 'Before I join the college,' he tried to sound eager, like he actually wanted to study at Silverfoot, 'there's something I need to do.' He hesitated.

'What's that?' Angelo sounded remote, like he had other things in his mind.

'My uncle Ian thinks that Dad was due to travel with … erm' he nearly blurted Jameson's name but at the last minute decided against it. What if they could put hoops and hurdles on his way, or even block his access to Jameson? So he said. '… a colleague of his – in fact, someone who might help me get in touch with my Dad.'

Angelo leaned forward, a glimmer of interest in his eyes. 'And do you know this person's name?'

'Well,' Geo replied carefully, 'I think so.'

Angelo frowned. 'You think so, or you know so?'

'I think so. But I'm not sure if it's right; I had to squeeze it out of my uncle, I have doubts about its accuracy, and it's probably not worth much.' He stopped, pleased with giving a good enough reason why he wasn't revealing Jameson's name.

'*Squeezed* it out of your uncle, did you? Hm!' Angelo's eyes creased in the corners, giving him an amused look. Geo wondered why. Perhaps Angelo knew Geo was fibbing, but was too polite to press him?

'Well, I have something to tell you, too,' Angelo added, his voice light. 'When your mother begged me to trace Max, seven years ago, I saw your aunt and uncle myself and, I'm sorry to say, failed abysmally to get anything out of them. I think your aunt was terrified of helping us – as though she had been threatened; which, knowing Cromund's people is entirely possible.

'Oh,' Geo breathed, 'I see.'

It made sense.

'But how do you propose to follow up this clue you found,' Angelo pressed on. He had pronounced 'clue' with a dismissive ripple in his voice, as though he thought the word was ridiculous and he had difficulty taking it seriously.

'How do you mean?'

'I mean, without any of the Dream Master's skills – not even at beginner level? How will you find this colleague of your father's?'

Geo wasn't exactly going to reveal his plans to dreamboard Jameson on the sly.

'S-so you're saying I should study at the college first?' he asked, trying, again, to sound keen.

'Naturally.'

'I – I liked the library,' Geo said, thinking he ought to act interested.

'The "Recent Past" one at the entrance lobby?'

'Yes.'

Angelo smiled. 'You know, the Library of the Recent Past is the least interesting one of eighty!'

'Eighty libraries!'

'Indeed. Hardly any of them contain books, mind you.'

'What then?'

Angelo gave a chuckle. 'The written word is, of course, a useful tool for us all, but it is dreaming with your eyes wide open and not merely reading that is the true mark of genius!'

Geo wasn't very sure what Angelo meant. 'How about The Hall of Records?' he asked. 'Is *that* one of your libraries?'

'So you already know about The Hall!'

'Hymal – my dreamcatcher's wolf told me.'

'I see. Yes, The Hall of Records is a library of sorts.'

'Could I maybe see that?' Geo asked, trying to suppress his excitement. Angelo nodded. 'Yes, well, there's no harm in getting someone to show you around,' he replied. 'I must warn you, however, that The Hall of Records may be a little advanced for you at present. You may be admitted as a visitor but not a user. But if you train hard, there's no reason why you shouldn't be allowed to use it in six or seven months.' He stood up. 'Now, we've talked for long enough, and I have urgent business to attend to. Any further questions before I see you out?'

'Yes. Um…who are you?' Geo asked as politely as was possible under the circumstances.

'Me? Oh!' He gave a self-deprecating laugh. 'Well, it says on my door doesn't it?'

'Yes.' Geo smiled. 'But how did you come to be here?'

'Ah! Well, like you, Geo, we are born, though in Oeska and not in Gaea. Of course most of the Marshals can live for thousands of years, which, to a human must seem as good as immortality – hence some unfortunate confusion about our supposed god-like nature. But as I said, the more contact we make with the earthly, temporal realm that is *governed* by time, the quicker we age and eventually die.'

'Right,' said Geo. His mind had already wandered back to his own problems. 'And could you help me track down my dad?'

'Geo, I should strongly discourage you from pursuing such a quest.' He sounded worried more than stern. 'I can't see how you can pull off such a feat, with so few dreamboarding skills. Dreamboarding can be a rather dangerous business, you know!'

'Why is it dangerous?'

'Look,' Angelo said tapping his fingers impatiently on the arm of his chair, 'you are here for an interview, not a crash course in dreamboarding. Just take it on trust. It's not safe, not without being experienced.'

Geo nodded, privately itching to get out of Angelo's office and get Hiker to show him The Hall of Records. 'But – just out of curiosity,' he added casually, 'what would happen if someone *couldn't* study here?' He was careful to put a lot of emphasis on 'couldn't' to give the impression that he was talking about someone who had no choice.

Angelo pursed his lips. 'You mean someone like you? A dreamcatcher bearer?'

'Yes.'

'A dreamcatcher bearer who can't study with us!' Angelo repeated, his voice barely a whisper. 'Well, that would be like letting a dull-witted goat-herd keep a high-tech spaceship in a cave with his goats.'

Angelo sighed. 'I hope this is not your wish, Geo.'

'No, of course not,' he cut in. 'I was just asking!'

'Especially now it is clear that Cromund wants the Hymal dreamcatcher – a move which, I must say, is a bit of a mystery to us all.'

'What? How do you know that?'

'The earthquake, Sadie Mandiball, Dysoedema, Bob Knock-Shaws, things Hiker has reported back, our own enquiries – everything points in that direction.'

Realising that he was gaping, Geo forced himself to close his mouth.

'You see,' Angelo carried on, 'an Oeskan dreamcatcher like yours, apart from being impossibly rare, can be used only by the members of the family it belongs to. Of course, if someone *gave* you his dreamcatcher because he wanted you to have it, it might work ... especially if the donor is genetically similar. But there is no way anyone could take it from you by force without destroying it in the process.'

At least that explained why Bob Knock-Shaws had tried to steal it while Geo slept but had avoided forcing it from him. And why Sadie Mandiball had tried to drug him before he could even claim it from the ruin.

'So why are Oeskan dreamcatchers so rare?' Geo asked.

Angelo glanced at his watch. 'Mmm? Oh, I suppose because they give ... um ... gaea-borns like you, unusual privileges.'

'Like?'

'Like dreamboarding and the freedom to travel from Oeska to the earthly realm – these are important privileges, available to the Marshals of Tide, as well very few members of their retinue. Everyone else – take Hiker for example – is only allowed entry to the earthly realm if he is posted there for a reason.'

'You mean Hiker has to have *permission* to cross over?'

'Absolutely!'

'Whereas the bearer of an Oescan dreamcatcher,' Geo said, finally realising his status, 'has powers a bit like the Marshals of Tide and Time.'

'A bit, yes, but don't let it turn your head. There are plenty of other powers that you do not and will never have. But at least, if you studied here at Silverfoot … Geo, I urge you to join us.'

Geo paused and stared at the garden. 'Yes, of course I will,' he said in a level voice.

Angelo pressed on, 'Yes, you must! How else would you use such a powerful talisman responsibly? How would you protect it effectively from the likes of Cromund? How would you join the ranks of those who dreamboard for the good of your world and not for petty, personal gain motivated by trivial human needs and desires?'

Geo was beginning to feel guilty. Before he could reply, he noticed Diam stepping out into the garden from the room next to theirs in her faded blue jeans, sandals and black tee-shirt, her straight black hair shifting slowly in a mild breeze.

'Ah, there's your friend,' Angelo gestured towards the courtyard. He snapped his fingers. The large glass pane overlooking the green yard simply vanished. Geo blinked in surprise. But he was in Oeska where natural laws were distinctly different.

They both stepped outside.

Diam smiled, looking relieved to see Geo.

'Look, there's a wooden shelter past those hollyhocks.' Angelo pointed at an overgrown part of the garden, past a screen of tangerine trees. 'Perhaps the two of you could wait there, to meet the guide that we've appointed to show you around. And, oh,' he added almost as an afterthought, 'before Leona went … um … away, she left this for you.' He extracted a folded piece of parchment from his pocket.

His pulse quickening, Geo took the stiff paper from Angelo's hand. His name was written on it in his mother's neat, calligraphic hand. It was scented with the faint, earthy smell of violets and sealed with red wax that bore a coin-sized coat of arms. When he looked at it more closely, he saw it was a seal-sized imprint of his dreamcatcher.

'Th-thank you,' he muttered, running his hands over it.

But Angelo had already turned on his heel and walked away. The glass of his study reformed behind him. Geo peered through just in time to see Angelo hurrying across the white floor and out of the door at the far end of his triangular tutorial room.

Two students, girls in their early twenties, got up from a white marble bench in the courtyard. It lay under the shade of a glossy-leaved orange tree, whose fruits hung from the branches like brightly coloured lanterns. Beckoning Geo towards the free bench, Diam sat down on it. Geo hurried towards her. They sat next to each other on the white stone, pleasantly warm in the dappled sunlight.

'What's this?' she asked, eyeing the envelope in his hand.

'A letter from my mother.'

'Oh, really? I'll leave you to read it in peace and quiet, then. Selini told me to wait for our guide at the shelter past those hollyhocks,' she added, pointing to her left. 'Meet you there in five?'

Geo nodded. Then, sliding his finger under the red seal, he unfolded the creamy paper and began to read.

CHAPTER TWENTY-THREE

Leona's Warning

My dear Geo,

I can't tell you how sorry I am for what's happened. My only defence is to explain that I had not prepared you for this for a good reason. I always worried that if I told you about Cromund, without any powers to show you how you can defend yourself against him, I'd have terrified you, or you'd think I was crazy, or both.

Since I've come back to Oeska, I've discovered my suspicions about Max and Cromund were right. Not in the way I had imagined it, though. You see, my dear, Max is not Cromund's prisoner, but his ally. Yes, that's right: your dad is not Cromund's prisoner, but his friend.

The letters blurred and crawled on the page. Ants, scorpions, cockroaches; Geo was too dizzy to read on. His insides felt as if they'd turned to water. Diam's Reality Check Cards flashed through his mind. She had said Max was in a 'prison' of sorts, but that the door was open – he could walk out if he wanted… and now this! But he didn't believe it. They'd got it all wrong. Who could have poisoned his mother's ears with dirty lies about his father!

He carried on reading, his eyes stumbling from word to word.

It must be hard to accept what I'm telling you. Perhaps, if I tried to explain how it came about, it'll be easier to take in. In recent times, Cromund's influence over the minds of mortals has grown many times over. Our side, the Guardians of Gaea, want to protect the life of the planet in any way we can. But the demon Cromund has learned to get under the skin of mortals. By dangling 'profit' and 'progress' under their noses, he's got human beings to put all their faith in his teachings. With their limited grasp of science, many act like thoughtless little gods, with no consideration for the well-being of the oceans, the forests, the creatures that inhabit the planet and even the unpolluted air that lets the earth cool.

Cromund's teachings have created a world divided into three sets – those who amass extraordinary wealth, those who are so poor they don't have enough to eat and a middle band who live in reasonable comfort. They don't have the fabulous luxuries of the first group. But equally, they don't live under the constant threat of starvation like the second.

It is this middle layer that Cromund targets most, because it is the largest, and so holds the greatest power.

My mission was to live on Earth for six years and to find out exactly how Cromund tempts so many people to do his bidding. To see my mission through, I befriended people who had direct dealings with him. Your father was one of them.

There are many stories about spies who fall in love with those they spy on and many tales about our kind falling in love with mortals. Max and I soon added our story to theirs. At first we used to laugh about it. Soon we stopped. Even in that first, blissful year when your dad and I went into hiding from

Cromund, I had already traded my true self for that of a mortal. I carried a child that was to be gaea-born – you. And I was the first from my world to break the new law that forbade intermarriage between us and mortals. My punishment? Exile: I would never see my family again, my friends and all the people I had loved and worked with back in my world.

Under cover, our little family then settled on the isle of Zonissos. But Cromund soon worked out who I was and why Max, his once faithful follower, had gone underground. Then Max disappeared from our lives, but seven years later, on the morning of the earthquake, he dreamboarded you with his life-saving warning. You can imagine my relief. It was the first time in seven years that I had proof that Max was alive.

But your father's warning also had an unfortunate side-effect. The Marshals were able to trace it back to Cromund. Positive proof that your father had rejoined Cromund! It's also the reason why I was brought in for questioning on the morning of the earthquake. So even I, who have been hunted and hounded by Cromund all my life, even I came under suspicion. As Max's wife, the Marshals now feared that I might have betrayed my own world to join ranks with my husband.

Of course, nobody was able to produce a shred of proof against me, so I was acquitted. But you can imagine my humiliation when I discovered that Max had switched sides and gone back to his old master. My only relief is the knowledge that you managed to claim the Hymal dreamcatcher as your own. Trust it. You are the new dreamcatcher-bearer. Nobody can tear it away from you without destroying it in the process. It can only be freely given.

I do worry though. What if Cromund finds some way to rob you? Why does he want it? What use could it possibly be to him? So I give you this advice: Geo, please join the college, so you can train properly and be able to defend what is yours.

But above all, I urge you, my boy, while Max serves Cromund, please do not go looking for your father. It is the most dangerous thing that you could do. So just don't!

With love,

Mum

Geo folded the stiff paper, stuffed it into his pocket and looked up towards the overgrown part of the garden, to where Diam had disappeared. His mind was churning. He couldn't get his head around his father's defection to Cromund. It just didn't ring true. He needed to know the truth about Max first-hand – never mind the rumours. He rose from his seat and made his way past the screen of tangerine trees to the wilder part of the garden.

He found the shelter soon enough, though it was hard to spot at first because its walls were teeming with wisteria and trailing roses. Diam was sitting inside it, on a circular bench, resting her elbows on a round table in the middle, looking deep in thought.

'So, how did it go?' Geo said, squeezing in next to her. 'Did that Selini woman offer you a place at the college?'

'She did!' Diam replied with a tearful smile.

'Hey, what's the matter? Was she horrible to you or something?'

'No, not at all, she was quite sweet ... but ... thing is, I got a bit carried away – I kept asking all these questions about my parents, and it was impossible to stop even though she couldn't tell me anything … and I made such a fool of myself.' Diam laid her head on the table and started crying into the crook of her arm. Geo put one arm round her shoulders, rummaging in his pocket with his free hand for a not-too-dirty tissue.

'I'm sure you did not!'

'I pressed her to tell me who my parents are, but she wouldn't. I think she knows, but isn't allowed to tell me!' Diam could barely speak with grief.

After a pause she managed to control her voice enough to say, 'Same thing happened to a friend of mine – the adoption agency had the details on file, but wouldn't give them to the one person with a right to know! It's so unfair!' She looked up at him, her eyes picking up a shade of gold, the corners of her mouth drawn down.

Geo didn't know what to say so he just hugged her, apologetically handing her an OK-looking tissue he'd fished out of his pocket. 'Your mum's letter did say to be patient and wait,' he said, his voice trailing off.

Diam nodded but let out a sigh, looking unhappy.

'Did you at least find out if your mum lives in our world?' he asked her.

She shook her head. 'The only thing I managed to squeeze out of Selini is that my dad is a working musician.'

'A musician?! Well, that's a lead at least. Perhaps we can make more enquiries,' Geo said.

'And she told me that you, Geo,' Diam said out of the blue, 'are one of the last gaea-borns and probably the bearer of the most powerful Oeskan dreamcatcher in the world. I'm very lucky to be your friend.'

'Aren't you exaggerating a bit?' Geo chuckled. 'So if your dad is a musician,' he asked, getting more curious about her parents, 'he might be the mortal – so could it be your mum who lives in Oeska?'

'I wish I knew. Anyway, how did you get on with Angelo?'

Geo told her about his interview, Leona's letter, Cromund and his mother's advice to avoid, at all costs, tracking down his father.

'So are you joining Silverfoot now you've found out all this stuff about your dad?' Diam asked.

Geo gave a loud snort and shook his head. 'I want to track down my dad even more now, just to prove them all wrong.'

She whistled. 'Really? But it sounds so dangerous!' Her eyes were very round and she looked flushed.

'Well, I don't want to study at this college – do you?'

Diam frowned. 'I can't make up my mind. When I asked Selini what I'd learn, she said, "how to dreamboard and help mortals take care of Gaea". It's not quite what I had in mind for a career.'

'So what do you want to do?'

'Get a job in a record store, set up a band, go to parties, you know! Maybe audition for one of those TV talent shows …' Her eyes went dreamy.

Geo smiled. 'Hm! So the musician thing runs in the family.'

'I haven't got a bad voice, you know, *and* I play the bass.'

'Really? You never told me!'

'Didn't come up.'

'Yeah, well, I play rhythm and lead,' Geo told her.

'Hey, why don't we play together, sometime,' Diam said, delighted, 'when I get my bass back? Maybe joining this college isn't a good idea – we'd be really missing out on other things.'

Geo's attention was taken by a slightly older teenager in a dark blue tee-shirt and white jeans walking down the path, holding what looked like a black shoebox. He had ivory-pale skin and Chinese features set off by short, spiky bleached-blond hair.

'Hi! I'm Chen, one of Lao Nai-hsüan's grandsons,' he said in perfectly accented English. 'And you must be Geo and Diam. I hope you are hungry.'

'Starving!' Diam peered eagerly at the box in Chen's hands. It seemed to be made of some soft, black cardboard. As Chen lowered it onto the round table, they saw a white gadget embedded into its lid. 'What's that?' she asked.

'We call it a v-pod as a joke,' Chen replied. 'The box is made of recycled vanilla pods. And the gadget on the lid is a vintage iPod – recycled. Watch!' He ran his thumb over the wheel beneath the gadget's screen. In the menu window, where song titles would normally display, a vast list of dishes appeared, starting with A: Andalucian Anchovies with Almond and Aniseed; Arabian Aubergine; Apple, Absinthe and …

'A food iPod!' Geo chortled. 'Can I try?'

'As long as you're gentle with it,' Chen said. 'The gadget is practically indestructible but the box is a bit fragile.'

His stomach rumbling, Geo picked up the box gently. The black material was as thick as felt and smelt of vanilla. 'May I?' he said, turning the v-pod wheel with his thumb until he reached 'Nut loaf with white sauce, roast potatoes and Mediterranean oven-baked vegetables.' He clicked his choice and a delicious smell wafted up from the box, bringing back memories of his mum and laid-back Sunday lunches. He breathed in, suddenly gripped by tremendous hunger pangs. He took the lid off. Served on a long, ceramic plate, piping hot, he found his favourite dish and, next to it, a tumbler of freshly squeezed orange with ice.

'Impressive,' he said. 'And it gave me a drink, too!' He took out the tumbler and plate with a murmur of appreciation and passed the box to Diam.

'Marshal Angelo let me borrow it from the High Table,' Chen explained. 'Is he trying to butter you up or something?'

Geo and Diam looked at each other.

'Probably,' Diam giggled, peering hungrily at the box. 'I want cheese puffs with filo pastry and a Greek salad garnished with feta cheese and Kalamata olives. Oh, and freshly squeezed pomegranate juice with ice.' The v-pod scrolled automatically up to her menu choice and served her order.

'Voice-activated too! How does it do it? Mmmm!' she said, already sampling one of the pastries.

'Some geek in Marshal Smythie's workshop made it,' Chen explained.

Geo nodded. 'But how does it work?'

'Well, it uses the basic quantum properties of matter. Of course, scientists on Earth have known about this kind of thing since 1982...'

'That can't be true,' Geo said.

'*You* can't be true! If you don't believe me, check Alain Aspect's name on the net. He is a distant cousin of my mother. So far, human scientists have only managed to transmit a few particles at a time. We, on the other hand, can beam up whole platefuls of filo pastry and nut roast from the kitchens – as you know! Plus you can instruct one of these v-pods to halve or quarter the calorific value of foods.' He leaned over the box and ordered, 'Double portion mango ice cream. Seventy-five calories or less!'

'You could make a fortune selling this stuff to slimmers!' Geo said.

Chen removed the ice cream from the box. 'Oh, no you couldn't! You don't smuggle stuff out of here unless you want to end up strapped onto a rock with eagles nibbling your liver...'

Geo stopped chewing and looked up. 'Has that really happened to someone? What on earth did he smuggle out?'

'Fire?' Diam suggested. 'Like Prometheus who cheated Zeus and the Olympians?'

Chen looked at Diam approvingly and nodded. 'Just like him,' he said. 'But, oh dear, we're running late,' he added, insincerely, as though speaking for the benefit of a hidden microphone. 'We'd better make a move!'

And with a mumbled word, he pointed at the empty space in front of him. At once, a Bubnatch formed at the tip of Chen's nail and grew big, soon filling the entire space in the shelter and sucking all three of them up with a soft belch. For a few seconds there was chaos inside it, Chen's Bubnatch being much more cramped, thick-walled and wobbly than Hiker's.

'Did you have to?' Diam yelled. 'I spilled my juice everywhere.' The floor of Chen's Bubnatch wobbled again and she fell forwards, losing an ice cube down her tee-shirt and swearing loudly. It was like being in a bouncy castle, only more unstable. 'I hate being cooped up in small spaces!' she shrieked.

Chen brought his finger to his lips. 'Listen! There's a good reason why we're in a Bubnatch. Now – promise me you won't tell a soul about it, will you? See, I don't want any of the Silverfoot tutors to overhear us – and a Bubnatch's the only soundproof space I could think of. So – promise you won't tell?'

'Sure,' Geo replied.

'Hm,' Diam grumbled. 'So what's the big secret?'

'Well, I've heard the gossip in the kitchens. It sounds like you two are quite important – there haven't been any other gaea-borns since the new law came in.'

'You mean the law banning intermarriage?' Diam said, leaning forward slightly, eyes narrowed.

'Yes,' Chen replied in a hushed voice. 'And if you two choose to stay on and study, then you'll be fine. But if you don't fancy the college – and believe you me, some of us don't – you don't expect them to let you return to your world without erasing your memory first, do you? Not to mention,' he added, glancing at Geo, 'deprogramming your dreamcatcher.'

CHAPTER TWENTY-FOUR

The Bogus Guide

Geo could feel his pulse quickening. *What sort of a choice is this*, he thought angrily.

He cleared his throat. 'Angelo said nothing about my dreamcatcher!' he croaked, raising his hand to feel for the tiny, furry head of Hymal. 'Why would they want to interfere with it?'

'Because they'd be stupid to let you have all this power without the training to know what you're doing,' Chen said, pushing his straight, bleached hair off his face and slurping his mango ice cream.

'Can we go to the college but still visit our world?' asked Geo.

Chen shook his head. 'We used to, but nowadays we're not allowed to come and go as we please. Until they brought in the laws forbidding intermarriage, anyone could nip down for fun. While now...' He pursed his lips and gave a disappointed nod. 'I'd give anything for a spin on Gaea! But the more we roam on the blue planet, the more chance ... you know ...'

'What ... you mean we might have babies with people who are wholly mortal?' Diam came in bluntly.

Chen nodded. 'Yep!'

'I don't get it, though! Where's the sense in introducing these laws *now*, after *centuries* of intermarriage?' Geo pointed out. 'So many humans must have *some* Marshal ancestry!'

'True,' Chen agreed. 'The Law against Intermarriage is only meant to prevent mortals from developing so fast.'

'A bit late now!' Diam said, taking a big mouthful of her pudding. 'The Marshals should have thought about the results of their actions long ago.'

'Perhaps they do have a point, though,' Geo said.

'Like what?' Diam demanded.

'Well, most people in our world don't give a hoot about how many species of animal and plant we manage to kill off – about fifty per day, I think! Not to mention pollution and climate change.'

'Well, nobody likes to even think about these things,' Diam said, finishing her plate. 'The other day I said that we're killing the oceans at someone's party, and you know, I got totally blanked out.'

'So what do *you* think?' Geo asked Chen.

'Me? Just a sec.' He poked the wall of his Bubnatch with his thumb twice, checking that the soundproof bubble was still doing its job. '*I* just spend my days hoping that one day I'll bump into someone like you – someone with a working dreamcatcher. So I can get out of here!'

Geo looked at Chen, trying to make up his mind about whether he trusted him. He could be just using them to get out of Oeska. He decided he'd discuss it with Diam later. She was, after all, a self-described 'good judge of character'.

'So with the help of my dreamcatcher you can get us out of here in one piece?' he checked with Chen.

'You can count on that!' Chen replied, eyes sparkling.

'So what's the deal?' asked Geo.

'From what I've heard, your dad disappeared seven years ago. And you're here to track him down, aren't you?'

'Well, yes,' Geo said cautiously, 'but various people including my mum, have not managed to track him down in Oeska. There's this place, though, The Hall of Records?'

Chen nodded.

'Can you take me to this Hall? Then I can do a new search, and that will help me trace him.'

'But how?' Chen asked eagerly.

'I just need to know if you can take us there?' Geo didn't want to give a direct answer. He believed that the key to tracing his father was Max's colleague, Jameson. Nobody had tried Jameson before. If he managed to dreamboard his father's travel companion, that had to be the best chance of solving the mystery of Max's disappearance.

Frowning, Diam gave him a piercing look. 'But this is crazy! Geo, you're supposed to *stop* looking for your dad, not keep going now you know what he's …'

'Diam!' he cut her off. 'I know what I'm doing. Please!'

Rolling her eyes, Diam gave an exasperated snort.

Chen raised his eyebrows in mock admiration. 'Oooh, a great horse impersonation!' he said with great seriousness, and they all laughed.

The mood lightened. Chen turned to Geo. 'So let me get this straight. You need help to track down a specific dreamer by breaking into The Hall of Records, right?'

'Yes,' he replied, his heartbeat quickening. He liked the sound of 'breaking into'. It sounded as if Chen could do it.

'Ge-o!' Diam said in a low, warning tone.

'Look,' Chen reassured her. 'It's no big deal. I can help you.'

Geo watched the young guy closely, the way his eyes twinkled with a confusing mixture of excitement, fear and mischief, and wondered exactly what this 'help' would consist of.

'But can you lead us to a specific dreamer?' Geo asked.

'Well, that's what The Hall of Records is for,' Chen replied, giving the Bubnatch a poke. Geo noticed it had snagged on a trailing rose. 'Ooops,' Chen murmured. 'This Bubnatch is about to burst on the thorns and, anyway, they'll be wondering what happened to us. Look, I'm going to have to move on – make a big show of giving you the tour.'

'You don't think they'll get suspicious?' Diam asked.

'If you do as I tell you, then no,' Chen replied. 'So who's the specific dreamer you want to dreamboard?' he asked Geo.

Chen's voice had been casual enough, but Geo decided that, for the time being, he wouldn't reveal Jameson's name to him, even if he did seem to be on their side. After all, what if the name was worth something to him? What if Chen had been planted to find it out? What if he was not as sincerely on their side as he seemed?

'A colleague of my father's,' he replied.

'So,' Chen said quickly, 'I'm going to take you to The Hall of Records *as soon as* we've done the tour. I'm going to burst this Bubnatch now, but please make no noise at all. We'll all creep out of the shelter. Then I'm going to take you around the college, where you will oooh and aaah and look impressed – but keep our little secret to yourselves. Ready?'

'Ready,' they both said, and Chen burst the Bubnatch with a long fingernail, making a soapy mess on the floor.

***

They visited the grand Council Chambers, ballrooms, dining halls, student libraries, gardens, courtyards, living quarters, common rooms, and kitchens. The only areas Chen didn't show them were a dozen specialist libraries, which he told them were 'exclusively for the use of the college tutors,' with their grand doors and oversized signs that warned students to not attempt entering.

Almost an hour had gone by. They were approaching a busy, grand-looking staircase with landscape paintings lining the walls, when Geo, desperate to go to The Hall of Records, said, 'So where's The Hall then?'

'Shh!' Chen grimaced, adding, in a hushed voice, 'I'll need to pick up some stuff, first.' He glanced around at a group of students who were within earshot, then motioned Geo and Diam to the stairs, saying, with an exaggerated concern, 'You really look like you need a break, you two!'

A few heads turned, but Chen was already leading them up the grand-looking stair. At the top they came to a wide landing with four doors.

'This way.' Chen pointed at the middle door. 'Have a rest. I'll see you in a couple of hours.' He pulled a key out of his pocket. 'Then I can show you the last library ...' he added, giving Geo a conspiratorial wink.

'But I...' Diam started.

Chen gave her a warning look – perhaps even the corridors were bugged?

He fitted the key, grinning. With the door slightly ajar, he turned and looked Geo in the eye. 'Just to clarify – if you feel tempted to try your dreamcatcher on any locks in the College, don't! They are dreamcatcher proof and you'd only succeed in setting off the alarm.'

They stepped into what looked like a small, cosy guest room, tucked under the eaves at the front of the building. A couple of wide sofas with plenty of cushions faced each other. A coffee table with a small v-pod labelled 'Snacks' stood in the middle of the floor between the sofas. Directly opposite the entrance, a pair of glass balcony doors gave views over the great blue lake in front of Silverfoot. Next to the glass doors a polished bureau with writing paper and a pen stood invitingly open. Chen opened the balcony doors and they all stepped out. The sun was riding high in the clear sky. Across the water, huge mountains rose grandly, perfectly mirrored in the azure waters of the lake.

'Awesome!' Diam said, rushing to stand by Geo's side.

'Listen!' Geo said. A noise like gravel rubbing against concrete wafted up from below. They both leaned down to check what it was and immediately realised that it drifted up from the stone sphinxes at the entrance of Silverfoot College.

The two statues were arguing about whether Geo and Diam looked handsome, bright and good.

'Sorry,' Chen said, mortified. 'It's the principal's idea of running an amusing college! I'll see you later.' And out he slipped.

'What did you make of him?' Diam mouthed the moment they were alone.

'Seems OK,' Geo whispered back.

He stepped back inside the room and picked up the writing paper pad from the bureau. He reckoned that if Chen felt he had to use a soundproof Bubnatch for privacy, they would have to be careful too. They were, after all, in a tricky position. His mother and the Marshals wanted him to stay and study. Chen wanted his 'spin' on the earthly realm. And Geo wanted to find out the truth about his dad.

Hoping that even if they bugged rooms they didn't have video cameras too, he began to scribble a message to Diam on the writing paper: '*Chen seems nice but u never know,*' he began to scribble. '*May be a liar. But there's a 1 in 2 chance he may be honest. What do u think – should we risk letting him help us?*'

'Yes.' Diam nodded vigorously, giving him a thumbs-up, 'Yes.' Then she proceeded to write down what looked like every phrase she'd picked up at that English mission in Greece: '*Coz if we're sure we don't want to study at Silverfoot, then we're in a pickle – up the creek without a paddle – and beggars can't be choosers.*'

Geo wrote, '*Aren't you exaggerating?*'

'*Not if Chen's telling the truth about the Marshals of Tide erasing our memories and de-activating your dreamcatcher!!!*' she wrote back.

CHAPTER TWENTY-FIVE

The Deteror Attack

'Ready to see the rest of Oeska?' Chen winked at Geo and Diam later that afternoon when he came to collect them from their room. They all knew what he meant: The Hall of Records.

Following their guide to the main entrance, Geo noticed that Chen's bleached blond hair was freshly spiked up with gel and that he'd changed; now dressed in light brown, khaki and green, he wore combat-style trousers with lots of big pockets, some stuffed with various lumpy objects.

In the garden, Chen took them to a remote spot, gave a furtive glance behind him, and then made another Bubnatch. By now, Geo was used to being snapped up by the squelchy bubbles with their loud burping and lip-smacking noises, but Diam looked as annoyed as ever. 'This Bubnatch, Chen,' she said, steadying herself inside his sagging vehicle, 'has the elegance of a drooping cow's udder.'

'Sorry!,' Chen apologised. 'Bit of a novice on the Bubnatch front. Can't quite get them to look even – they fly just as well, though …'

'As well as what?' Diam shrieked, falling on all fours, but Chen pretended he hadn't heard. They rose up and the Bubnatch moved towards the centre of Oeska, but as soon as Silverfoot disappeared from view Chen stopped poking it with his forefinger in the direction of the city and his Bubnatch partly sank, partly wilted down towards the canopy of trees.

'So,' Chen turned towards Geo and Diam, 'do you want

to keep up appearances, I mean, look at the rest of Oeska first? Or sneak off to The Hall of Records right away?'

'To The Hall of Records,' Geo said without hesitation, 'where I can trace my man.'

Chen nodded. 'So does he have a name?"

'Yes, he does.'

'And is there a reason why you're not telling me?'

Geo felt his face flushing, but stood his ground. 'Yes, there is.'

'You don't trust me?' Chen said, and his voice sounded frankly curious.

'I *want* to trust you. But sometimes trust has to be earned before it's given.'

Chen grimaced. 'Fair enough,' he said with a shrug. 'But I *will* need to use this name when we're inside The Hall. We'll have to get past the Deterors first, of course …'

'Who are they?' asked Diam.

'They're guards – warriors,' Chen explained. 'They defend The Hall.'

'Warriors! So how are we supposed to get past warriors?' Geo was starting to panic. This would not be as easy as Chen had made out.

'Just do as I tell you, and hope for the best.'

'Hope!' Diam said faintly. 'What good is *hope*?'

'Look, I didn't mean it flippantly,' Chen replied. 'I meant "believe" that the best that can happen will. It's far easier to succeed if you believe you can. I'm sure we'll be able to get around them.'

Geo decided it was better not to think that far ahead. Perhaps these Deterors would not be a problem. Chen sounded like he knew what he was doing.

But Diam would not let it rest. 'Why are they called "Deterors"?' she asked, frowning.

'They are mind-erasers who disable your free will,' Chen replied. 'You know, I wouldn't normally risk breaking into

The Hall. But the prospect of a spin on Earth with you two – it's just too tempting! And the reward's really worth the risk. But, as I said, you shouldn't worry because I know what I'm doing. Trust me.'

They all fell silent for a while, Geo wondering about Chen. If his Bubnatches were anything to go by, perhaps he was, just, a useless bungler. Then again, even though they were not exactly relaxing and cosy, his Bubnatches managed to fly, so Geo decided to set his misgivings aside. Taking a few deep breaths he distracted himself with the woodland to their left. They now flew cautiously under cover of trees, next to the blue lake, until they reached a very quiet, sleepy harbour, hidden in the folds of a valley, where they landed. Through the wobbly wall of the Bubnatch, Geo couldn't see anyone around.

'Right! From now on we'd better go on foot,' Chen told them. 'We don't want to be spotted arriving by air.' He punctured his horrendous Bubnatch and they all tumbled out in a tangle of legs and arms.

The harbour was tiny – only a dozen fishing boats, a wave breaker and, tucked away next to it, a beach where several people dozed under sunshades.

'So could we board the dreams of any of these people?' Diam asked.

'Well, they're not people, strictly speaking, but spectral bodies of dreamers. You can tell, look,' Chen added, giving a gentle poke to an old man, asleep in a deck chair, which made him mutter and disperse like a cloud. 'And the answer to your question is yes, of course we could dreamboard any of them with Geo's dreamcatcher. But you've got to be careful. Random outdoor dreamers could lead you to a beach in Hawaii or a park in Berlin. Which is not exactly the best place for us to be right now …' He paused and turned to Geo. 'Now, is the man you're looking for in England?'

'London, hopefully…' Geo replied, hurrying after Chen

up a rocky path. It led through fields covered in yellow stubble and then to steeper ground between two large, dry-looking hills.

'But, Geo, why can't we just dreamboard your uncle Ian, and simply get back to Brighton,' Diam suggested after a few minutes of silent marching into the hills. 'Why risk dreamboarding your dad's colleague? What if he doesn't live in England anyway? What if we get stranded in – I don't know – Siberia, or the Antarctic, or something?'

Geo shook his head. 'Because I *have* to find out what happened to my dad. And that's the only lead I've got.'

'I know, and I don't mind helping you!' She gave him a sidelong glance. 'But can you at least promise me that you won't go chasing after him if it's as dangerous as your mother says?'

'I'm not a six-year-old,' Geo snapped. 'Why should I listen to my mother?'

'Well, why not? Why would she have said it otherwise?' Diam insisted.

'Look, the deal is this,' Geo said, his words clipped. 'I'm here to trace my dad. What happens after I do depends on what we discover.'

'But how about Cromund?' Diam reminded him. 'What about the danger to you and your dreamcatcher?'

'Well, Cromund can't have it!' Geo replied more angrily than he'd intended. 'Unless he kills me first, but that will also destroy my dreamcatcher!'

The others went quiet. Geo marched up the sloping, dry hillside that rose ahead of them. He was baking hot. And he was puzzling out the problem about his dad. He was desperate to make up his own mind about Max. He couldn't stop wondering about what had really happened to him. But he was convinced he had to find him first, to hear the truth from his father's mouth. Besides, even if everyone was right, even if his dad had switched sides as everybody seemed to think, and no matter what he had or had not done, he had been a great father before Cromund took him away – kidnapped him probably!

On the other side of the hill they found themselves on the outskirts of what looked like a northern African village built on a steep hillside. Chen motioned for them to all hide behind a boulder and he looked out, checking for danger, Geo supposed. The village consisted of a huddle of small, white dwellings, with wide, stepped lanes leading down the hill to a stretch of scrubland and then desert. However, less than half a mile across the sand, Geo could make out one of the grandest monuments of the ancient world. It was enormous, with two statues of Egyptian deities or Pharaohs towering up on either side of its temple gates, each the height of a five-storey house. He was sure he'd seen it before, perhaps on TV. But in this place it was not an ancient ruin, but immaculate and far bigger than he recalled.

'Duck and run!' Chen suddenly shouted, breaking into a sprint down the hill. Heart drumming, Geo raced after him, Diam at his side, until, under the cover of town houses, Chen slowed and then hurried them along a maze of lanes in the direction of the monument.

It had to be The Hall of Records, Geo guessed.

They reached the sandy strip at the bottom of the hill, where the last village houses stood. Geo peeked around the corner of the last building.

'Don't worry!' Geo said. 'They didn't see me.'

'Stay under cover!' Chen warned pulling him back. 'What did you see?'

'Soldiers – warriors of some sort – guarding the temple gates – about a dozen of them.' Compared to the size of the monument, the warriors had seemed no bigger than cockroaches, crawling by the Pharaoh's gigantic feet.

Chen swore. 'I don't come on the sly normally – I should have told you to … ach, never mind now.' He peeped round the corner carefully. 'Heck! They've caught our scent!'

'What's happening?' Diam asked, her voice tense.

'They've left two guards behind – ten coming to meet us,' Chen replied, his face twisted with worry.

'Why don't you make another Bubnatch?' Diam shrieked.

'They'll bring it down,' Chen replied. 'They're armed with the latest gear. But we're going to freeze them. Or try, at least.'

'What! How?' Geo asked, his voice high-pitched.

'Just watch, and do as I do!' A muscle was pulsing uncontrollably under one of Chen cheekbones.

'What makes you think we can copy you?' Diam cried out.

'Because you're both gaea-borns with serious Marshal ancestry. Let's get on with it!"

Chen quickly dug six tiny, elaborate weapons from one of his many pockets. They were as long as matchsticks but thicker. He shared them out equally.

'Watch!' he said, placing one in the middle of each palm. He made fists with both hands, released just his index fingers, and leaning around the corner pointed at the Deterors, muttering nervously, 'Come on! Get in my range!'

Behind Chen, Geo peeked round the corner too. Ten warriors had stopped about two hundred yards from them, raised their thin, narrow shields, each with a transparent viewing screen at the top, and poised their javelins at the ready.

'Go!' Chen yelled.

Four thick beams of electric blue spurted from Chen's hands and he was suddenly holding two full size alien-looking guns, exact copies of the miniature ones he had put in his fists. The beams of light hit the band of approaching Deterors, but bounced off their shields.

'What the …' Geo's heart leapt in his chest as ten homing javelins came whizzing round the corner. One of them grazed his arm; he barely had time to duck and roll along the ground to avoid being skewered by another. He lay flat in the dust, crying out with the shock.

He caught a glimpse of Diam, activating her own guns, then leaping behind a low parapet to her right. Seconds later, another volley of homing javelins, their silver spearheads flashing in the sunlight, hurtled round the corner five inches above their heads.

Chen crawled along on his belly and lifted both his hands up again. His two weapons shot out four bands of electric blue that this time pulsed and looped around some of the warriors. 'Remember! Just do what I do!' Chen screamed at Geo and Diam. 'Diam, can you deal with the guards at the temple gate, while we distract the defence squadron?'

'I can have a go,' Diam said, and ran off among the buildings to their left, by-passing the fighting.

Geo tried uselessly to copy Chen as another javelin came whizzing round the corner.

Shaking, he opened his palms to check that the miniature guns were still in his fists. They were. He peered out and saw the Deterors now only eighty feet or so away. Chen cursed as a new volley of javelins shot past, just missing his head.

Geo concentrated on the Deterors' feet. He reckoned that, to get a strike, Chen would have to aim very accurately at the warriors' feet, as their shields seemed to resist all his attacks any higher. Geo pointed with his index fingers, just like Chen, and this time *willed* his guns to work. At first there was nothing, but then he noticed something happening to his hands, which appeared a little darker and more angular. Two faint, almost invisible bands of ruby red trembled out of his right hand, then quivered and vanished like wisps of cloud. He tried again, this time with every drop of concentration he could muster. Although he dared not look up, he guessed The Deterors were no more than twenty strides away now. Geo took aim again, though it seemed impossible to get a clear view of their feet. All of a sudden a blurred but colourful picture turned up in his mind. It showed a large gun in his hand spewing out a lasso of light. Then, miraculously, the two small guns grew enormous in his hands, while two ropes of ruby red flew out of them, straight and true, and looped around the nearest Deteror's foot, pulling him down. That was when he realised what he had to do. 'Aim for their toes!' he hissed at Chen, steadying his shaking hands.

But even though he'd managed to trip up one of the Deterors, the warrior soon scrambled to his feet and came roaring and charging at them with the force of an enraged bull.

Ten strides, nine, eight, seven. Chen rolled next to Geo on the ground just as the squadron leader bounded round the corner. 'Get his ankles,' Geo repeated, feeling a sudden surge of power that seemed to rise from the soles of his feet, sweep through his body and crash into his brain like a wave.

His hair stood on end. His eyes took in the same scene but perceived it differently: he could see auras and energy fields, bands of azure, spirals of indigo and cardinal red streaked with bright yellow. Suddenly he felt connected with Chen in a way that was impossible to explain. There was no longer any need for words between them. They just worked together, each knowing what the other would do, which Deteror they would bring down next. A silent flash of indigo, followed by spikes of fiery red, swept the ground. Had the fireworks been produced by Geo, or Chen or both? Not that it mattered. It was a direct hit! The Deterors' leader looked stunned, his whole body going rigid before smashing onto the ground with a thud.

Chen gave Geo a thumbs-up. 'Nice one!' he yelled.

Another Deteror – the second-in-command, Geo guessed – took the lead. Reaching the corner, he flew at them, grunting like a rhino. With lightning speed, Geo rolled aside, counter-attacking with the same trick he'd used on the leader. Like a film going into painfully slow motion, the second warrior now crunched to a standstill.

The rest of the warriors had reached them now, pulling out axes, daggers and machetes. Geo leapt and bounded, vaulted and thrashed about on the ground to avoid their blows, yelling while shooting ruby red lassos of light at their feet. He found it easier to target their ankles at close quarters and, as he tripped them up, Chen could shoot behind their shields and freeze them with a blast of darker blue.

Geo had no idea exactly how his weapons worked, but they certainly did: soon, the remaining Deterors looked as though they were wading through treacle. Their movements became increasingly slower. Their heads strained, eyes rolled, their mouths grunted unrepeatable curses. Their growls were the last to fade away. It made Geo think of a film's sound track going wrong and finally grinding to a halt. Eight of the Deterors fell stiffly like toy soldiers to join the others, while two remained standing, frozen like grotesque statues.

'Wow,' Chen said, his weapons growing smaller and ghostlier in his hands. 'If only we could fight like this on Earth ...' he added with an impish grin.

'What is that supposed to mean?' Geo panted, taking deep gulps of air. His guns were beginning to shrink, too.

'None of this could happen outside Oeska. The realm of Gaea has different natural laws.'

But Geo had more urgent things in his mind. 'Diam!' he cried out, turning sharply towards The Hall of Records. Now the battle was over, he spotted her at the foot of the temple gates. Dwarfed by the sheer size of The Hall, she was waving and shouting at them.

'Done it!' she yelled, cupping her hands round her mouth. 'Come and see!'

They found her with the two remaining temple gate

guards, who were standing stiffly to attention, eyes glazed, unconscious of anything around them.

Chen gave an appreciative whistle. 'What kind of attack did you use, my gifted friend?' he smiled.

'Well, I just kept reminding myself what you told us!'

'Which bit?'

'About being the two last gaea-borns with serious Marshal ancestry. And the other thing you said, "Just do as I do."' Grinning, Diam shook one of the Deterors' massive armoured hands. It fell with a clank against his side. 'They'd make an excellent tourist attraction,' she added with a little smile.

CHAPTER TWENTY-SIX

Dreamboarding with Geo

'That was epic!' Chen said with a laugh. But the moment he tried to push open the temple gates, his mood changed.

'They won't budge!' He ran his hand through his bleached hair. He turned to Geo. 'Well, don't just stand there. We don't have long before the Deterors perk up!'

'They *what*? How soon?' Geo asked, horrified, realising they were wasting time.

Chen rolled his eyes. 'At this rate, before we've even broken into The Hall.'

'So what do you want me to do?' he asked quickly.

'You've got the best door-opening tool in town,' Chen snapped, 'and you're asking *me* what to do?'

Of course! Geo went through the usual routine of grasping the spider web ring charm with one hand; then he touched the temple gate with the other. He hadn't even got past the first word of the chant when he heard several bolts sliding upwards and sideways on the other side. Perhaps because it was just a door and not a towering castle wall, Geo found it much easier than breaking into Oeska.

'Great!' he cried out, as the right-hand gate whirred and then clicked open, leaving a gap wide enough for them to squeeze in one at a time.

But the moment Geo's eyes adjusted to the dim light inside the building, he stopped dead in his tracks. There was nothing there. The cavernous interior of The Hall stretched for what seemed like miles, shadowy and completely bare. The building's far wall disappeared into the gloom beyond. All they could see was a stone bench in the middle of the floor, about a quarter of a mile from the entrance.

He stood on the spot, staring. 'How can this be a Hall of Records? Where are the flipping records?'

'I'll show you later!' Chen sounded really on edge. 'For now, can you just give me a hand?' He pushed the gate with all his weight, and Diam and Geo heaved either side of him.

When they managed to shut it, Diam tied her long black hair on the nape of her neck to cool down. 'Phew! This should keep them out!' she said, helping Chen and Geo push the bolts across.

'Yeah, for all of two minutes,' Chen panted, then ran ahead into the immense room. 'Hurry up!'

They followed, their footfalls echoing in the empty space.

Geo could see no windows, only occasional skylights cut in the high roof. They let in beams of light that slanted across the stone bench they had seen from the entrance, and towards which Chen now led them. Closer by, Geo saw that it was a finely crafted stone seat with detailed engravings of tiny human figures flying, without wings, in and out of clouds. The scent of cinnamon and cloves wafted deliciously around it. *Where is that coming from?*

Chen already sat on the stone bench, palms upturned and resting on his knees. He looked up to the beams of light that poured into the immense building through the skylights. Geo and Diam joined him and he gave Geo a nudge. 'So – let's start with the guy's name,' he murmured. 'And his age.'

'Right.' Geo scratched his head, embarrassed by how little he knew about his dad's colleague. 'He's called Jameson. I don't know his age, but he's a grown man.'

'Now, listen carefully.' Chen sounded very business-like, all of a sudden. 'Going to the earthly realm,' he added slowly, 'is safe enough. But if, at any stage, you get *any* chance at all to enter Cromund's kingdom, no matter how tempting or safe this chance seems to be, you must not give into it. OK?'

'But why?' Geo asked.

'Because, if you go in, there's no telling what might happen.'

'What do you mean?' Diam asked.

'I just said: there's *no telling*,' Chen replied, his voice clipped. 'We have no idea what natural laws operate inside it. For all we know, in his own realm, Cromund may have some means of hijacking Geo's dreamcatcher without damaging it.'

'So it's dangerous?' asked Diam, her voice tense.

'Yes!' Chen replied bluntly. 'It could be deadly.'

Diam, who was sitting next to Geo, pushed her hair off her face and took his hand in hers. 'No matter what information we come across about your dad,' she said, the pupils of her eyes huge in the subdued light, 'promise me that you won't be tempted to go into Cromund's kingdom. Promise me.'

'I'm not stupid,' said Geo, squeezing her hand.

'Ah – that was not a promise!' she said, spotting his avoidance tactic.

'Well, I promise I *won't* take you into Cromund's kingdom,' he reassured her; and before she had a chance to nit-pick and argue that he had not included himself in his promise, he clapped his hands, adding, 'So what are we waiting for, the Deterors to wake up?'

'Geo,' said Chen, '*you* sit between us. Now use your thumb and forefinger to hold on to the wolf-head. Gently!' he added, as Geo's fingers clamped the wolf-head in an anxious grip.

Chen raised his arms and looked up at the golden beams of slanting light. 'We look for the one named Jameson,' he said, his voice amplified in the echoing space. 'A grown man.'

Geo and Diam gasped as hundreds of wafer-thin slates popped out of the walls like drawers. Hovering above half of the slates Geo could see the ghostly shapes of men fast asleep. The empty ones, Geo guessed, were ones whose occupants were awake. He realised there were way too many people to choose from here. They had to narrow it down.

'Say an Englishman!' Geo whispered hoarsely, hoping that Jameson was actually English.

'We look for the one named Jameson; a man who comes from England.'

Many of the drawers snapped shut back into the walls of the building. But there were still at least a hundred open.

'This is impossible!' Geo said. 'Try *Doctor* Jameson,' he whispered. 'And say London!'

'We look for the one named Jameson – a man who comes from London and is a doctor,' said Chen, fixing his eyes on the shafts of light. Dozens of drawers slid shut, leaving only five.

'Still too many of them!' Geo said in dismay. 'But he's not a medical doctor. Say "an academic".'

'We look for the one named Dr Jameson, a man and academic who lives in London.'

Geo jumped as a thunderous crash exploded from the temple gates. He turned to see the bolts throbbing and rattling under violent strikes. Five thumps boomed through The Hall, and then a sixth. The air vibrated with the Deterors' roars and war cries.

But the temple gates remained shut. Their bolts were holding fast.

Geo turned back to The Hall and realised, with some relief, that only one figure now remained: his father's colleague, he hoped. Chen pointed at the man's sleeping figure with his index finger, tracing a line in space as though he were using a touch-screen.

Geo swung back to check on the gate. He saw axes beginning to tear through the thick wood of the door.

Meantime, the thin platform holding Jameson — his Jameson, Geo hoped —came out of the wall and floated gently down to the level of Geo's chest. On it was a tall man with sallow skin and thinning hair, in stripy blue and white pyjamas, fast asleep.

The noise from the temple gates was deafening as more axes bashed against them.

'Go on then!' Chen said. 'Link arms and use your spider charm!'

Geo linked arms with Chen and Diam, gripping the ring with his right hand and squeezing the tiny spider web between his thumb and forefinger. With his left hand, Geo reached out and touched the forehead of the sleeping man between the eyes. His mind was at first overcome by the noise of the Deterors' axes and then went completely blank.

At the edge of his field of vision, Geo saw a long, narrow panel come off the door and fall into the room. Armoured limbs poked through the opening; bodies began to squeeze through.

Words slipped and slid around in Geo's brain, as he struggled to remember the correct phrasing.

'Say it! Say the chant!' Diam pleaded. 'Have you forgotten? *Spiders know nothing of closed doors* or something … Geo, say the spell!'

'Shut up, you're making it worse! *The spider knows nothing of a closed door. She'll come into your house anyway.*' Nothing! He hesitated, furious with himself. '… *she'll get inside your house anyway.*' Nothing.

The Deterors were trickling through the smashed-up door into the hall by now, their snarling, barking voices, excruciatingly amplified in the echoing space. He saw a glint of metal as they angled and poised their javelins ready to throw. '*The spider …*' Geo took a deep breath, closing his eyes and telling himself that of course he knew the exact word sequence, knew it with every cell in his body. When he reopened them, javelins were arcing towards them. '*The spider,*' he intoned in the deep, low-pitched drone he'd first heard from Hymal, '*knows nothing of closed doors. She will come into your house anyway...*'

As the javelins closed to rain down on them, Geo felt himself falling and at the same time collapsing into himself, shrinking to the size of a doll, a thumb, a dust particle, an atom. He funnelled down into Jameson's head, as if he was being swirled in a gentle whirlpool, dragging the others with him.

Far, far away, as if in a deep cave, he heard the clang of high-tech javelins denting the stone floor in The Hall of Records. Behind him, Diam and Chen were shrieking and whooping like kids going down a rollercoaster.

***

'What if the Deterors follow us?' Diam yelled.

'Jameson would have vanished back into the wall,' Chen replied, standing up. They seemed to be in an odd, cramped place, squashy and padded, and lit by a flickering, bluish light. 'If they don't know his details they won't be able to trace him.'

'Can't they do a search?' asked Geo.

'Can a rhino surf the net?' Chen chortled. 'Besides The Hall doesn't keep a record of its own history.' He turned round full circle to examine his surroundings. His eyes seemed wide with curiosity and wonder. Geo didn't find this very reassuring.

Diam stretched out her arms and felt the space around her, trying to orient herself.

'What now?' Geo asked Chen, his voice a bit panicky.

'What do you mean? *You're* the dreamcatcher-bearer.'

'B-but you said-'

'That I was desperate for a chance to meet someone

like you, with a working dreamcatcher,' Chen reminded him. 'Hell, are you really *that* inexperienced?'

Geo felt like hitting him. 'Well, you said you knew what you were doing,' he snapped. 'Now – let me think.'

Geo trawled through everything he knew about dreamboarding, trying to make sense of what was going on: he had used the spider charm, the key that unlocks doors. By using it, they had unlocked the first door that led to Jameson's dreams. But there was a second door and he had to find it. 'We're probably in Jameson's brain,' he concluded slowly. 'So I think we should look for Jameson's memory.'

'Do *you* know how to do that?' Diam said, looking hopefully in Chen's direction.

'Your guess is as good as mine,' he replied, his manner casual.

A colourful assortment of swear words rushed into Geo's head but he managed to restrain his anger. Studying their surroundings, he took a couple of steps to his left towards a small field of thick, mushroom-coloured twisting tubes, stuffed with soft fleshy tissue that throbbed gently in rhythm with Jameson's heartbeat. In the distance he could hear the ebb and flow of the sleeper's blood pumping through his arteries. The light kept flickering and changing hues. The gloom was studded with little electrical flashes; some were like small blue fireworks, others bright fountains of silver and purple that blossomed, sparked and died out against the darkness.

'Probably the electrical impulses in his brain,' Geo guessed. He'd read it in his last biology book.

'Well?' Diam said. 'What next?'

'I guess we've got to work out a way to get inside his dream,' Geo replied.

'I wonder if we could use these light fountains – I mean electrical impulses.' Diam asked, her voice uncertain.

Chen was crawling about on all fours checking out a forest of fleshy nodes that waved about like heads of corn.

Geo put his hand over one of the spark-emitting nodes. At once, the image of a large, unfamiliar classroom flickered into his mind.

'Wow, yes,' he said. 'I think I just got a glimpse of a dream.'

'Great! Is it possible we could just jump into one of the spark fountains?' Diam suggested.

'Maybe!' Geo leaned over the largest of them. A bluish tentacle of brilliant light spurted out of it, winding itself round his neck like a warm scarf. He tried not to flinch. Squinting, he stared at the well-lit centre of the spark fountain. He realised that what he had seen was not a classroom so much as a small lecture theatre with a stream of students strolling in and taking their seats.

Geo's heart leaped inside his chest as he watched. This is what he'd been hoping for – to gain access to Jameson's dreams, hoping he might be able to question the dreamer about his dad.

'Right! I'll jump first.' Without waiting for a response from the others, Geo dived headlong into the nearest fountain of blue.

'Wait for me!' he heard Diam call out behind him.

***

Geo and Diam floated gently down to the floor of the small, noisy lecture theatre, and turned to see Chen landing smartly on his feet behind them. The teacher had not arrived yet. The students were a gruff-looking lot in huge white trainers and jeans so baggy that the crotches had slipped down to their knees. Some played cards, some chatted and swore, some talked on their mobiles, complaining about the college being rubbish, the teachers crap, and the computers a pile of old junk.

Geo, Diam and Chen sneaked off to the back row, hoping no one would notice them.

A tall, thin teacher turned up by the door, dressed in a

smart jacket with nothing underneath it except a pair of crumpled boxer shorts. He staggered slowly to the podium with a pile of handouts wedged between his chin and his clasped hands. It was Jameson.

He plonked his pile of papers on the table, pulled up his boxer shorts and turned to his class.

'Good morning and welcome!' he said with a forced smile. Most students ignored him and carried on with whatever they were doing; the few who didn't ignore him, pelted him with paper aeroplanes.

Then a voice full of contempt seemed to waft up from the underside of Jameson's desk. 'Plenitude and Platitude,' it spat out, 'the most boring subject in the known universe. A two-year course of drivel in Winnydung College for Insipid Morons. Job satisfaction: nil. Capacity of average student brain: pea. Brain capacity of highest academe: cherry tomato. Capacity of local genius: small, rotting tangerine.'

A wind began to blow and Jameson's dream turned into a nightmare. Torrents of his handouts folded themselves into darts and began to attack his students. Paper aeroplanes crashed into the ceiling, changed direction and escaped out of an open window. Exam papers swirled madly in whirlpools. Sheets of closely-typed notes blew everywhere as if caught in a hurricane.

Manuscripts and lecture materials crammed the voids under Jameson's table, blocked the windows and jammed the gaps under the doors. Handouts got scrunched up, stuffed themselves into Jameson's mouth and wriggled up his nose. Paper folded itself into origami birds that flew up his boxer shorts, or into caterpillars that slid into his ears.

All the time, Geo watched on, bewildered.

With surprising decorum, Jameson peeled the handouts from his face. 'Silence! Silence in the room!' he addressed his students, who were laughing hysterically.

'What's going on?' Diam whispered.

'We seem to be in the middle of a weird teacher's nightmare,' Geo replied.

'But why is he in his underwear?' Diam hissed, stifling a laugh.

'I don't know! Maybe it's an anxiety dream?'

'But whose was that creepy voice that said the students are all morons?' Diam asked.

Geo gave a shrug. 'No idea.'

'Could be Jameson's mind-chatter,' Chen whispered. 'You know, words and phrases that float about in your mind while you sleep?'

The paper storm was now abating. 'Waste of effing time!' a tall student grumbled, marching out of the classroom.

'Wish this college would employ someone who can teach for a change,' said a short, tubby guy who followed the tall one. The rest of them soon marched out of the classroom too, leaving Jameson behind, sifting through the ruins of several lecture plans.

'But how do we get to Jameson's memory store from this place,' Geo whispered to Chen. 'I need to try and access stuff about my dad.'

'I've heard that the memory store is where recurrent anxiety dreams are kept,' Chen replied. 'And this looks like a recurrent anxiety dream, if I ever saw one!'

'Silence at the back!' Jameson glared at them, banging the table with a frying pan that had somehow materialised on his desk. Then he barked, 'You! I've never seen you in this class before. What are your names?'

Geo got up and strolled over to the front of the lecture theatre. 'You haven't seen us because we've never boarded your dream before,' he said evenly, deciding it would be only fair to tell the truth. 'I am Geo,' he added. 'Max Cleigh's son. I think you knew my father.'

Jameson stepped back as if he'd seen a scorpion. 'Oh!' Then he leaned forward, ogling Geo's face, his eyes bulging a little. 'And whatever makes you think I knew your father?'

Geo frowned. After all they'd been through, did they have the wrong man?.

But the voice that had come from under Jameson's table now crept down the walls, filling the space with sighs. Long strings of words slithered around the room. Ghostly whispers slid across the floor, slipping under the desks, until, out of all the confusion of sounds, the scornful disembodied voice spat out a few words that rose above everything else:

> 'Max's son had a wolf in hand
> Until he met his match,
> Who fetched a gun
> And a frying pan
> And served his brains
> To Cromund.'

CHAPTER TWENTY-SEVEN

The Inverted Pyramid

'But why would you want to do that?' Geo asked Jameson calmly, taken aback at the aggressiveness in the words.

Jameson clutched his head as though he had a migraine. 'Whatever did you do that for?' he bellowed.

'Did what?'

'Remind me of stuff I'm trying to forget.'

'I need you to tell me everything you know about Max Cleigh,' Geo replied evenly, while Jameson staggered about like a drunk, clutching his head. Geo began to feel seasick. The room spun and now he, like Jameson, found it hard to stand up. He grabbed hold of the table, but it slid off the podium and he tumbled onto the floor with it. He pushed himself back up and tried to walk in a straight line. The room was blurring and tilting. In the distance he could hear Jameson's heartbeat and the loud rumble of his snoring.

'Chen! Diam! Where are you?' The tilt became so bad that it threw him to the floor again where he rolled across the classroom floor, towards the door.

'No worries, Geo, he's only turning in his sleep!' Geo recognised Chen's voice, though he couldn't see him.

'Where are you?' he called out.

'With Diam. We think you're about to dreamboard an older event,' Chen replied. 'Stay exactly where you are. Stay with Jameson.'

Geo's heart gave a kick as he rolled into a stuffy room. The place was crammed with odd bits of furniture, dusty plants, tourist souvenirs, ugly ornaments and dozens of framed pictures. There was so much stuff everywhere, he wondered if he had entered some chaotic second-hand shop. But at least the floor was no longer tilting.

He sat up and saw Jameson sitting right in front of him in an armchair, wearing corduroy trousers and a brown shirt. He was talking to someone and Geo had to look behind him to see who it was. It was his father! Max stood with his back to a fireplace, his powerful face preoccupied, looking exactly as Geo remembered him when he was just a boy. Geo's heart boomed at the excitement of it and he leapt up from the floor, his whole body flooding with joy.

'Dad!' he shouted, trying to catch his eye. But Max looked away, completely ignoring him. 'Dad! Hello?' Geo moved so close, he could have tweaked his dad's nose and still Max took no notice. He waved his hand over his father's face. Nothing!

'Can't you see me?' Geo stared into the mirror above the mantelpiece, which reflected the back of his dad's head. No reflection of Geo's own face stared back.

So he wasn't really present in this room, and could only watch the action. But why? Perhaps because it was just a fixed dream memory?

But he had more urgent things to work out. Clearly, there was no point in trying to talk to his father – he was invisible to him. But he could at least try to gather information. He looked around him at the cramped, messy, overheated living room that smelt of burnt toast and musty clothes. He noticed three children sitting huddled in front of a TV at the far end, eating crisps and watching what sounded like Saturday morning cartoons, while their mother –Jameson's wife? – trudged around, sifting and sorting through piles of stuff, anxiously muttering, 'Has anyone seen my wallet?'

Looking annoyed, Jameson got up from the armchair and made a dive for the front door, squeezing past a mound of anoraks and shoes, signalling to Max to follow him.

Then Jameson turned in his sleep and Geo felt himself being tipped, rolled and ejected into another dream.

He was half-swimming, half-flying behind a hot-air balloon that travelled across an intensely blue sky. Geo's heart leapt – perhaps it was the balloon that Uncle Ian mentioned! Were they in Egypt? The balloon carried three passengers: Max, Jameson and a third man who wore western clothes with an Arab head-dress, and who looked at the desert through a pair of binoculars.

A map flapped in the breeze, wrapping itself round Jameson's head; another gust blew it off his face and tore it into tiny, fish-shaped shreds that floated lazily around the balloon. The third man took out a fishing rod and caught the bits of map one by one from the sky. Geo swam through the air faster, trying to catch up.

The desert stretched out beneath him – a vast, empty sea of sandy waves, barren hills, harsh sunlight and shifting shadows. Except for an occasional word exchanged by the three passengers, he could only hear the flapping of a rope against the balloon. The air smelt dry, hot and dusty. He looked up at the balloon. The map had somehow pieced itself back together again and Geo saw his dad doing a quick calculation in the left margin and pointing at a flat, round mound in the desert.

Then Jameson wrote some co-ordinates in the right margin of the map in neat black ink.

Geo swam furiously through the air, managing to grip the gondola of the hot-air balloon to pull himself closer. He listened in.

'There! Can you see the outline of The Buried City?' Max asked Jameson, who glanced at the map, picked up the binoculars and looked through them.

'Just about,' he said. 'What's that faint circle around the ruins?'

'Aziz,' Max addressed the Arab, 'do you think that may be the city wall?'

'It is,' said Aziz. 'But it's almost sunk under the shifting sands…'

'We are lucky to be able to see it at all,' Jameson added.

'When the north wind blows,' Aziz explained, 'it disappears altogether. But November is the season of the south winds, which is why you can just about see it.'

'Have there been any archaeological excavations in the area?' Jameson asked.

'No,' Aziz replied. 'The shifting sands make it almost impossible to excavate here. And there's no road access. Once upon a time the city had plenty of water. There were trees, gardens, even pastures. Caravans crossing the desert used it as a stage-post. Not any more, though,' he added, pursing his lips.

Geo waited patiently, as his dad and Aziz grounded the balloon inside the city wall. The Arab jumped out of the gondola first. Jameson passed him spades, pickaxes, torches and a length of rope. Max consulted his map and took some measurements from the west wall to a huddle of crumbling buildings in the middle of the Buried City.

'Here!' he said, and all three of them grabbed spades and began to dig at the spot Max had indicated. It was late afternoon and the sun was setting. In the west, the sky turned rich orange and then faint lilac.

Geo sat cross-legged, a few metres away as the men kept digging, until they unearthed a square slab of dark stone about a metre wide. It was smaller than the Zonissos stone that had appeared in place of the fountain, after the earthquake, but it was similar. The deeper they dug, the more it became clear that the stone tapered narrower towards the bottom. Geo's heart gave a lurch. This was clearly the upturned pyramid Uncle Ian had talked about! The object destined never to find itself in a museum, which his dad had been so determined to find. Had he really found it? Was all this based on Jameson's memory? Or was it just nonsense from some random dream?

The sun was sinking behind the dunes. Against the vivid red colours of the desert sunset, his dad stepped into the middle of the upturned pyramid base. Jameson and the workman stopped digging and looked on, seeming puzzled.

'What's up, Max?' Jameson demanded. 'What are you doing?'

His dad planted his feet firmly on the square stone, opened his arms towards the setting sun and murmured something. Geo gasped, as a powerful gust of wind blew, then two lines of fire raced diagonally across the square base of the pyramid, which divided into four equal triangles and began to open slowly inwards, like a trap-door. Max raised his arms above his head like a diver about to take the plunge. Then, bringing his palms together so they touched, he let himself slide down into the engulfing darkness underfoot.

The wind grew stronger, blowing sand over the lines of fire, which soon died out. The stone closed up as smoothly as it had opened. Where had his dad gone? What was inside the upturned pyramid? Jameson and the local man leapt onto the stone, cursing and shouting, trying to prise it open with their spades. But it would not budge.

The wind blew even harder. A violent sandstorm rose with uncanny speed. Jameson and Aziz ran for shelter behind the remains of the low stone wall of a ruin.

Geo crouched behind a small boulder, waiting for the storm to blow over.

***

As Geo sheltered, Jameson's dream broke into a million specks of colour. Darkness engulfed him; he closed his eyes and breathed deeply, feeling scared and drained, exhausted and even a little tearful as he went over what he'd just witnessed. Was the inverted pyramid meaningless, or was it a real memory woven into Jameson's dream? He knew his father had been searching for it. But why did he have to go somewhere so remote to find it? Could it have lead Max into Cromund's kingdom?

The floor tilted again. He guessed that Jameson was probably tossing and turning in his bed. The darkness melted. Geo felt himself floating gently, like a leaf caught in a breeze, down, down to the floor of the lecture room. The desks were empty except for one at the front, already occupied by Chen and Diam, much to Geo's relief.

'Any luck?' Diam asked Geo.

'Tell you later,' he replied, 'got to do something first.' He jumped onto the podium, where Jameson, still in his smart-jacket-no-trousers outfit, was filling his register with a look of immense concentration. Geo tapped him on the shoulder but Jameson ignored him and carried on working. He was marking all his students 'present,' Geo saw. 'Students,' he wrote neatly in his teaching record, 'were asked to conduct library research for their current project.'

'Yeah, right!' said a voice creeping from under the tables.

'Dr Jameson?' Geo said.

'Sssh!' Jameson hissed.

'What do you really know about my father's expedition?' Geo persisted. 'Oh, come on now,' he said, his voice pleading. He grasped his dreamcatcher, hoping that if his spider web charm could open actual doors, perhaps it could help Jameson open up a little and answer his questions. He had no idea how else he'd get him to talk. Grasping the spider charm between his thumb and forefinger, he touched Jameson lightly on the arm and whispered, 'The spider knows nothing of closed doors. She will get into your house anyway.'

At once, Jameson's face changed to a trusting, open expression. He stepped down from the podium and showed Geo to a seat at the back of the class. Geo followed quietly, not daring to speak in case he broke the spell, sat down and bent his head slightly to the side, like someone about to listen to a confession.

'The dream memories you've just seen,' Jameson murmured, 'were from the time when Max Cleigh invited me to take part in his expedition. It was a time before I knew about the other realms and before I even knew of the dreamcatcher belonging to the Cleigh family. All Max had told me when he visited me was that he needed help with his research. I thought we were going to co-author a travel book. He told me he had a publisher waiting for it.

'He did not tell me that the inverted pyramid was the portal to the Kingdom of Prince Cromund. There are seven such portals, each leading to a different realm. I have since only discovered two of these realms, the one named Oeska and one known as The Colony, the realm of Prince Cromund. The portals are generally stable. But occasionally they move to a new area. When this happens, they turn up in a village or town where there is a spring, or other natural source of water. For some reason which I don't I understand, when a portal rises, the source of water dries up at the same time. This is how The Buried City in the desert died.

'To stop humans from asking too many questions about these supernatural events, the Marshals and, increasingly, Cromund, often "piggyback" whatever earthquakes they can use to cover up these portal relocations.'

For a moment, Geo lost all concentration, thinking back to the quake that had demolished his house, his mother's anxiety about Cromund and her excitement when she heard about The Fountain and The Stone. So the Marshals piggybacked the earthquake to create a portal to Oeska!

When he managed to focus again, Jameson was saying, '... the more ruthless of these beings, like Prince Cromund, can also induce earthquakes if it will serve their ends.'

So had Cromund *induced* a whole earthquake? Just to destroy his home?

He lost focus again, and when he regained it, Jameson was saying, '...Max had been very clever at locating the portal you saw in The Buried City. He probably used knowledge he'd gathered from his wife, who has powerful Marshal ancestry and knew about such phenomena. He did vast amounts of research in London. Max is very good at breaking codes. Before he married and went into hiding with Leona in Greece, he worked as a mathematician, highly skilled in using the latest theories of probability and computer intelligence, which make it possible for traders to come up with complex predictions about future values of shares. By using his considerable mathematical skills, not to mention code-breaking, computer-hacking and his personal contacts in the City, he studied trade patterns associated with the activities of the Prince: distribution networks of certain drugs and the supply of the global weapons trade. He worked out that the heartland of some of these operations was neither in London, nor any other world capital, but an obscure country with a large desert area – but not Egypt as everyone thought at the time of his disappearance.'

'I found out all these things after our expedition to the desert, when I had the honour of meeting the Prince myself. You see, it was not his Excellency the Great Prince who was after Max Cleigh, but the other way around. And that was the purpose of the journey you have just seen: for Max to make contact with the Prince.'

'But why?' Geo blurted out.

He knew, even as the words flew out of his mouth, that he had made a big mistake. He had disrupted Jameson's obedient description of events at a most unfortunate moment. As Jameson looked up, Geo saw a different face: cold again, and hard, furious.

'Money, I suppose, and power. I guess that your father, being nothing but a stock exchange gambler before he married, needed more cash. By the time you were nine years old, he probably needed a top-up, what with buying a villa and all that land in Greece, and earning nothing for ten years.'

'My father was a travel writer,' Geo defended angrily.

'Oh, really?' Jameson sneered. 'Well, he certainly squandered a fortune on his travels, yeah; but as for making money from his writing ...' he gave a loud, scornful laugh. 'You must live in cloud cuckoo land if you think a travel writer can actually make enough to live on. But talking of money, Geo,' he carried on in a smooth voice, 'you can, if you like, make a tidy sum by swapping your trinket for some very juicy information.'

Jameson stared at his neck, making Geo shudder. In the rush to get away from the Deterors he'd forgotten to tuck the Hymal dreamcatcher back under his tee-shirt.

'That's not for sale,' he said quickly, hiding his talisman from view.

'Who said anything about selling it? But you might want to *swap* it for something of far greater value! Something priceless.' Jameson's voice had gone soft and oily, while the indistinguishable voice of his mind-chatter crept around the room like a whole nest of hissy serpents.

'As I said – the trinket stays with me,' Geo repeated.

Jameson leaned forward, the murmur of his unconscious mind slithering around them. 'You tell me you're refusing to part with your dreamcatcher, even if you could have your father in its place?'

Jameson sprang up from his seat and began to write something on the whiteboard, while Geo absorbed what Jameson had just said.

Diam and Chen rushed to the podium and grabbed Jameson by the arm, but it was too late to stop Geo from seeing the all-important coordinates.

The room was suddenly steeped in sounds, mathematical symbols and numbers. Longitudes and latitudes showered down from the ceiling in ribbons of light, filling the space above like a laser show. Snippets of information flickered across the board with the dizzying speed of a fast-forwarded video. Image after image of Cairo, Alexandria, the Valley of the Kings, a 'Welcome to Sana'a Airport' sign; a view of the Buried City from the hot-air balloon. And then a still picture floated across the whiteboard, showing Max Cleigh's map with the coordinates marked in the margin in neat, black fountain pen.

'Quick boy! Memorise the figures! They will lead you to your dad,' Jameson called to Geo. 'Have it on me! Have it as a freebie,' he yelled, his face contorted and his mouth speckled with spit. And he began to shout out the map coordinates from the board that would lead Geo to Cromund's kingdom.

'Don't look! Don't listen! Don't go there! It's a trap!' Diam yelled, throwing herself between Geo and Jameson. The whiteboard splintered and fell on the floor. There was a loud hiss. Thick grey mist poured into the room through the windows. The lecture room blurred and went out of focus. The floor juddered. The sound of Jameson's heartbeat became loud and clear. Geo felt as though an invisible hand grabbed hold of him, hoisted him out of Jameson's head and flung him into what seemed to be a forest of thick vegetation, rife with ravenous fleas and armoured dust mites.

CHAPTER TWENTY-EIGHT

The Bedsit Alarm

Speck, pin's head, thumb, doll, boy!

It took about three seconds for Geo to shoot back to his normal size. He glanced around him, surveying the bleak and dingy bedsit where he now was: *definitely back in my world – Earth – realm of Gaea,* he reckoned. It looked like he was in Jameson's room, a kingdom of chipped furniture, grubby rugs, smelly socks and alarm clocks. Opposite a bay window, Jameson, half-asleep in a single bed, was muttering to himself under the covers. Next to his feet was the door to the room. By his head, in an alcove, was a kitchenette, brimming with unwashed mugs and plates. The window overlooked a long street lined with little terraced houses. A depressingly grey dawn light filtered in through the dusty window panes.

In the bay itself, a faded armchair squatted in front of a television set. Empty beer cans, ashtrays, wine bottles and charred bits of foil littered the floor between the TV and the armchair.

Geo's eyes fell on Jameson's bedside clock: 5.34 AM. His stomach tightened. What had happened to Chen and Diam? They should have followed him out of Jameson's dream now. Should he wake the man up? Would it be safe? Perhaps not – what if a dreamboarder got stuck in someone's dream? And … what if a dreamer was to actually die in his sleep?

He decided not to think about that. But his mind wouldn't stop racing, wondering whether his friends were safe.

'Dig it all up!' Jameson said in his sleep. His eyelids twitched – it looked as though he was at the tail end of a waking dream. 'Dig it all out. There's treasure down there! Poxy gate! Damn you Max, give us that key, will you? What does that brat of yours want then? Like father, like son… Come out, boy! Give me that!'

All of a sudden, Jameson sat up bolt upright. He blinked and stared at Geo in a daze. He rubbed his eyes and muttered something that sounded like 'zleebum!' as two tiny specks shot out of his head. Geo leapt aside. The specks hit the carpet, exploding outwards and upwards into figures – Chen and Diam! They staggered towards the door like a couple of drunks.

'Ou-outuvhere. Run! *R-run!*' Chen stammered. Diam struggled with the door latch, rattling, banging and pulling it without effect. Striding forward, Geo fiddled with it and pulled out a matchstick, which had been jammed into the latch. He released the lock. Jameson glared at them groggily from his bed but so far hadn't made a move to come near them.

Then several things happened at once: Jameson raised his arm and pulled a red metal triangle that dangled from a strap next to his bed like an emergency alarm. Geo flung the door open for Diam and Chen, who bolted out of the bedsit. Just as Geo lurched out, he felt a claw-like hand grab him by the neck and drag him back into the room. He screamed in shock, but Jameson slammed him against the floor face-down and kicked the bedroom door shut.

His face pressed into a filthy carpet, at first Geo thought he'd heard the noise of a flick-knife, then he realised it had only been the door latch, locking with a loud snap. With Jameson's weight bearing down on his back, he couldn't think how to wrestle his way out of the man's grip. If only the tricks he and Chen had pulled off against the Deterors would work here! But this was a different realm that obeyed the mundane laws of normal, day-to-day life.

'Give me the trinket, boy! The dream gadget!' Jameson hissed, shoving his knee into Geo's back. At the edge of his field of vision, Geo could see Jameson in the bleak light of the dawn: grey face, teeth bared with the effort, and bloodshot eyes. With a surge of strength, Geo groped behind him, dug his nails into Jameson's thigh, and twisted hard. Jameson yelped.

A searing pain hammered through Geo's head as Jameson landed a heavy blow on his left temple.

Far away, as if he was in a deep well, he could hear Diam and Chen pounding on the door. 'Geo! Are you okay? Jameson, let him go! Geo! Say something!'

'Help me!' The thick, salty taste of blood filled his mouth. The ache in his stomach became a cramp. As the world came back into focus he realised that he was lying face up now. The pain in his stomach was Jameson's knee, pressing down on him, while a pair of bony hands tore at his neck, trying to yank off his dreamcatcher.

Through the fog of his mind, Geo realised one of his hands was free. Though the angle was awkward and his strength weakened, he lashed out, landing a punch on the side of Jameson's face. With a furious yell Jameson rolled off him and snatched a pair of long, pointed scissors from his bedside table.

Geo's world kept coming in and out of focus. His ears felt stuffed with cotton wool. He just managed to scramble up to a half-sitting position against the wall before Jameson pinned his head against the skirting board and forced the scissor tips towards his throat.

'This is the end,' he thought when, with a splintering crash, the door got kicked in and Chen and Diam burst into the room. But they froze in their places when they saw the glint of metal at Geo's throat.

'The dreamcatcher, boy,' Jameson said, the scissor tips digging into Geo's skin. He felt a drop of blood trickle down his throat to the top of his chest. 'Undo it!'

'It won't come off!' Geo lied. 'Anyway – if you kill me, my dreamcatcher will die with me!'

Jameson frowned deeply, pursing his lips. 'Who says I want to kill you?' he said, his upper lip curling slightly. 'Just take it off!' And he moved the scissor tips to Geo's eye in his clenched fist, ready to ram.

'How can I undo it, squashed against the skirting like this?' Geo heard his voice come out in a half-choked gasp.

Jameson shifted reluctantly to give him more room, one eye on Chen and Diam. Someone else flew into the room – a half-dressed guy in pyjama shorts, about his age with a baseball bat, Geo thought perhaps a neighbour who'd got curious about the noise in Jameson's room. Then he heard him say, 'I reckon breaking his friends' kneecaps might help him undo it,' and Geo realised with a horrible shock that the blotchy legs at his eye level belonged to Bob Knock-Shaws.

'Who's going to be first then?' The glee in Bob's voice made Geo's stomach churn. The baseball bat twitched in the boy's hand, as he edged closer to Chen. But what was Bob doing here? Had they played right into Cromund's hands? Did Bob Knock-Shaws know Jameson? He must do! How else could they be here, together?

What a moron I am, Geo thought dimly, *what sort of a sucker would fall into this trap?*

'Hey, boy! Wake up! You want to see Bob's bat in action? He's very good at it!' came Jameson's delighted voice. He was grinning and fumbling with the clasp of Geo's dreamcatcher, his thin lips drawn back into a snarl, his chin flecked with spit, his breath hot and rancid against Geo's face.

Diam gave a scream like a war cry and lunged for Bob's baseball bat, already in mid-swing. And then she kicked Bob savagely on the shins, her deafening screams making Geo's ears ring as she yelled, 'You watch *your* knee-caps. Jerk!' Then, holding on to the bat with both hands, she lost her balance and crashed onto the floor, dragging its owner onto the floor with her.

With Jameson briefly distracted by Diam's spectacular performance, Geo managed to gather both legs to his chest and aim an almighty kick at his opponent. Jameson fell backwards and landed beside Chen, who didn't waste a second: grabbing hold of Jameson's hair from behind, he wrenched the man's head back as hard as he could. Jameson screamed, and Chen used his other hand to yank the scissors off him.

Someone else ran into the room, a squat man in a baggy vest and a pair of horribly tiny underpants.

'Dysoedema!' Geo breathed, his heart sinking. Everything happened too quickly after that: Bob Knock-Shaws kicked out at Diam, rolling her sideways towards Dysoedema's feet; Geo flew at Dysoedema but felt a heavy, stinging blow and a numbing pain in his side. The shock of it took his breath away. He stumbled across the floor, dazed, only able to watch as Dysoedema picked up Diam with his trunk-like arms, threw her over his shoulder and left the room.

'*Do* something, Chen!' Geo screamed.

Chen knocked Jameson out of his way with a punch that sent him crashing into the under-sink kitchen cupboard in a floppy heap. Then, picking up the only chair and using it both as shield and weapon, he charged at Bob and knocked him over. Geo grabbed the baseball bat from Bob who was cursing, trapped under the chair. Then he dived out of the door, leaving Chen to deal with Bob and the unconscious Jameson.

The corridor was empty. Geo padded along, listening for any sound of movement. His pulse drummed in his ears. Where had Dysoedema taken Diam? And how on earth did they know Geo had boarded Jameson's dream?

There were four doors, including the one Geo had just left. The first two Geo tried were locked, but even before he got to the last one it was thrown wide open before him. The squat outline of Dysoedema filled the doorway, blocking what little light came from a window at the far end of the room. Geo froze when he saw that Dysoedema held a gun, and it was pointing straight at Geo's face.

'Welcome!' he said, his piggy eyes assessing Geo coldly. The limp red mouth with its oversized, shark-like teeth rearranged itself into an ugly grin. 'And I don't play games,' he added, pointing at the baseball bat. 'So come in, drop that down and put your hands up.'

Dysoedema backed into the room, so Geo could follow him in. Inside, on the vomit-coloured carpet, lay Diam, bound and gagged with wide silver tape. Sadie Mandiball knelt next to Diam, her perfectly proportioned doll's face glistening with a sweaty sheen.

She looked up as Geo dropped the bat. 'You will hand over your dreamcatcher now, dear, won't you?' she said. She yanked Diam by the hair and pressed a small silver pistol to her head.

Without another thought, Geo began fumbling at his neck to unfasten the dreamcatcher.

CHAPTER TWENTY-NINE

Another Kingdom

Geo fiddled with the clasp of his dreamcatcher, not daring to keep it on and not wanting to take it off. All the while, he stared at the dark spout of Dysoedema's semi-automatic, still pointing at his head. Mouth dry, heart racing, Geo could feel a vein throbbing in the side of his neck.

And then something happened, something so unexpected it felt as though the heavens themselves had opened up to help him out. A myriad of images, postures, holds, kicks and tricks from every martial arts film he'd ever seen, every fight he'd had in the school yard, every kick-boxing class he'd attended as a child came back to Geo and he suddenly remembered how to breathe – long and deep. *It's probably just the adrenaline*, he thought, as his vision became as detailed as a camera zooming into the tiniest crease, fold and speck of dust. He could hear like he had never heard before – the faintest of sounds, distant voices, shuffles, creaks, the breeze ruffling the grass in the garden.

'I'll count to ten...' Dysoedema's voice. 'If your dreamcatcher isn't off by then, Sadie shoots and the girl gets it. Easy. One...'

Geo knew everything he needed was there – locked up in every sinew and cell of his body.

'Two.'

His eyes travelled from Diam's trembling eyelids to Sadie Mandiball's pistol.

'Three.'

He took in the grubby floral curtains.

'Four.'

He registered the single bed with its matching floral bedspread.

'Five.'

His eyes moved on to a chipped desk next to the bed. 'Six.'

And there they stopped.

'Seven.'

He had caught sight of the first useful object in that room.

'Eight.'

A heavy, blue glass paperweight in the shape of a tortoise.

'Nine.'

He finished unclasping his dreamcatcher and tossed it so that it hurtled way above Dysoedema's head into the dark corridor behind him. Cursing, Dysoedema ran after it, while Geo did two things with one flowing move. He kicked backwards fiercely at Sadie Mandiball's hand with his left foot, so that her silver pistol arced up into the air and down towards him. With a flick of his wrist, he snatched the pistol up, then swept up the glass tortoise from the desk and hurtled it with all the speed and strength he possessed at the returning Dysoedema, smashing it into his gun-holding hand. The man roared as the semi-automatic flew off him, fell on the floor and spun towards Geo, who trapped it under his foot and picked it up in a flash. He now had the silver pistol in his left hand, pointing at Sadie Mandiball, and Dysoedema's black semi-automatic in his right, pointing at its owner.

'I'd like my dreamcatcher back, please!' he said, unable to quite believe the position he was in. Something odd had happened to him. As though an angel had guided his hand; as though the universe itself was on his side. *Perhaps,* he thought, his heart flooding with brief, ecstatic joy, *Oeska has rubbed off on me.*

He could hear Diam making excited noises through her gag. Sadie Mandiball glared at her silver gun now in Geo's hand, squealing. He kept it trained at the woman's head, using the semi-automatic to control Dysoedema who stood in the doorway with his beefy, wrestler's forearms held limply up, the dreamcatcher in one hand. His face was so red he looked ready to explode.

'Be my guest! Shoot! Get the armed police swarming all over you,' he growled.

'Just hand over my dreamcatcher, will you? Oh yes, I forgot: *Sir!*' Geo grinned and fired a glancing shot at the carpet beside Dysoedema's shoe. It came out no louder than the thud of a book on the floor. 'Oooh, a silencer! No armed police to come swarming then, is there? Now – give it back!'

Geo saw a muscle pulsing uncontrollably in Dysoedema's right cheek, but still he would not hand over Geo's dreamcatcher. A door slammed, there was the sound of running feet and Chen appeared behind Dysoedema, skidding to a halt, his forehead glistening with sweat.

'Wow!' he blurted, seeing Geo with the two guns. 'Hey, this belongs to my friend.' He snatched the dreamcatcher from Dysoedema, who stood gaping. Then, as Geo's hands still held both guns at their enemies, he ran across the room and snapped the dreamcatcher back in place around Geo's neck. Pulling a Swiss army knife out of one of his many pockets, Chen freed Diam next, found the reel of thick silver tape on the floor that must have been used to tie up Diam and started to bind Dysoedema with it.

'Where's Jameson?' Geo asked.

'A bit tied up,' Chen grinned. 'With the Bob guy.'

Just then Geo heard a door open with what sounded like a kick. A cold draught drifted up the stairs.

'What was that?' Diam rushed out into the corridor, but Geo indicated that she should close the door, take charge of the silver pistol and keep an eye on Sadie Mandiball. Chen finished tying Dysoedema and Geo covered the door with the semi-automatic.

Muffled steps sounded outside. A putrid smell drifted into the room even before the door burst open. A tall man with a large, corpse-like head filled the doorway. His hooded eyes leered at Geo as though he was plotting to suck away his last breath.

'Your Excellency,' Sadie Mandiball murmured, falling to her knees and dropping her gaze to the floor. 'Prince Cromund,' she added breathlessly, 'Your Grace!'

The very air around him tasted of decay.

Geo stared. Cromund carried no weapons. His face was curiously unmarked by smile and frown lines.

'Shoot!' Chen yelled as the man strode towards Geo.

Looking into his eyes, Geo was in no doubt that he had to fire.

Once, twice, three times, he aimed right through the heart. To his horror, only a tear of colourless liquid dribbled out of the bullet holes but Cromund didn't seem at all affected. In fact he didn't even flinch or break his stride as the bullets hit, but closed in, reaching out first for the semi-automatic and then the pistol. Confused, Geo shot again just as uselessly, before Cromund wrenched the weapons from him.

You!' He addressed Geo in slow, heavily accented English, full of guttural harshness. He didn't even bother to point the guns at him. 'You come with me.'

Geo was shaking uncontrollably. It took all his willpower to control his voice enough to say, 'You want my dreamcatcher, right? Well, it can't be taken. It can only be given.'

Cromund gave him a piercing look as though considering whether to kill him on the spot. A repulsive grimace made the skin across his face stretch. 'You will come with me,' he said, 'to meet your father.'

'Give me one reason why I should believe you,' Geo said, his throat dry.

'Sadie...' Cromund nodded in the direction of Mrs

Mandiball. 'Tell him.'

Sadie Mandiball straightened up and said, slowly, 'You are offered an incredible opportunity, Geo. Unmissable. Take the path of no resistance and we promise to take you to your father.'

Geo's mind was ticking fast. He mulled over Sadie Mandiball's words:'take the path of no resistance'. So they didn't want to force him. They wanted him to go willingly, of his own accord and without a fight. It was becoming obvious to him that they had learned their lesson. What had his mother written in that letter? *You are the new dreamcatcher-bearer. Nobody can tear it away from you without destroying it in the process.* So the more they tried to force it off him, the more they risked ruining it.

'Right,' he now said, trying to stop his voice from quivering. He cleared his throat, tying to think, mulling over the surge of power he'd felt during his fight with Dysoedema and wondering if he was changing; perhaps his dreamcatcher was making him better at fighting, stronger, with a clear purpose and an uncluttered mind.

Perhaps he would be able to fight back, once Chen and Diam were safe.

'If – if I agreed to your request,' he said slowly, 'would you let my friends go?' He pointed at the window, which, from this room, overlooked back gardens and a park. He saw the London Eye arching in the skyline a couple of miles down the road. 'That's the deal,' he added. 'Take it or leave it.'

Cromund gave a slight nod, pulled out a knife from a pocket and cut off Dysoedema's bonds. He handed Dysoedema the semi-automatic, saying:'Get his friends to jump over the garden wall, so he can see them leave.'

'Don't go with them! This is madness,' Chen hissed at Geo, as he was pushed out of the room at gunpoint.

'I'm not going!' Diam snarled at Dysoedema, but that was before she was dragged, shrieking, to the door. As she stumbled past Geo she shot him a livid glance and spat out, 'Don't be a fool! It's a trap, can't you see?'

Dysoedema manhandled her out into the corridor and slammed the door behind him.

Geo soon saw his friends being shoved over the garden wall and into the park at the back of the house. Dysoedema kept his semi-automatic trained on them from the end of the garden until they ran off and disappeared into a clump of trees.

'What if his friends fetch the Marshals and they trace him?' Bob asked Sadie, sounding sincerely curious.

'Are you stupid?' Sadie Mandiball hissed. 'He's getting an anti-trace injection right away.' She pulled a syringe out of her bag. 'Hold him still, will you?'

Geo flinched as the tip of a needle pricked his right shoulder. He stayed slumped on his chair, wondering exactly how an injection like that worked.

'Isn't going to interfere with his trinket?' Bob asked in a low voice.

'Will you stop criticising?' Sadie snapped. 'It's just a two-hour injection - until he's in The Colony.'

Then Dysoedema came back and Geo let himself be led to a large four-wheel drive with black tinted windows, waiting at the front of the house. He didn't resist as Bob Knock-Shaws bound and blindfolded him, then bundled him to the floor of the vehicle. He heard the rumble of the engine and they set off, Geo hoping he hadn't just made the biggest mistake of his life.

CHAPTER THIRTY

The Strangest Meeting

They drove on through the busy London traffic. Without a chance to see anything or get up from the floor, Geo's world shrank into a confusion of sounds. In case it could help him retrace the car journey, he tried to memorise the underground train vibrations, the wail of sirens, the squeal of carriages as commuter trains screeched in and out of stations and the muffled thunder of planes crossing the sky above the great city.

From the front of the car he could hear Sadie Mandiball trying to make small talk with a man of few words; it could be Dysoedema. They got stuck in a traffic jam, then, for perhaps twenty minutes – he wasn't really sure – picked up speed along a stretch of smoother road, until they slowed down and went round a large, even loop. It led to what felt like a maze of streets with frequent turns left, right, left, left again. This area sounded quiet and residential, judging by the occasional twittering of birds. A few minutes later, they made a slow, sharp turn to the left. A gate clanged shut and the car went down a slope – an underground garage, he presumed – where they stopped. Someone pulled Geo up, leading him out of the car, into a carpeted corridor, up a lift and into a room.

Someone cut off his bindings. His sweaty blindfold was torn away and he blinked, looking around and trying to orient himself. Geo was in a grand room with a high ceiling, cornicing, deep sofas, armchairs and thick carpets. Right in front of him, their legs apart, two beefy men in dark suits cracked their knuckles and glared at him as though he were a fly they could swat with a slap. Sadie Mandiball was in the room, too, sinking into one of two armchairs on his left. She pointed to a seat just behind Geo, a plush sofa set in front of a long bay window. Its curtains were drawn though, so that neither the radiance of the sun nor any hint of what might lie outside came into the room. In front of him was a coffee table. Directly across the floor from his sofa was a large door, on either side of which the two burly men now moved. On his left next to the armchair where Mrs Mandiball sat was a writing bureau, a smaller sofa and a couple of wall paintings. On his right two tall bookcases stood in the alcoves on either side of a black marble fireplace; a huge, gilded mantelpiece mirror, set above it, reflected most of the room.

With Chen and Diam safely out of the way, Geo toyed with the idea of escaping, hoping he might be able to dredge up the same odd kind of energy he had experienced during his fight with Dysoedema. But the problem was, he wasn't sure he *wanted* to escape; he reckoned that if Cromund had told the truth, he was about to have the one thing he wanted more than anything else in the world, the longed-for meeting with his father.

He decided to wait until he had seen Max. He was so close now! How could he possibly *not* meet his father? He sat drumming his fingers on the arm of the sofa, with Sadie Mandiball sitting opposite as though this were some cosy social gathering. He found this idea so depressing that he pulled the hood of his sweatshirt over his head, folded his arms, hunched his shoulders and kept his gaze on the floor. He had imagined the reunion with his father so many times, but now that it had finally arrived, everything was wrong. There was a tightness in his chest as though a fist had lodged itself there. Never before had he wanted and at the same time dreaded something so much. A sick feeling gurgled in the pit of his stomach. Until now, he had refused to believe the story of Max's defection to

Cromund. For the first time, he wondered if it might turn out to be true.

The door opened, Geo held his breath... and his father walked in.

'Max!' Sadie Mandiball got up from her seat, smiling and greeting him with a hug like an old friend.

'Ah, Sadie, I see you've rounded up my wayward son.' His dad smiled with the easy charm Geo remembered well. The tightness at the top of Geo's chest became unbearable; he could hardly breathe. 'I hope you don't mind...' Max gave him the slightest of glances. 'Perhaps the guys could wait outside?'

There was a note of unmistakable command in his voice. Mrs Mandiball nodded and trotted obediently out of the drawing room, taking the two guards with her.

'So, Geo, first things first,' Max said, taking the armchair on which Sadie Mandiball had been sitting and dragging it closer. 'How was your journey?'

From the shadows of his hood Geo stared back, mystified. He had no idea what was going on, but he did know one thing: he had not expected to hear words like 'wayward son' or to sit facing his father like a kid pulled in before the headmaster. No hug, no handshake even. This wasn't what it was meant to be like.

'You've no idea what I've been through to get here,' Geo said, his voice croaky with distress and anger.

'Tell me everything. But first – if you don't mind – I'm not used to talking to people in hoods.'

'That's too bad,' Geo said. 'But as for telling you "everything", I reckon it should be you who does the talking. Like, why you left when I was nine without a word, and never came back or kept in touch, and how come people talk about you as the guy who changed sides to Cromund.'

'Geo! Don't speak to me like that. And take down your

hood. It's hard to hold a conversation with someone dressed like a street robber.'

'Really?' Geo burst out. 'Look who's talking, the guy whose "friends" shot tranquiliser darts at me, tortured me with sleep deprivation, hunted me down, ambushed me, threatened to shoot my friends, and are still trying to blackmail me to get hold of the dreamcatcher. Have you got any idea what I've been through? And all for what? A dreamcatcher they can't even have? Why don't you just *take* it if it'll make your friends so happy? I'm just sick of this whole thing.' He put his hands to his throat to unfasten the dreamcatcher. He really had had enough of everything.

'Geo, no!' The colour faded from his father's face. He fixed his eyes on the marble fireplace before speaking again. 'Giving it in resentment,' Max said, his voice sounding dull and unemotional, 'won't work for you or us. There are good reasons why Prince Cromund wants you on side. But until you are able to show a bit of goodwill, there's no point handing over your dreamcatcher. Of course, I'm sorry if they've been a bit heavy-handed. You're clever and stubborn and won't give in easily. I expected no less from my son. I'll have words with them.'

'Oh, I like that.' Geo gave a bitter laugh. 'You'll have words with Cromund's thugs! Like it was just a bit of playground bullying! And it was much more than "heavy handed".'

'But you're here, now, safe, and the most important thing for you is to be happy, and only do things that you want to do…' It was as if Max was trying to sound upbeat, but not making a good job of it. He glanced furtively towards the black marble fireplace again.

'Oh, I see. So now your buddies finally worked out – after weeks of hunting me down – that they can't just snatch the dreamcatcher off me, and that you have to make me happy first, so I give it away *willingly*, is that right?'

'No! It's because it's the best way,' Max protested, giving him a smile; but Geo could not read his eyes.

'Well, it may be the best way for you and your – your *buddies* – but not for me. You know, Dad, I thought you cared! I thought you had risked everything to come to my rescue in that earthquake. I thought you were someone amazing, magical even ...' He folded his arms and pulled his hood lower over his forehead.

'I am honoured that you ...'

'*Don't* be,' Geo cut in harshly. 'It wasn't meant as a compliment. Anyway, you still haven't told me why you left in the first place.'

There was a pause, and Geo couldn't resist looking up. His dad's face was deathly pale against his flawless night-blue suit. Max took a deep breath.

'I left,' he said, 'to meet with Prince Cromund. He led me to the portal in the desert, the gate to his kingdom.'

'And once you discovered what fun it was to be back with him, you didn't want to come home any more?'

'If you really want to know, Geo,' Max snarled, his lips thin with anger, 'nine years of living as a mortal had taken their toll on the charm and grace your mother had when we'd first met. Very little remained of the woman I had once fallen in love with. I'd been completely taken in by her when I'd first met her, which was why I agreed, against my better judgement, to live with her on that obscure Greek island. By the time you were nine, I'd been really missing ... my real work.'

'So Jameson didn't lie to me,' Geo cut in, 'not about that, at least. You were some rich stock exchange gambler before you met Mum?'

'Gamblers are losers, Geo...'

'While you were the winning type, right?'

'By some people's standards!' Max shrugged, looking nonplussed. 'And words like "rich" mean very little in that world. There are always people far richer than you – even so, after I left the island, I carried on sending your mother money from a secure Swiss bank account.'

'Oh, cheers, Dad, that was really decent of you!'

'I see you are skilled at sarcasm. So, what did you think? That Father Christmas dropped credit cards down your mother's chimney? And how do you think Leona managed to maintain an 18th century villa and a whole olive grove?' He gave a cheerless laugh. 'By painting unicorns and dragons?'

'I'm not interested. Just tell me why you never came back.'

'I think I told you already. I went to serve Prince Cromund. When I left, things were already difficult between your mother and me. Living in that Greek backwater had lost its appeal. When I found myself in Prince Cromund's sphere of influence again, I realised what I'd been missing.'

Geo looked at his father's pale face. Max reminded him of an actor who had learnt his lines well, but didn't quite believe in what he said…

'So you abandoned me and Mum for …'

'Not if you check your mother's bank statements, I did not!' he cut in angrily. 'But she was being difficult. She couldn't accept that I had moved on. And so she convinced herself that the Prince was somehow keeping me captive.'

'Yeah, but you could have at least told me the truth and I'd have believed you. You could have written, phoned, emailed, even visited. You have no excuse, Dad, and you know it.'

He shrugged. 'Sometimes grown-ups do things they are not proud of. And the longer they leave it the more difficult it gets to do the right thing. But the fact is, when it came to the crunch, when I found out your life was in danger, I did what it took to be there for you.'

Geo mulled this over for a moment. 'So how *did* you appear when you came to warn me about the earthquake?'

Max looked at Geo, his brows furrowed, then he said, 'It was not easy – and it only worked for a short spell ...'

'So that's something that your lot can do?'

Max didn't meet his eye. 'My lot, your mother's lot ... the only difference is that your mother and her chums think they have the moral high ground.'

'While your lot only ever think of how to make the fattest profit and which rainforest to chop down next!' he retorted.

'I won't argue against any of that nonsense, Geo, except to say that it's unfair and uninformed. So!' he leaned back, crossing his legs. 'Tell me about your travels – how did you end up here?'

'Why not ask your chums – seeing as they've been hounding me for weeks, they'll know. Although I still don't know exactly why. Why does Cromund want me here?'

Half of his father's face seemed hidden in shadow. 'Look, why are you being so hostile, so *rabidly* against the Prince?'

'Because I don't understand what dealings my own dad could possibly have with ... with that evil walking, talking corpse.

'His name is Prince Cromund, Geo,' Max repeated evenly. 'And you'd better start to show respect. Whatever you've heard about him and me from your mother's lot, he is nothing more and nothing less than a business partner with a great instinct for what sells, and a track record of success in anything and everything he touches... Are you listening?'

But Geo was not; or at least, not to the words. He was listening, instead, to a little voice in his heart. Thinking through the little clues his father had been giving since he'd walked into that room – tiny gestures, small furtive glances towards the fireplace, the pallor of his skin, his toneless voice. And he listened out for other things, too; things which, Geo guessed might be beyond the usual hearing range of anyone without a dreamcatcher. Which was how he heard the almost inaudible gasp of impatience from somewhere to his right, where the fireplace was, and he suddenly knew that someone was watching him – no, not him, *them.*

Geo looked up at his father, keeping his face in the shadow of his hood. His eyes flickered in the direction of the mantelpiece mirror as if to ask, *Are we being watched?* And Max raised his eyebrows and gave the slightest of half-nods.

The whole conversation had been a sham. Cromund was watching. So was his father double-crossing Cromund? Was he only pretending to be on Cromund's side? If that was the case, then it also meant Max was really on Geo's side.

He felt his head swim as he tried to digest this. 'Look,' he said, keeping his face still, despite the churning of his brain, 'why don't you just tell me why I am here and exactly what your Prince wants from me?'

As Max opened his mouth to speak, the door burst open and Cromund swept in with Sadie Mandiball and the two thugs.

'I think you ought to leave,' Cromund said, glaring furiously at Max. 'Get out!'

'But …'

'Now!'

'No,' was all Geo had time to say. 'Wait!'

A jab in his side. This time the tranquiliser struck home.

Knees buckled. Everything came in waves – of nausea, of cold sweat, of greyness; waves of noise; too much noise; his father's protestations as Max was forced out of the room; the squeaky wheel of something; strong hands grabbing him from the back. Someone yanked up Geo's sweatshirt and tied it by the sleeves over his head so he could see nothing.

'Don't upset him,' someone was saying. 'It could damage the Key to Dreams. See? Under his tee-shirt.'

'How can upsetting him damage it?'

'They say that it's, like, connected to him. Like his heart or something.'

'Somethin' else.'

There was laughter.

'Here. Sit him in the wheelchair.'

'Look, he's not passed out, not completely. I can see his eyes moving.'

'Don't underestimate him.' Sadie Mandiball's voice.

'Would another tranquiliser help?'

'Best not,' Sadie Mandiball again. 'His dreamcatcher might …' Her voice lowered and Geo heard something like 'rake'. *Break?* he thought dimly. Maybe that wouldn't be a bad thing.

'Oi, lad, don't thrash about like that. It's bad for you.'

Were they talking to him? Was he having a fit? Arms twitching, he was being wheeled across a bumpy floor at speed, pushed into a lift that went a long way down, then out to a much cooler corridor and into a room that reeked of mould.

Someone loosened the sweatshirt tied around his head, cut his wrist bindings, then tipped him out of the wheelchair onto a smelly earthen floor. Though he was weak and drowsy, he threw the sweatshirt off his eyes and staggered up. His vision adjusted to the dingy light of a bulb just in time to see the metal door slamming shut.

He was in a bare cellar with a high ceiling. Eyes drooping, he saw that the room was long, so long in fact that it disappeared into the gloom beyond. He felt nauseous and very tired. Maybe he should lie down and sleep. Then he heard several bolts sliding, and glanced at the metal door again. A square window, the size of a letter-box, slid open and Geo saw the eyes of Sadie Mandiball peer through.

'Ah. You've come round!' she said in a cheerful voice, her face filling the square. 'So! Welcome to Prince

Cromund's kingdom!' Her eyes were wide with glee, her red mouth grinning.

'Whaart ... kindorrm?' Geo's speech, affected by the tranquiliser, came out slurred, while his dazed brain threw up a memory of the London Eye he'd seen from the back of Jameson's house. 'Arrr... aren't we in London?' he faltered.

'Yes ... yes,' she said with a giggle. 'But, you know how it is. London, being a world capital, has so many embassies! 'And, well, Geo, you're in one of them! This territory belongs to Prince Cromund. It counts as another country, kingdom, another world or realm or call it what you will! So its rules are, guess what, *different*! And,' she added with a pout, 'best part of it is, down here in the dungeons, you will find that the *natural* laws are different, too.' Her smile widened; he saw a streak of blood-red lipstick running down one of her teeth. Then, with a deafening smash, she slid the metal flap closed and was gone.

CHAPTER THIRTY-ONE

Lyke

Geo rested his forehead against the cold prison door and forced himself to breathe. He was trapped here; and he felt full of remorse. He deserved nothing; not his friends, not his parents and, least of all, the astonishing gift of his dreamcatcher. His last fight with Dysoedema had given him a completely false sense of confidence, of self-importance. How arrogant he'd been! It was his arrogance that had led him to make some terrible decisions. And now it was payback time. Now he was getting what he deserved.

A cold draught rose somewhere behind him, bringing with it the stench of rotting flesh. His pulse quickened as Geo turned around and saw something detaching itself from the gloom at the far side of the cell. Veiled by shadow, two eyes stared out of darkness. He met their gaze without blinking, his fists clenched in preparation for a fight that he knew would be only an empty gesture. The figure advanced silently; he had no doubt it was Cromund.

The window in the cell door slid open again and Cromund beckoned to the person on the other side. 'Bring it in,' he said quietly. 'It's quite safe now.'

Keys, catches, mort-locks and bolts clanged, and Sadie Mandiball came in, carrying a red silk cushion upon which lay another dreamcatcher. Geo suppressed a gasp: it looked like an exact copy of his own.

'Don't make my friend Max Cleigh ashamed when you could make him proud!' Cromund's voice was low but harsh with its clipped, guttural precision.

'Now – this,' Sadie Mandiball said airily, glancing down at the red cushion, 'belonged to your family. It was given as a gift to his Excellency.'

'And … how do I know that's true?' Geo asked, glancing down at the red cushion. He found it hard not to sound disdainful. 'This dreamcatcher could be anyone's,' he added. 'It's probably a fake.'

'Really!' Sadie laughed off his remark. 'But can you not see the quality of the workmanship, the hallmark of its three charms, and, of course, the detail on the three emblems? This wolf-head, together with the spider web ring and feather are as good as your family's coat of arms!'

'So it is,' he said, his voice cold. 'But if my parents gave it of their own free will, then why isn't anyone wearing it?' Geo cast a furtive glance at Cromund. He sensed the demon studying his features. He didn't really think the dreamcatcher in Sadie Mandiball's hands was a fake. Yet, the more he looked at it, the more aware he became of two differences between his and the one on the red cushion. They were so insignificant they would have probably escaped anyone who was not himself a dreamcatcher-bearer, but to Geo they were clear. The other dreamcatcher was the tiniest bit smaller than Geo's Hymal. And the expression in the eyes of the grape-sized wolf-head was passionate but not fierce like Hymal's. For some reason, this wolf made the hairs on Geo's neck stand on end.

Sadie Mandiball was still talking and Geo pulled his attention back to her. '… have brought it for his Excellency to use!' She did an absurd little curtsy before Cromund, who picked up the second dreamcatcher from its silk cushion, but still made no attempt to wear the talisman. Sadie Mandiball walked to the door and stood by it like a servant in the presence of royalty, waiting for permission to depart.

Geo, anxious to delay the moment when he'd be finally

alone with Cromund, kept his eyes on Sadie Mandiball and, gesturing in her direction, asked, 'But I don't get it: if, as you say, your people are all such good mates with my dad, why set Knock-Shaws on me, and Dysoedema and Jameson and… and even your gardener? Why not just get my dad to do all your dirty work?'

She looked at Cromund, as though asking for permission to respond.

'You can explain.' It seemed that Cromund wanted to let her do all the talking while he was happy to sit back, watching Geo's reactions.

'His Excellency,' she said from the doorway, 'thought it was important to observe the properties of your dreamcatcher. Think of everything that's happened until now, Geo, as a rehearsal. We were merely noting how this particular talisman performs in different conditions. But the rehearsal is now over. The real thing is about to commence.'

What was she talking about? He didn't like the sound of it. What, exactly was about to begin?

'Sounds like an elaborate scam,' he said dismissively, keen to buy time.

'More of an experiment,' Sadie Mandiball replied. 'You see, no two human beings behave in exactly the same way, and this also goes for dreamcatchers. But, my dear boy, even here, in the embassy of the Prince's kingdom, where you have no hope, no hope at all, of preserving your talisman, his Excellency is still willing to give you a chance. Your father awaits you upstairs in a splendid drawing room, sipping delicious drinks and listening to music. On the feather cushions by his side are clean clothes for you. In the room next door a bath is filled to the brim with hot water and aromatic oils. Do you not want to join your father and start a new, privileged life? Have you not longed all these years to be reunited with him? Are you not willing to hand over your dreamcatcher to the

Prince in exchange for a life most young men of your age can only dream of?'

'I see,' Geo said, doing his best to sound reasonable. 'Can you give me a moment to think about it?' He was bluffing, of course, but he briefly toyed with a new idea. Should he *pretend* to fall for their proposal and let them have the dreamcatcher? But how would he get it back? Besides, he didn't trust himself to act as though he was on their side. His father seemed to manage it, somehow; and his mum had come to Gaea from Oeska to spy on Cromund in the first place. But could he pretend to be one of them?

Even as this thought entered his mind, Geo realised he was being naïve. He'd never be able to pull off such a thing. He was too impulsive, and anyway, once the dreamcatcher was safely in their hands, they could murder him, plain and simple. Unless they could not take his life, even here in Cromund's realm... was it possible that they needed him alive to operate it? But what then? He'd be condemned to live as a slave trapped in their kind of luxurious, empty lifestyle that made his stomach churn – and what sort of an existence would that be? As satisfying, he reckoned, as selling his soul to the master of slavery and self-loathing.

'No, I won't hand it over willingly,' he said after a long pause.

Cromund immediately took a step forward. 'Willingly is best,' he said, thrusting his hand into Geo's face, palm wide-open, fingers spread out. 'But to requisition it in my own kingdom, that will also do!' He gestured to Sadie Mandiball to leave the room, his face full of rage at her failed, last-ditch attempt to coax Geo to their side.

Geo flinched in shock as a small black flame shot out of the demon's hand. It had the shape and look, but none of the warmth, of fire. He leapt back flattening himself against the cold brick wall of the cell that felt slimy with damp. The flame darted towards him, staying close to his eyes. At first it felt no worse than the warm tongue of a cat, licking Geo's eyelids, creeping across the bridge of his nose and sliding down into his nostrils. Then, with a sudden 'whoosh!' it burst out all over his body, bringing with it a pain so cruel that he thought he was being skinned alive. In its grip, he blacked out.

***

When Geo came to, he was slumped on the floor of the dungeon. Cold hands were searching at the back of his neck for the clasp and a harsh voice cursed and muttered chants, commanding his dreamcatcher to unfasten.

He tried to roll away from the hands. Grasping the tiny golden spider web fixed inside the dreamcatcher's ring, he held it between the pad of his thumb and forefinger, hoping against all hope that it might transport him to the foothills of Mount Olyska as it had in the past. But there was no fall through the enchanted night, no waves lapping on the faraway shore; only Cromund's scornful laugh and the closeness of his withered lips.

Cromund's cheeks puffed out to bursting point. Then he began to blow. A wind rose, a wind so loud and powerful that Geo felt as though he were caught in the slipstream of a jet-plane. His whole body seemed to vibrate with the thunderous noise, until, amid the pandemonium, his dreamcatcher began to pull violently away. He felt its hoop straining so hard he thought it would slice his neck. Just as he could bear it no longer, the Hymal dreamcatcher snapped with a loud crack and, vaulting through the air, fell into Cromund's waiting hands.

Geo lay frozen at the base of the wall. A horrible pain had clamped itself to the top of his spine and was spreading agony to the back of his skull. He felt as though his brain was getting crushed in the coils of a python. He could not move at all. All the same, he kept his eyes on Cromund, who now rammed the smaller dreamcatcher, the one he'd picked up from the red silk cushion, inside Geo's Hymal. The demon arranged the two hoops at right angles, then set them whirling in the palm of his hand like a spinning top. They turned so fast, they became a sphere of gyrating grey with a rim of ruby red swirling around them like an evil spirit.

That was when Geo heard the roar of a thunderstorm, though not one that came from the skies above, but a subterranean drawl drifting up through the ground from the guts of the earth. In spite of the pain that pinned him to the floor, the night of the earthquake stirred in his memory, the hollow boom thundering up from the foundations of his house, the terror of a presence locked up deep underground and now let loose. Then, from far, far away, Geo picked up another sound, which he recognised as the scrape and clash of immense links, the pull and push of the titanic chains that anchored Oeska to the Earth.

Suddenly everything hushed, before a ringing whisper rose and peaked with the blast of exploding metal.

'Good riddance, guardians of Gaea,' Cromund jeered.

Another peal of trembling, searing thunder rolled underground, and Geo heard the heave of granite, coal, iron ore, and then another crash. The time he had first seen the castle of Oeska came to his mind; it was floating like a vast spaceship in the sky anchored to the mountain top with dozens of chains; he had listened, awed by the boom and crash of the titanic chains, scraping and groaning eerily amid the silence of the mountains. This, he now realised, was what Cromund was doing, though Geo had no idea how: breaking the chains! Another chain, let loose. One more anchor that had held Oeska to the Earth gone!

He knew that Cromund wouldn't stop until he had destroyed all the anchors. Taking deep breaths, Geo fought back the excruciating pain and tried to reconnect with his previous sense of clarity, the feeling that had guided his hand during his fight with Dysoedema. Instead, the memory of Diam leapt into his mind, sudden and vibrant as though she were there with him. He saw her sitting cross-legged on the floor of Linda's attic room, reading her Reality Check Cards for him, the sun streaking her jet-black hair with a red glow. *'Immense danger,'* she had said. *'Offer two libations to the great mother. Seek her help.'* And then the explanation he'd found in the dictionary: *'libation: liquid poured out in honour of a power beyond human understanding.'*

Concentrating hard, Geo managed to breathe in and wipe his mind clean of all thought, regret and pain. It didn't take long – perhaps it took no more than one second. Or it might have been only a fraction of a second; but it had been enough. He felt his spirits rising free of fear and self-blame. In the short time between one breath and the next, his muscles relaxed enough for him to turn over, so he now lay on the earthen floor face-down. He tried to scramble up, but the excruciating pain at the back of his body burned fiercer than before and spread into his every bone. He had nothing to offer; nothing except two swelling tears that slid down his eyelashes and splashed against the dark soil of the floor. 'I'm sorry,' he murmured, more tears streaking down his face, putting all his focus in making his worthless libation count, as Diam had said. He tried to visualise the energy field of life that runs through every leaf, root and living cell; the unknown forces that bring snow and rain, making leaves die and trees wake up again in the spring, giving fruit and causing lambs to be born in the fields. Then he murmured, 'Gaea, help me!'

Geo watched the black, compacted earth suck in his tears. And then he felt – or thought that he felt – a subtle current of air rise gently out of the ground and glide towards his skin. As it landed, it swept Geo clean of the unbearable pain Cromund had inflicted upon him. It was odd: Geo could move again, think, act and even see, quite clearly, what to do and how to do it. The pain had gone. He stood up and pointed in the direction of Cromund, who was still chanting and spinning the two dreamcatchers on the palm of his hand.

'I call to you, my wolf,' commanded Geo. 'Return to me!'

The gyrating ball of ruby-red in Cromund's palm came to a standstill. Cromund could only watch as the two dreamcatchers split from each other and one of them came whizzing like a frisbee towards Geo. To his astonishment, however, the talisman that had answered his call was not the Hymal dreamcatcher, but the smaller of the two. Before Geo caught it in his hand, something furry broke out of it and, in the blink of an eye, grew into a short-haired grey wolf who landed by his feet and looked up at him. Slick, sinewey and young, he was a creature quite unlike the grumpy Hymalayan who'd shown him the way to Oeska. This one had two long, dark leathery wings neatly folded up on the sides of the wolf's body.

'You can fly?' Geo whispered.

The creature gave a nod, his amber eyes widening.

'Lyke!' the wolf growled his name in Geo's mind just as Hymal had first spoken his. But his eyes seemed to be smiling; and with one, magnificent clean strike of insight, Geo knew, as surely as he knew that some shoes fit and others don't, that Lyke had always been meant for him. This was why it had been Lyke and not Hymal who had answered to his master, Geo, when he had been called.

Rapidly coming to the same realisation, Cromund changed form. His human features wavered and he shrank, stooping, eyes red, ears more pointed, skin sodden with a sickly, corpse-like yellow sheen, until he looked more demon than man, Prince of terror, evil eye, brutal master. Lyke crouched, growled and leapt at the demon, but Cromund was quick to raise one arm in defence. A streak of red, a blood-soaked rope lasso, uncoiled out of Cromund's hand but, before the rope tightened around his neck, Lyke looped it with his front paw, pushed it to the floor and leapt at the demon once again.

But Cromund wasn't done. With a whispered command, he created a cage of fire, a large blazing cube that caught Lyke mid-leap, trapping him mid-air and rising to the ceiling where it swung above their heads. From inside his prison, Lyke bared his teeth, flattened his ears and spoke again in Geo's mind.

'Sword!' he uttered, at the same time as Geo heard a loud crackle next to him. He looked across: a sword of burning fire had tumbled into his hand, its blade glowing molten red. But its hilt felt like velvet in his palm – not hot, not burning.

'The other dreamcatcher, give it back to my new master!' Lyke growled at the demon.

Cromund gave a nasty laugh and raised his arm again. Before he could create another weapon, Geo struck the floor of the enchanted cage with the sword of fire; it cut through it as easily as a knife slicing through butter. With a muffled explosion, the cage dissolved, and the wolf's leaping figure arced down towards Cromund, who now charged back at him, with a frenzied snarl.

Holding the sword with both arms above his head, Geo stormed at the demon, bringing it down to strike. But a shot of dark red unfurled from Cromund's hand into the space between them, hitting Geo squarely on the chest. He let out a terrified gasp. He couldn't breathe. The world around him spun. Sounds became muffled. Then a whine started inside his head, a loud, high-pitched wail that made him feel like he was made of glass, and would surely shatter. He felt two trickles of blood ooze out of his nostrils and drip onto his shirt. His chest burned as if his lungs were being ripped out. The sword slid out of his hand, clanging onto the floor. Everything turned grey, flat and empty. He was sure he was dying. If so, he thought dimly, would his new dreamcatcher die with him? Would Lyke die?

He could hear Lyke yelping in pain and snarling next to him.

This is it, he thought dimly, his knees buckling. But the voice of Lyke thundered into his mind, gentle, firm: *'Come back. Don't faint. Not now.'*

Eyes barely open, Geo felt the strong smell of fur in his nostrils and realised that he had somehow managed to pull himself onto Lyke's back. His wolf reared, stretched out his odd, leathery wings and soared into the air. With Geo's arms wrapped around him, Lyke dived down, kicking Cromund with his hind legs before rising again. Geo looked down – the kick had caught Cromund on the side of the head, and slammed it against the wall of the cell. The impact only seemed to stun the demon, but in the seconds that it took him to recover from the blow, Lyke dived down again towards the door. Instinctively, the unlocking command burst out of Geo's lips, the door flew open, and, with Geo still clutching onto Lyke's back, they zoomed down several corridors. As they sped on, guards hurled sprays of crimson machine-gun fire that brought down whole sections of wall and ceiling, yet left them untouched, cocooned in some protective shield of Lyke's making. Past the lifts, they shot up a long spiral stairwell, reached the ground floor, knocked a dozen gun-wielding men aside like toy guards and kept climbing higher to the building's top floor, where Lyke smashed out of a skylight into pelting rain.

When Geo dared look down, he saw they were flying above the capital. Below them, crowds crammed into tube stations and streamed out onto pavements, their multi-coloured umbrellas competing for space. He saw the roofs of cars and red buses stuck in slow-moving traffic queues, glistening in the August rain. Geo wondered how soon they'd be spotted, but it looked like everyone down below was too busy keeping dry under umbrellas, bus shelters and shop entrances to bother glancing up at the bucketing London sky.

Rainwater drove against Geo's face, flattening his dripping hair and trickling down his collar. His shirt stuck to his body, but he didn't mind. Shaking the droplets from his eyelashes he checked anxiously over his shoulder, but saw no-one following. He suppressed his rising sense of relief, thinking it was too early to give in to the words now playing in his mind like a triumphant chorus sung by a thousand choristers – 'Done it! No idea how, but we've done it!'

And now, like a great bird, Lyke double-backed on himself, spiralling downwards on a current of air that led to a complicated maze of streets behind a busy London market, before landing on a rooftop terrace. Whether from his relief, his injuries, or the sheer exhaustion that suddenly came over him, Geo felt himself go floppy, his head against Lyke's neck. A chilling, all-engulfing darkness came over him, as he finally allowed himself to pass out.

CHAPTER THIRTY-TWO

Tamcrow

Geo's head hurt and the blinding fireball on his left made it worse. He covered his eyes, turned away from its brilliant glare and went back to sleep. All he wanted was to be left undisturbed, not caring whether he would ever wake up. He was drifting through a jumble of shots, explosions and shouts. As the demon's eye drew closer, his lungs burst with pain. But it was the weeping that eventually woke him. He sat up, staring wildly around. The fireball on his left had been the rising sun. He put a hand to his face – it was wet. He must have been crying in his sleep.

He couldn't see anyone else. It seemed he was alone, but where? Cromund's kingdom? Oeska? Home? Too weak to stand up, he lifted his eyes to the sky. Tree branches with small, jagged leaves fluttered in the breeze many feet above his head. They looked like the leaves of an oak. He had been sheltering under a tree. Turning his head to the left, he saw a wide strip of grass, a steep drop, and beyond that the sun, riding high in the sky. The salt smell of the sea mixed with wild thyme and oregano drifted in the air. Was he somewhere on the side of a mountain?

He listened. There was the murmur of water running downstream and the calls of birds. Behind him, he heard the sound of feet wading through dry grass. Heart thumping, he turned around. The familiar figure of a tall man in a long, scruffy coat had emerged from a wood of pines. Reaching Geo quickly, he sat cross-legged on the ground, a short double-headed serpent staff poking out of his coat pocket.

Geo's eyes widened. 'M-mmrrshall Angelo!' he mumbled, feeling so weak that his words came out slurred. 'C-Cromundshh g-got the dream c-catchers,' he stammered like a drunk, 'And he is breaking th-the anchors …'

'…that chain Oeska to the Earth?'

Geo nodded.

'But he can't be. Look, the Lyke dreamcatcher is right here.' A smile lit up Angelo's eyes as he pointed to the top of Geo's tee-shirt.

'Huh?' Geo grimaced, bringing his hand up to his neck. Sitting in the hollow under his Adam's apple he found the tiny, soft wolf-head of Lyke. He ran his fingers over it, hardly daring to trust his senses. 'Lyke has gone back to his dreamcatcher?'

'And why not!' The voice of Lyke piped straight into his mind – cheerful, amused.

'Ah!' Geo allowed his face to break into a huge grin. His new talisman was such a perfect fit he was no more conscious of its weight round his neck than of the presence of his nose on his face.

'B-but the chains?' he asked Angelo. 'What happened to them?'

'We lost a handful of weaker ones…' Angelo murmured. 'But we still have ninety out of a hundred doing their job perfectly well. So I, for one, have no concerns.'

'But can the broken ones be repaired?'

'Ah, now …' a fleeting sadness passed in his eyes as he said, 'some things can never be repaired.'

'B-but the other talisman?' Geo asked eagerly, feeling more wakeful now. 'Hymal?' You see, I'm pretty sure Lyke was mine – I mean – intended for me, well, kind of. We, you know …'

'Bonded?' Angelo smiled.

'Yes! It felt like it, anyway. But the other one, Hymal, he is my mum's, really – he was on loan, I suppose, to help me on my way.'

'Mmmm!' Angelo nodded, frowning. 'It would seem so.'

'So where *is* Hymal?' Geo pressed.

Angelo pursed his lips. 'It won't be easy to explain,' he replied. 'But I've brought something to show you.' He pulled a book out of the folds of his coat. It was bound in red silk and bore the title, '*The Tale of Tamcrow*'.

Angelo tapped it twice with his thumb. The pages fanned quickly towards the end, revealing many blank pages in the middle. 'The unwritten section,' he explained, 'spans the last seven years, when your father was in Cromund's kingdom.'

'Who is Tamcrow?'

'Ah, yes. Now, Tamcrow, Geo, is a code name of sorts. If you could think of your father as a double agent — that would be helpful. Such a good one, in fact,' he added with a chuckle, 'that even we got fooled for a while, thinking he had switched sides.'

Geo's heart leapt, and his grin returned. 'I knew you were all wrong. Max has scammed the scammer — Cromund. Right?'

By way of an answer, Angelo opened the book. 'This transcript,' he explained, comes from one of our libraries at Silverfoot. These volumes are programmed to record events in your world, and *only* in your world. What I mean is that we cannot "look" into other realms, including the Colony — Cromund's territories. You see, as your father was operating from the demon's realm and not from yours, we lost the ability to trace him. We could not tell whether he had been kidnapped, gone on a self-appointed mission or joined ranks with the demon. However — remember when you flew out of Cromund's so-called embassy?'

Geo nodded.

'Well, Diam and Chen had the readiness of mind to alert us as soon as they were off Dysoedema's radar. We couldn't track you down at first. Cromund's kingdom is impenetrable to our detection. But once you were out, we traced your journey back to his base in London.'

'And have you caught him?'

Angelo drummed his fingers on the side of his scruffy old coat, pursed his lips then rubbed his chin looking, Geo thought, unhappy. 'Not quite. But we *have* turfed him out of an important foothold in your world. As a result, he's had to go into hiding deep in his territories, leaving some of his associates behind, without cover. Now, let me show you something!'

Geo's heart beat faster as Angelo turned to page two hundred and sixty-one of '*The Tale of Tamcrow*'. The book was like nothing Geo had ever seen, with writing on the left-hand page, and a tiny 3-D stage on the right, where Geo noticed something that made him gasp with surprise.

'That can't be!' he said, bending over the page to look more closely. 'Wow!'

A real, living, breathing thumb-sized Max was staring at the view out of a large floor-to-ceiling window.

'We're not, strictly speaking, allowed to take these books out of Silverfoot,' Angelo was saying. 'But your service to Oeska has been exceptional and I was granted special permission to show you a short section from it. You may find it of interest.'

'I … I am … th-thank you,' Geo stammered gratefully, taking the book.

His dad didn't do much at first, except walk from the window to a desk where he consulted a semi-circle of a dozen computer screens, then back to the long, floor-to-ceiling window through which Geo could see a green river twisting through many buildings. Geo read the writing on the left, hoping it would give him a clue to what he saw: *'Tamcrow stared at London sloping gently down, past the domes of the Naval College. The Thames gleamed in the sun, snaking in front of the steel and glass structures of the City.*

He had already made a few calls early in the morning: Toronto, New York, Singapore. He had talked to Research, consulted his

Bloomberg screens and re-scanned the morning volatility of markets, planning his afternoon. Money-making was second nature to him. His hands would fly over the keyboard – clickety-clack thwack! – setting the cash-engine in motion, and whoosh! Thousands would pour into the various company accounts.

Cromund's operation was smart, sleek, well-planned, and Tamcrow knew how to make himself useful. But that day he couldn't settle down in front of the screens. Instead, he pulled a sheet of A4 paper from a drawer and started to write. He only put pen to paper rarely, when his loneliness and his need to confide got the better of him. And he only ever wrote this kind of thing by hand, careful not to leave any electronic trace of his real thoughts.

1st September.

Geo, my boy, there is nothing you can do for me now without destroying everything your mother and I have worked for. Unbelievably, things have gone very well. You have reclaimed Lyke and that's all that matters now.

Please, forgive and forget everything that I said to you in Cromund's 'Embassy'. As you probably realised, it came from a script because we were being watched. But the truth is this: I never wanted to leave you and your mother. I've had to sacrifice everything that is dear to me to safeguard your lives.

You would know our story by now. Your mother chose to disobey the Marshals' new laws against intermarriage and had to live as an exile from her world, having to rely only on the kindness of her friends for protection. There was, however, a limit to the number of favours she could call upon. Too much help would endanger her friends' position among the Marshals of Tide and Time, who are meant to do a greater bidding, beyond their personal desires and compulsions.

I had problems, too. Before I'd met your mother, I used to work for Cromund. But whether a man joins a bunch of gangsters, the mafia, or Cromund's cult of rapacious greed, it's almost impossible, once you've taken this road, to turn your back to it without expecting retaliation. And so it was with me. Leona and I went into hiding in Zonissos. After a few blissful years raising you, Cromund managed to track us down and I was made to choose between your lives or having to go back to his employment. I kept my humiliating secret to myself. I was afraid your mother would do anything in her power to stop me – or worse, follow me. But Cromund was very clear about one thing: if I kept any contact with you, any contact at all, you and your mother would have been killed long ago. And so I had to leave you in order to serve my old master.

It is now clear to me that the real prize for him was not your life, but your dreamcatcher: as August of this year drew near, I got wind that something was brewing. There were too many secret meetings, too many rumours. It's only now that I realise it was Cromund himself who leaked the information about the 'earthquake' to me, using a young man, a trainee, who was working in my office. I felt I had no other choice but to warn you. I had no idea that the Marshals would be able to trace the source of my warning back to Cromund, that they'd pull Leona out for questioning, or that you would be left out in the streets without protection – which was what Cromund had intended and wanted all along.

The reason he set me up was that he wanted to

study the properties of the Hymal dreamcatcher when it came to your possession. Luckily for us, like the stolen Lyke, he wasn't able to take Hymal unless it was willingly given. However, who knows by what dark means, he discovered an unusual way to enslave and misuse both dreamcatchers yoked together. With you in close proximity and the two dreamcatchers in the wrong hands, immense negative energies were generated in Cromund's kingdom, releasing power of a strength that could destroy even the links between Oeska and the Earth.

Amazingly, you managed to reclaim Lyke and frustrate Cromund's plans. Therefore Hymal is now in the demon's service but drained of its power. It's nothing but an object in his hands, a trinket, gathering dust, completely useless to the demon or anyone.

Now that your attempt to track me down is over, Geo, you must put this dangerous quest to rest. Please. Your presence near me is the only thing that can, and does, make me vulnerable. In this game of espionage, counter-espionage, double-dealing and second-guessing, my boy, I cannot afford to be ruled by anything except logic.

I repeat then: don't look for me. There's nothing you can do for me now without endangering everything your mother and I have worked for. Trust me. Things have turned out well enough. Lyke is powerful, well-matched to you and as close to the heart of wisdom as anyone of your age could hope for.

I send my love, as ever,

Your father.'

'And now,' Tamcrow wrote next in his journal, *'before I burn these papers, it's time to make offerings to Marshal Angelo: Great Messenger, hear my voice. Convey this to my son. And if you can, mediate for me, that I may be with my family again, some longed-for day.'*

Then, having offloaded his feelings, he burned what he had written. He couldn't afford to leave any evidence behind. Even walls had ears in Cromund's service.

Geo rubbed his temples. The effort of not crying was giving him a headache. Angelo withdrew the book gently and put it away.

'So you see …' he murmured, 'as long as you stay clear of your father, everything will sort itself out. Max knows what he is doing, Geo. What could be better?'

'Having my mother back?'

'Well, I do have news of her,' Angelo said, pulling a wafer-thin, phone-sized screen out of his pocket. 'Have a look!'

Geo's heart gave a jolt as a 3-D hologram of his mother's head appeared.

'Mum, you're out of regeneration!' he exclaimed. He leaned back a little, startled. 'You look great.' His praise had been understated; Leona looked about twenty years younger and glowing with health.

She gave a laugh. 'Thanks! You look great, too, considering …'

'Considering what?'

'… what you've been through! Congratulations, by the way, on reclaiming Lyke. You should be very proud of yourself!'

'When are you coming home?'

She sighed. 'When some bureaucrat in Delaciel's office …'

'Sorry, who's Delaciel?'

'Marshal Angelo's boss – when he decides there's need for me to be assigned to my next task. But why don't you join me here? I hear you've already made friends with Chen.'

'I don't know yet, Mum,' he said evasively. 'I'll let you know as soon as I've decided.'

'Stop sounding so grown-up,' she teased.

He chuckled. 'Yeah, well, either that, or I'll have to sneak in and kidnap you!'

'Well, I hope that erm... a potential kidnapper, would do me the courtesy of asking if I'd like to be snatched out of here first.'

'So what would you do if I just came along without asking, hit me with your handbag?'

'I might!'

'Mmm! Shame that,' he tried to laugh it off, but underneath he was as amazed as ever about how his mother never failed to exasperate him.

'Thank you,' he said returning the wafer-thin phone to Angelo after they had said goodbye.

The Marshal gathered his long, scruffy coat around him, looked up into the sky and said, 'I'm running out of time. But remember this, Geo. Both your parents have made sacrifices to safeguard your life and dreamcatcher. Trust in them. Nothing's gone to waste and all will be well in the end.'

Geo stroked the tiny wolf-head at his neck. He took a deep breath and hauled himself up from the ground.

'I'm going for a walk to clear my head,' he said, although standing up made him dizzy and nauseous, he realised.

'You're shivering. Are you cold?' Angelo asked, helping him to steady himself.

'Yes.' Geo could barely walk a few paces without his legs buckling. 'How long have I been here?'

'Almost a week; you've been very ill, I'm afraid... But,' he added cheerfully, 'one cannot see any visible evidence of your so-called civilisation from this spot, which makes it the perfect place for healing!'

Geo shuffled to the other side of the oak tree. Behind its enormous trunk they found a sunny spot. Geo sat on a flat rock, warm in the sun. It overlooked a glowing ocean, and a couple of islands, like rags of scrunched velvet, green and blue, against the satin of a perfect sea.

'Greece!' he exclaimed, astonished, as always, by the flawless beauty of his second homeland. 'But where exactly?'

'Not far from the foothills of Olympus.'

Geo noticed that Angelo was impatiently drumming his fingers on his coat pocket but decided to ignore it. He still needed some answers. 'But how did I get here? Did you rescue me?'

'Certainly not! Once you had reclaimed Lyke, the balance of power shifted. You fought Cromund and in the confusion found a means of flying out of the embassy dungeons.'

Geo nodded, recalling how he and Lyke had burst out of Cromund's kingdom into the pelting rain. He let the memories flow through his mind, smiling faintly to himself. 'And what about Diam and Chen? Are they safe and well?'

'Of course! They're staying with your relatives in Brighton.'

'Ian and Linda? Amazing!' Geo chuckled. 'How did they manage to get my shrew of an aunt to put them up?'

Angelo gave a low chuckle. 'They must be highly skilled in the art of persuasion.'

'But it was you who rescued me once Lyke and I got out of Cromund's embassy, right?'

'The only person who rescued you, Geo, was you. By Lyke's account, you acted faultlessly and on pure instinct. You showed signs of impeccable intuition!'

Geo rolled his eyes. 'All I did was get stalked, mugged and almost killed, nearly taking Oeska with me!'

'But that was not your fault. None of us had predicted the power of both the dreamcatchers in the wrong hands.'

'You hadn't?'

'Do you think that Einstein knew his elegant mathematics would, one day, be used to launch a nuclear attack on Hiroshima?' Angelo said, with a steady gaze.

Geo didn't know the answer to that. He just gave a shrug, feeling awkward.

'Men much older and wiser than you would give their eye-teeth to achieve the mastery you seem to possess so naturally! When it came to it, you acted brilliantly. Don't you see, what you did was a stroke of genius for someone so inexperienced. You should be celebrating what you have achieved.'

Geo looked seawards, not knowing what to say. It had been a narrow escape. If it had not been for Lyke, he would be dead, and his mother's world annihilated. But after some thought he had to admit that he had, at least, stood up to Cromund. For the time being he'd have to put his quest to rest. The enemy had retreated to his territories, underground. That had to be a good enough victory.

But what he secretly felt most proud of was that he had learned to dreamboard, not by studying but by fighting for the truth about his father. He sensed that he had gained the respect of the Marshals and that he would, sooner or later, find a way to get his mother back. Until that day, Leona, Max and Geo would have to stay connected by nothing more – or less – than the unbreakable threads of love.

He realised that Angelo was drumming his fingers again, this time on his staff, which was sticking out of his coat pocket.

'You look anxious. You probably have better things to do,' Geo muttered. 'Can I just ask you one more question, before you go?'

'Not better things to do, Geo, *other* things to do. What's your question?'

'Well ... what next?'

CHAPTER THIRTY-THREE

The Unceremonious Awards

Geo had only seen Angelo in his human form before. Now he began to shape shift so subtly that at first Geo didn't realise what was happening. But he blinked; and when he looked again, something appeared to be wrong with his eyesight. Perhaps he was seeing double – or was it triple?

Against the glowing sea in the background, Angelo gave the impression of being wrapped in light, the outline of his body becoming blurred and merging into the blue of the sea and the sky behind him. Geo stood up in surprise. He blinked again. Angelo's human shape grew fainter but his aura became stronger, electric blue and buzzing with a low hum like electricity running through wire, until he looked like nothing more than a flickering brightness, a hypnotic voice, a harbinger of news, a vibration of light. Instinctively, Geo shielded his eyes and listened to his words: 'What next, indeed, Geo… I'd say that sleep is in order next, and more rest.' Then he added, as though he could read Geo's mind, 'But you may stay, if you prefer, in the earthly realm and be schooled by life...'

A great drowsiness came over Geo. He keeled onto his side and fell into a deep, enchanted sleep.

***

Geo had no idea how long he had slept for, when he felt someone shaking him awake.

'Get up, sleepyhead! Wow, what on earth is this?' came the familiar girl's voice.

Someone prodded and poked at his side.

'This is the *weirdest* sleeping bag I've ever seen!'

'Diam? Chen?' His eyes shot open. In spite of feeling hellishly groggy and clumsy, he scrambled to a sitting position, his heart drumming with excitement. 'You're here! But how did you find me?' he croaked, squinting at the sun.

Chen gave a laugh. 'Angelo's fault. *He* told us where to find you.'

'So, *so* good to see you!' He tried to stand up but found it impossible. His legs felt heavy as lead and he could not control the lower part of his body very well.

'Geo,' Diam chuckled, pointing at his feet, 'do you have any idea how freaky you look?'

He glanced down at where his feet should be. 'What?' he burst out laughing; from waist upwards he appeared to grow out of the ground.

Chen gave a whistle. 'Looks like Angelo has lent you his Chameleon Sleeper!'

'Is that what it is?' Geo gave up trying to stand up. Instead, he crawled out of the sleeping bag, which was impossible to distinguish from the grassy soil.

Diam gave Geo a big hug. Her long hair that smelt of elderflowers tickled his arms. Then she let go of him and wriggled into the bag, making delighted noises. 'Wow! How comfy!' She exclaimed. 'And makes you feel sooo sleepy.'

'I'm so thirsty!' Geo grumbled. 'Is there anything to drink around here?'

Chen passed him a plastic bottle labelled 'ICED TEA,' though it had the colour and temperature of wee.

'So where's Angelo?' Geo asked, taking a swig, hoping it would taste better than it looked.

'Rushed off his feet.'

'Doing what?' Geo asked, taking a bag of pretzels from Chen and stuffing his mouth with a few.

'Preventing more olive forest arsons; pulling the local

economy from the brink of another collapse; trying to stop financiers from paying all the government subsidies to themselves in bonuses; while the Marshals of Tide are sending messages to thousands of officials ...'

'What kinds of messages?' Geo asked.

'Dreams.'

Geo spluttered into his not-so-iced tea. 'Is this the best they can do?'

'Yeah, that's just sooo useful, isn't it?' Diam said, rolling her eyes. 'Rather like using smoke signals in the age of mobile phones.'

'That's unfair,' Chen protested.

'No it's not!' Diam laughed. 'I mean, unless they modernise, they don't need Cromund to sever Oeska from the earth, they're doing it DIY style!'

'That's so not true,' Chen disagreed.

'Oooh! Standing up for the Marshals, huh?' Diam teased him, scrambling out of the Chameleon Sleeper. 'I thought you hated being stuck in Oeska.' And before Chen had a chance to say anything, she turned to Geo. 'So what happened to you? You've got to tell us *everything*!'

Geo swallowed another mouthful of pretzels and told them about Lyke, his fight with Cromund, and why it was so important for the safety of his father that he should put his quest to rest.

When he asked what they'd been doing, Chen explained they'd tried to get on with their lives. They'd had no other choice. Linda had grumpily agreed to put them up. Diam told Geo how she'd got a job in a record shop in Brighton, when Chen cut in.

'Got a job? Don't make me laugh. I was there, I saw you. You practically hypnotised the poor man into hiring you!'

'Rubbish!' Diam exclaimed with a frown. 'What do you mean?'

'Hypnotised, that's what! *Mesmerised* the poor bloke with your pretty eyes, so what choice did he have?' Before

Diam had a chance to get even, Chen changed the subject to himself. 'And I,' he said, his dark eyes sparkling, 'got myself an old acoustic guitar. Bought it for a tenner from a junk shop and managed to make some money doing a solo act in a pub on Brighton Pier.'

'Well, if you've been having such a great time,' Geo said a bit resentfully as their enthusiastic tales of Brighton nightlife became increasingly longer and louder, 'why bother to come here at all?'

'To get *you*, fool!' Diam replied. 'Also, I need to go to Salonica, to pick up my bass guitar from home – well, what *used* to be home, anyway. Haven't quite decided what I'm doing next. But I'm definitely not going back to that dump with Anthon!'

'And I've come to say my goodbyes,' Chen added, biting his lip. 'Got to get back home – to Oeska…'

'Seriously!' Geo chortled. 'But how about your solo act then, and the Brighton nightlife, and your fans?'

Chen grimaced, slouching and looking annoyed. 'That's all very well for you to say, but my parents have kicked up a right old stink about me running away!'

'But …' Geo started.

'You two should count yourselves lucky you don't have pushy parents,' Chen said. 'No worries, though, I had a great spin this side of the tracks. Such a shame I got to go back now!' Then he looked up at the sky. 'Not bad, this place,' he winked mischievously, 'for "commuting" to Mount Olyska!' He sat on a rock and stared down at the sea. 'Man, I'm going to miss you …'

'We'll miss you too,' Geo said. 'You've been awesome. Come to stay with me in Zonissos any time…'

'So you persuaded Angelo to let you off studying, did you?' Chen asked.

'I think so,' Geo replied.

'Lucky you!' Chen looked impressed. 'A free-range dreamboarder, huh?'

'Better free range than cooped up,' Geo said, then turned to face Diam. 'But maybe *you* could come to Zonissos with me?' In the pause that followed he added, 'I mean, Brighton is great, but we could just as well play music on a Greek island?'

'Yes, sure,' she grinned, ''cause you got a lovely house in Zonissos, Geo, and the kindest of neighbours.'

'No, seriously! The house is ruined, but we've still got our land. Why can't we set up a caravan next to the ruin in the olive grove? And if Sadie Mandiball's still around, perhaps Marshal Angelo could re-instate the defences?'

'Oh, I wouldn't worry about her,' Chen intervened, 'there's a rumour that they've moved out. She's left her husband and gone underground to live with Cromund.'

Geo choked on the last pretzel. 'A match made in heaven!' he said, when he could speak again.

In the growing twilight Diam spread out Angelo's enchanted sleep-inducing bedding. 'I'm bushed,' she said. 'I'm going to need at least nine hours sleep to feel normal again.'

They all squeezed in together, and within seconds were sleeping like babies.

***

Chen wanted to make his way back before dawn. He'd set his alarm, and woke them when it was still pitch black. Blearily at first, but then with increasing energy, they followed him up a moonlit path that wound its way along the side of a valley, leading towards the rugged peaks of the mountain. Below them, in the light of the setting moon, Geo could see a wide plain with a couple of villages and a faraway beach. By the time they'd reached the steep, craggy rockface at the top end of the valley, bright morning sunlight was glowing behind the horizon and the ink-blue sea had turned into a pale, milky aqua-marine.

Chen pulled a flat package out of one of his combat-trouser pockets. It contained a pair of finely crafted, although rather worn, sandals, the leather soles of which were fitted with long straps that served as tie-ups. Chen ran his hand through his bleached-blond hair, rolled up his trouser legs and began to fasten the first sandal.

'Not such a great terrain for wearing sandals!' Geo remarked.

'Ah, but these are not just *any* sandals,' Chen said, giving him a daft smile and raising his eyebrows twice in quick succession.

Gazing at the peeping sun in the east, Geo and Diam sat on a nearby rock and waited for Chen to finish the laborious business of tying on his sandals.

Except for the faint rustling of leaves in the breeze, the place was silent. Watching the sunrise, Geo felt a rush of fierce joy sweeping through him. It was not only because it felt so good to be up this early in the morning. It was also that as the disc of the sun rose out of the sea, the water broke into a billion stars of ruby light and for a moment the sea, sky and land became as strange and mysterious as Oeska.

He thought of his father, hunched over a computer, making in one day more money than many people make in a lifetime, yet how poor he was in other ways. He thought about everything that had happened to him since the earthquake, and how he had lain in Marshal Angelo's Chameleon Sleeper and dreamt that the earth was pulsing under his own heart as though it had been alive. He realised that even though he had no plans, he was, at least, ready to accept that it was possible for a common mortal as well as an Oeskan to act not just for selfish gain and blinkered desire, but for the good of Gaea.

'Better say goodbye,' said Chen, both sandals now securely strapped on.

For a few moments the three of them stood on the track, looking to the east at the sun, now risen in full splendour. The blue dawn sky arched overhead, the colour of Arctic ice.

Geo, in the middle, slipped one arm through Diam's and the other through Chen's. 'Odd!' he said. 'It feels like I'm dreamboarding.'

The others smiled and nodded. 'Yes,' they both said.

Below their feet, in the villages, metal and glass caught the morning light – windowpanes, the patch of water in a village pond, the windscreen of a fast-moving car.

Chen gave each of them a quick hug and climbed onto an outcrop of rock. 'Don't leave it too long. To complete your training, I mean!' He gave them one last wave, his face shining in the morning light.

Geo looked at Diam. 'What does he mean?' he said in a hushed voice.

Diam cleared her throat: 'I'll tell you in a sec.'

Then Chen began to rise, light as a leaf, in his finely crafted sandals that seemed to glow a little, his arms casually outstretched.

He ascended slowly, as though an invisible thread was pulling him up by the head, higher and higher, until he was just a black speck against the blue; then, nothing: only sky.

'Sandals!' Diam chortled after a moment's silence. 'Good job we've seen odder gear. Oh, by the way, Linda gave me this,' she added, producing a white envelope from her small back-pack.

Geo took it from her, wondering what kind of a surprise his grumpy aunt had in store for him – cat-poo? A dead rat? But then he saw that Diam's name as well as his was written in a neat, calligraphic hand on the white envelope.

'Linda said it got delivered by some unshaven weirdo in a long dark winter coat,' Diam explained.

'Sounds like Marshal Angelo,' Geo said, his heart quickening. Perhaps some news of his parents? But then why would the envelope include Diam's name too?

'He said we should open the envelope together,' Diam added.

Geo squeezed the white paper with his fingertips. Inside, he could feel two soft cylinders, each the size of a large rolled-up napkin.

They opened the flap together and pulled out a couple of scrolls, made of some sort of soft, creamy papyrus. One had 'Geo' scrawled on it; the other was for Diam. Geo examined his scroll, which bore a red wax seal embossed with a coat of arms. He instantly realised it was the crest of Sileverfoot College and that it displayed a pair of sandals like the ones Chen had just used for his commute to Mount Olyska.

Unrolling his scroll, he read:

BEGINNER'S CERTIFICATE IN DREAMBOARDING

The bearer of this certificate George Cleigh has demonstrated competence

Against the following Silverfoot Objectives at Beginner Level I

Located dreamcatcher and crossed over to Oeska.

Gatecrashed Dreams.

Engaged in combat with agents hostile to Oeska.

The learner has also achieved one

Advanced Level Dream Master's Competence at Level 4:

Successfully evoked Chi to his aid

George Cleigh is hereby awarded

The Level I in Dreamboarding.

Grade: **Distinction**

Signed

Silverfooted Selini

Principal

'What on earth is 'Chi'?' Geo asked.

'Life energy – life-force– it's a Chinese word.'

'How do you know these things?'

'Chen told me.'

'Right! So let's see *your* certificate then.'

Diam (Diamondheart Katharophtalmi actually, according to her Silverfoot College certificate) was awarded a very similar Level 1. She too, had attained a Level 4 competence in 'Structured Insight,' so her overall grade was also a 'Distinction'. Her 'instrument' was the Reality Check Cards and some of her dreamboarding skills had been achieved 'by proxy,' through usage of Geo's Oeskan dreamcatcher.

Diam gave a laugh. 'Why are they fixated on qualifications?' she asked, rolling up her certificate and chucking it over the edge of a precipice into the valley below. 'Don't look so shocked,' she added, glancing at Geo's face, 'it's only papyrus. You know, tree bark? Completely biodegradable!'

Geo smiled, but didn't follow her example. He had, after all, made an important realisation, when he watched that morning's sunrise. And whichever way he looked at it, he had to admit that he had two choices: to let the Cromunds of this world take charge and override every aspect of human life down to our most precious thought and desire. Or to join ranks with those who worked for his mother's world. So if it really was possible to have on-the-job training without being stuck in that boring college, then he was happy to go along with it. He would try to go to Oeska as often as was necessary, but would do his bit from the realm of Gaea.

Diam gave him a sideways glance. 'Go on, then, throw it away,' she dared him.

But Geo slipped it in his pocket. Then, squinting at the rising sun, they carried on east. 'You know,' he told her after a few minutes, 'I'm serious about setting up a caravan in the olive grove...'

'And about music? Did you really mean that?'

He stopped and looked at her. 'Yes!' he replied. 'Of course! And there's my friend Evangeli who plays rhythm, and a couple of school friends we sometimes jam with. You'll love it. Just bring your bass guitar!'

'You can count on it!' Diam beamed.

Smiling, Geo slipped his arm through Diam's.

The two of them meandered down the track that led from the foothills of Mount Olyska to their beloved, everyday, earthly life.

The End

If you enjoyed this book and would like to visit
I. Rosenfeld's weekly blog about creativity,
please go to **https://creativityandus.wordpress.com**